THE SAINT GOES ON

FOREWORD BY STEPHEN GALLAGHER

THE ADVENTURES OF THE SAINT

THE SAINT GOES ON

LESLIE CHARTERIS

SERIES EDITOR: IAN DICKERSON

Text copyright © 2014 Interfund (London) Ltd.
Foreword © 2014 Stephen Gallagher
Preface from *The First Saint Omnibus* (Hodder & Stoughton, October 1939)
Publication History and Author Biography © 2014 Ian Dickerson
All rights reserved.

Published by Thomas & Mercer, Seattle

www.apub.com

ISBN-13: 9781477842737
ISBN-10: 147784273X

Cover design by David Drummond, www.salamanderhill.com

Printed in the United States of America.

To Prosper Buranelli,
A small souvenir of many gallons of pre-Repeal wine,
and many nights of superbly useless argument
which I shall always love to remember

PUBLISHER'S NOTE

FOREWORD TO THE
NEW EDITION

This is how he was, back in the day. Though you wouldn't guess the age of these stories from the style alone.

For me, the Saint of the early 1930s is as modern as the character gets; he's hard, he's principled, he seems to take nothing seriously, but he can turn in a second. It's all an act. And underneath it is a very, very bright guy indeed.

Scratch any "clubland hero" of the era, and underneath the jaunty exterior you'll find a deeply conventional product of Empire, with sport-based principles and an eleven-year-old's grasp of womankind. A public-school background and, most likely, a touch of the aristocracy somewhere in the genealogy. The officer class in civilian life. That's how it was with the Bulldogs and the Tigers and so many other of those dated Hodder Yellow Jacket heroes.

The Saint may have been born within that tradition, but he subverts it in a way that makes him always fresh to the reader. Leslie Charteris kept a deliberate air of mystery around the Saint's early life, but I'm sure that if Simon Templar ever attended a public school, he was kicked out of it. If he saw military service, he achieved single-handed victories while treating orders as optional. And should there be any aristocracy in his bloodline, it would be of the black-sheep, bastard strain.

Think about that one. All the kingly graces and none of the privileges, living by his wits, and living well, with no debt to tradition or the status quo, free to follow his own belief in what constitutes a just world. At ease in the upper echelons of wealth and society, but never at home. One of the reasons you have to love the Saint is that, in the classical/mythological sense, he's a bastard loose in the court. He can move where he chooses, but can never drop his guard.

In *The Saint Goes On* we have three novellas from the character's first decade, two of them originally published under other titles in a British weekly publication, *The Thriller* ("The Paper with a Thousand Thrills"). "The High Fence" was originally titled "The Man Who Knew" and "The Elusive Ellshaw" appeared as "The Race Train Crime," while "The Case of the Frightened Innkeeper" was written for the book.

It was a prolific time for Charteris. These were far from early stories, but the Saint is still very much as the author conceived him. He's yet to be modified by historical change (Charteris did some rethinking of his hero's relationship with authority in the context of the Second World War), the author's success-driven lifestyle (where the globetrotting good life led him to replace familiar London landmarks with more exotic locales), or the blurring of Templar's in-print character with his differing incarnations in radio, film, newspaper comic strips, and eventually TV episodes.

In *The Saint Goes On*, this is the Saint as I've always liked him best. Here, he's a man with a complete disregard for authority and a rigorous code of personal fairness. He lives high on money that he takes from thieves and the greedy rich. He appears to seek a life of luxury and entertainment, while nothing entertains him more than righting an injustice done to an innocent. But every now and again, we get a glimpse of the utter steel underneath. We may get the sense that something really bad happened to him early in life, and it made him who he is. We never find out what that might have been, and it's important that we don't.

This is London between the wars—its street names, its criminal underworld, its Metropolitan police force under Lord Trenchard (whose moustache gets a nod in the text). Whenever Simon Templar has a run-in with the police they're usually represented in the figure of Chief Inspector Claud Eustace Teal, a dour and serious older man whom Simon delights in baiting. Teal endures the teasing with heroic stoicism. Though he's a comic creation, he's no fool and Simon knows it. They're natural opponents in a game with rules, and on rare occasions they can set aside the rules and work as allies when there's a powerful reason to do so. The bottom line, though, is that Templar's disregard for the letter of the law means that Teal wants to see him behind bars. He knows that Simon's personal code makes him capable of anything, including murder.

Then there's Patricia Holm, sometimes described as the Saint's girlfriend, but their relationship is way more subtle and complicated than that. Sex is occasionally implied, but they're not a couple. It's as if Charteris had invented the concept of "friends with benefits" way before anyone else dared to think of it. She'd have him if he were a normal, available guy, but she knows him well—probably better than anyone—and knows that he isn't. Whatever shaped him, it's made that hard core impenetrable. You can get up close—and Patricia Holm gets closer than anyone—but there's no way in. So she dates other men and knows he has flings with other women. Sometimes she worries about him as a mother might. If she were in danger, Simon would move the earth to save her. And God help the person who did her any harm. She doesn't play a featured role in every story, but in these early years she's a consistent thread in Templar's life.

Also appearing here is Hoppy Uniatz, a boneheaded and thickly accented gangster from New York's Lower East Side who serves as the Saint's London sidekick in a number of stories. Hoppy is largely comic relief, loyal to Simon, rendered in broad strokes and mostly defined by his appetites for booze and busting heads. Along with the minor but memorable Orace, a taciturn former military valet who's the caretaker of Simon's country hideaway (and no, he's not featured here), for me these three characters represent the core of the Saint "family."

There were a zillion "Gentlemen Outlaws" in '30s fiction, and none of them had the genes for survival we find in the Saint. That shouldn't be too hard to understand—Leslie Charteris's own description of him as "the Robin Hood of modern crime" pretty much tells us all we need to know.

And then . . . coming up in these pages, there's Junior Inspector Desmond Pryke. He's a bit of a . . . well, just be careful how you pronounce it.

Charteris always knew exactly what he was doing.

—*Stephen Gallagher*

THE SAINT GOES ON

PREFACE

I am rather well aware that the Saint Saga is somewhat noticeably sprinkled with a large number of allusions to the British Public School, the Public School Man, and the Public School Spirit, and that all of these allusions are so conspicuously devoid of proper reverence that it begins to look as if I might have a complex on the subject. But I had to re-read the next story in our collection, which plays the same tune with more than ordinarily concentrated consistency, to realise that the time might be coming when some astute reader would be liable to pounce on me for an explanation of this violent prejudice.

Whereupon I also realised that I should also have to be very cautious in my choice of the explanation I gave, since a study of what I proudly call my fan mail statistics reveals that a large percentage of my most faithful readers are either past or present members of some British Public School.

The more deeply I pondered the various horns of this dilemma, the more clearly I saw the fact that there was positively no explanation I could give (since any definitive explanation must, a priori, involve a statement of my own personal opinions on several broad but very ticklish subjects) that would not be doomed to expose me to the undying hatred of just about as many readers as it would deathlessly endear me to. And I therefore hereby give notice that any future questions addressed to me on the subject will be tactfully but ruthlessly ignored.

But since on this one occasion something inescapably had to be said about it, I have taken refuge in that sublime genius for equivocation and diplomacy which was so tragically stolen from the world of politics when my first publisher accepted my first novel. I propose, as my last public utterance on the matter (until next time) to tell a very short story which is also scripturally true.

This was during one of my last months at one of the Public Schools which we are talking about. The class was devoted to the study of English—a language which, to judge by the curriculum and the hushed whispers in which it was referred to, became extinct quite early in the nineteenth century. The crucial point was an exercise in composition on some dreary subject such as An Appreciation of the Humour of Shakespeare's Clowns.

Feeling, at the time, somewhat full of oats, I had ventured, for perhaps the first time in my academic career, to kick over the traces of what my British Public School considered to be the inviolable commandments of respectable English prose. I was waggish and disrespectful. I pulled the wisecrack and the long nose. I cannot say that I wrote anything that would have held any interest for the passionate commentator; on the other hand, I am equally sure that nobody else in the class did, either. But I am no less certain—even after so many years—that any editor of any popular publication would have read more than the first paragraph of it, which is more than he would have read of any of the other theses submitted.

Returning my opus to me, with many indignant blue-pencillings of my choicest epigrams, and with the lowest marks at his disposal written in the largest figures that there was room for, my instructor peered at me over his spectacles and said severely:

"My advice to you, Charteris, is to confine yourself to the subject you are supposed to be studying, and get rid of the idea that you are starting on some sort of literary career of your own."

—*Leslie Charteris (1939)*

THE HIGH FENCE

1

Apart from the fact that neither of them was a productive or useful member of the community, Johnny Anworth and Sunny Jim Fasson had very little in common. They did not own allegiance to the same Dear Old School; they had no meeting-ground in a passion for the poems of William Wordsworth, no shared devotion to collecting birds' eggs or the rarer kinds of cheese. But the circumstances in which they ceased to adorn their usual places in the files of the Records Office at New Scotland Yard had a connecting link, which must be the chronicler's excuse for reciting them in quick succession.

Johnny Anworth entered a jeweller's shop in Bond Street during the Easter holidays of that year, and omitted to pay for what he took out. He entered through the ceiling, from an apartment on the floor above which he had rented temporarily. It was a pretty neat job, for Johnny was a sound worker in his line, but it had his personality written all over it, and Headquarters put out the routine dragnet and in twenty-four hours duly brought him in.

He was taken to Market Street Police Station, where he was seen by the Divisional Inspector. The awkward part of it from Johnny's point of view was that he had most of the proceeds of his burglary on him when he was caught—at any rate he had all the precious stones, which had been prised out of their settings, carefully packed in a small cardboard box, and done up with brown paper and string. What he had not had time to do was to write an address on the package, and for this reason the DI was very gentle with him.

"You were going to send that stuff to the High Fence, weren't you, Johnny?" he said.

"I dunno wot yer talkin' abaht, guv'nor," answered Johnny mechanically. "I fahnd the stuff lyin' in the gutter in Leicester Square, an' I did it up to send it to the Lost Property Office."

The Divisional Inspector continued to be gentle.

"You've been in the stir six times already," he said, consulting a memorandum on his desk. "If we wanted to be hard on you now, we could have you sent to the Awful Place. You could go to the Moor for seven years, and then have three years' preventive detention waiting for you. On the other hand, if you told us who you were going to send this parcel to, we might forget about those previous convictions and put in a word for you."

Johnny considered this. There is honour among thieves, but it is not designed to resist bad weather.

"Orl right, guv'nor," he said philosophically. "I'll squeal."

This story might have ended there if the station shorthand writer had been available. But he had already gone out to lunch, and the Divisional Inspector was also hungry.

They put Johnny Anworth back in his cell with instructions to order anything he wanted to eat at the DI's expense, and an appointment to make his statement at two o'clock. His lunch, which consisted of roast beef and cabbage, was delivered from a near-by restaurant by an errand-girl who deposited it in the charge-room. Almost as soon as she had gone, after some flirtatious exchanges with the charge-sergeant, it was picked up by the gaoler, who carried it in to Johnny. He was the last man who saw the talented Mr Anworth alive.

The girl had taken the tray from the chef in the kitchen, and no one had stopped her or spoken to her on the way. The chef had had no unusual visitors. The only people in the charge-room when the girl delivered the tray were the gaoler, the charge-sergeant, and Inspector Pryke. And yet, somehow, somewhere on the short journey which Johnny Anworth's last meal had taken, someone had contrived to dope the horseradish sauce with which his plate of roast beef was garnished with enough cyanide to kill a regiment.

The murder was a nine days' wonder which provoked its inevitable quota of headlines, newspaper criticisms, and questions in Parliament. Every inquiry seemed to lead to a dead end. But the Criminal Investigation Department has become phlegmatically accustomed to dead ends, and Chief Inspector Teal was still working methodically on the case, six weeks later, when Mr James Fasson clicked to the tune of five thousand pounds' worth of gems to which he had no legal right whatsoever.

The assets of Sunny Jim Fasson were a smile which made children and hard-boiled business men trust him instinctively, a wardrobe of prosperous-looking clothes, some high-class American luggage plastered with a wonderful collection of expensive cosmopolitan labels, enough ready cash to create an impression of affluence at any hotel where he stayed, and a girlfriend who posed as his wife, sister, niece, or old widowed mother with equal success and distinction.

On this occasion he stayed at the Magnificent, a hotel which he had not previously honoured with his presence. He was a wealthy American on his honeymoon, and for a few days he and his charming wife were quite happy seeing the sights and making a round of the theatres. One day, however, a small rift appeared in their marital bliss.

"I guess she's feelin' kinda homesick, or something," Sunny Jim confided to a clerk at the inquiry desk. "Whaddaya do when your wife gets moody, son?"

"I don't really know, sir," confessed the clerk, who was not employed to answer that kind of inquiry.

"Y'know, I always think a woman wants some kinda kick outa life when she feels that way," mused Sunny Jim. "Some lil thing that makes her feel good with herself. A noo hat, or a fur coat, or—a diamond bracelet . . . That's what she wants!" he cried, recognizing divine inspiration when it breathed on him. "A diamond bracelet! Say, what's the best store in this town to buy a diamond bracelet?"

"Peabody's, in Regent Street, are very good, sir," said the clerk, after a moment's thought.

Sunny Jim beamed.

"Ring 'em up and tell 'em to send some of their best diamond bracelets around," he said. "I'll have the man take 'em right up to her room, and she can pick what she likes. Say, I bet that'll put everything right."

Whether it put everything right or not is a question that the various parties concerned might have answered differently. The hotel was glad enough to oblige such a lavish guest, and Mr Peabody, the jeweller, was so impressed with their brief account of Mr James Fasson that he hurried round in person with six diamond bracelets in his bag. After a short discussion, Mrs Fasson chose the most expensive, a mere trifle valued at a thousand pounds, and Mr Fasson rang for a pageboy to take his cheque for that amount round to the bank to be cashed.

"You must have a drink while you're waitin' for your money," said Sunny Jim, turning to a bottle and a siphon which stood on a side table.

Mr Peabody had a very small drink, and remembered nothing more for another hour, at the end of which time Mr and Mrs Fasson had left the Magnificent for ever, taking all his six diamond bracelets with them. Nor did Mr Peabody's afternoon look any brighter when the bank on which Mr Fasson's cheque had been drawn rang up the hotel to mention that they had never carried an account for anybody of that name.

This episode was the subject of a hurriedly assembled conference in the Assistant Commissioner's room at New Scotland Yard.

The other two men present were Chief Inspector Claud Eustace Teal and Junior Inspector Pryke. Mr Teal, who was responsible for the conference, explained his point of view very briefly.

"Anworth and Fasson used to be fairly well acquainted, and if Anworth was using the High Fence there's a good chance that Fasson will be using him too. I know exactly where I can lay my hands on Sunny Jim, and I want permission to try and get a squeal out of him unofficially."

"What is your objection to having him arrested and questioned in the ordinary way?" asked the Commissioner.

"He'd have to be taken to Market Street, wouldn't he?" meditated Teal aloud. His baby blue eyes hid themselves under studiously sleepy lids. "Well," he said dryly, "because I don't want him murdered."

Junior Inspector Desmond Pryke flushed. He was one of the first graduates of Lord Trenchard's famous Police College, and he usually gave the impression of being very well satisfied with his degree. He was dark, slim, and well-manicured, and the inventor of that classic experiment for turning gentlemen into detectives could certainly have pointed to him as a product who looked nothing like the traditional idea of a policeman. Mr Teal had been heard to thank God that there was no possibility of confusing them, but there were obvious reasons why Mr Teal was irrevocably prejudiced in favour of the old order.

"It's in your manor, Pryke," said the Assistant Commissioner. "What do you think?"

"I don't see what there is to be gained by it," said the other. "If Fasson hasn't been too frightened by the murder of Anworth to talk anyhow—"

"What does Fasson know about the murder of Anworth?" demanded Teal quickly, for the official statements to the Press had contained certain deliberate gaps.

Pryke looked at him.

"I don't suppose he definitely knows any more than any other outsider, but it's common gossip in the underworld that Anworth was murdered because he was going to turn informer."

"You look as if you spent a lot of your time picking up gossip from the underworld," retorted Teal sarcastically. He caught the Assistant Commissioner's chilly eye on him, and went on more politely: "In any case, sir, that's only another reason why I don't want to take him to a police station. I want to try and prevent him thinking that any squeal could be traced back to him."

There was some further discussion, through which Teal sat stolidly chewing a worn-out lump of spearmint, with his round pink face set in its habitual mask of weary patience, and eventually gained his point.

"Perhaps you had better take Inspector Pryke with you," suggested the Commissioner, when he gave his permission.

"I should like to, sir," said Mr Teal, with great geniality, "but I don't know whether this can wait long enough for him to go home and change."

Pryke adjusted the set of his coat delicately as he rose. It was undoubtedly part of a resplendent suit, being of a light fawn colour with a mauve over-check, a very different proposition from Teal's shiny blue serge.

"I didn't know that Police Regulations required you to look like an out-of-work rag and bone man," he said, and Chief Inspector Teal's complexion was tinged with purple all the way to Hyde Park Corner.

He resented having Inspector Pryke thrust upon him, partly because he resented Inspector Pryke, and partly because the High Fence had been his own individual assignment ever since Johnny Anworth put his knife and fork into that fatal plate of roast beef six weeks ago. For a lieutenant, when necessity called for one, Mr Teal preferred the morose and angular Sergeant Barrow, who had never been known to speak unless he was spoken to, and who then spoke only to utter some cow-like comment to which nobody with anything better to do need have listened. Chief Inspector Teal had none of the theoretical scientific training in criminology with which the new graduates of the Police College were pumped to offensive overflowing, but he had a background of thirty years' hard-won experience which took the intrusion of manicured theorists uneasily, and at the entrance of the small apartment building in which Sunny Jim Fasson had been located he said so.

"I want you to keep quiet and let me do the talking," was his instruction. "I know how I'm going to tackle Fasson, and I know how to get what I want out of him."

Pryke fingered his MCC tie.

"Like you've always known how to get what you want out of the Saint?" he drawled.

Mr Teal's lips were tightly compressed as he stumped up the narrow stairway. His seemingly interminable failure to get anything that he really wanted out of that cool, smiling devil who passed so incongruously under the name of the Saint was a thorn in his side which Inspector Pryke had twisted dexterously before. Whenever Chief Inspector Teal attempted to impress the rising generation of detectives with his superior craftsmanship, that gibe could always be brought up against him, openly or surreptitiously, and Mr Teal was getting so tired of it that it hurt. He wished, viciously, that some of the smart infants who were being pushed up under him could have as much to cope with as he had had in his time.

But Sunny Jim Fasson was quite a different problem from the blue-eyed bantering outlaw who had occupied so much of Mr Teal's time in other days, and he felt a renewal of confidence when he saw Sunny Jim's startled face through the slit of the opening door and wedged his foot expertly in the aperture.

"Don't make a fuss, and nobody's going to hurt you, Sunny," he said.

Sunny Jim, like Johnny Anworth, was also a philosopher, in his way. He retreated into the tiny bed-sitting-room without dropping the ash from his cigar.

"What's it about this time, Mr Teal?" he inquired, with the sang-froid of old experience.

He did not even bother to put on his cultivated American accent, which saved him considerable trouble, for he had been born in the Old Kent Road and had learnt all that he knew of America from the movies.

"It needn't be about some diamond bracelets that were stolen from Peabody's—unless you want it to be," said Teal, with equal cold-bloodedness.

Sunny Jim raised his eyebrows. The gesture was mechanical.

"I don't know what you mean, Mr Teal."

"Would you know what I meant," replied the detective, with impregnable drowsiness, "if I told you that Peabody has identified your photograph and is quite sure he can identify you, and half the Magnificent Hotel staff are ready to back him up?"

Sunny Jim had no answer to that.

"Mind you," said Teal, carefully unwrapping a fresh slice of chewing-gum, "I said that we needn't go into that unless you want to. If you had a little talk with me now, for instance—why, we could settle it all here in this room, and you needn't even come with us to the station. It'd be all over and forgotten—just between ourselves."

When Sunny Jim Fasson was not wearing the well-trained smile from which he had earned his nickname, his face fell into a system of hard-bitten lines which drew an illuminating picture of shrewd and sharp intelligence. Those lines became visible now. So far as Sunny Jim was concerned, Teal's speech needed no amplification, and Sunny Jim was a man who believed in the comfort and security of Mr James Fasson first, last, and in the middle. If Teal had arrived half an hour later he would have been on his way to Ostend, but as things were he recognized his best alternative health resort.

"I'm not too particular what I talk about with an old friend, Mr Teal," he said at length.

"Do you sell your stuff to the High Fence, Sunny?" Fasson held his cigar under his nose and sniffed the aroma.

"I believe I did hear of him once," he admitted cautiously. The appearance of bored sleepiness in Chief Inspector Teal's eyes was always deceptive. In the last few seconds they had made a detailed inventory of the contents of the room, and had observed a torn strip of brown paper beside the waste-basket and a three-inch end of string on the carpet under the table.

"You've already got rid of Peabody's diamond bracelets, haven't you?" he said persuasively, and his somnolent eyes went back to Sunny Jim's face and did not shift from it. "All I want to know from you is what address you put on the parcel."

Sunny Jim put his cigar back in his mouth till the end glowed red.

"I did send off a parcel not long ago," he confessed reminiscently. "It was addressed to—"

He never said who it was addressed to.

Mr Teal heard the shot behind him, and saw Sunny Jim's hand jerk to his brow and his head jar with the shock of the bullet. The slam of the door followed, as Teal turned round to it in a blank stupor of incredulity. Pryke, who was nearest, had it open again when his superior reached it and Teal barged after him in a kind of incandescent daze, out on to the landing. The sheer fantastic unexpectedness of what had happened had knocked his brain momentarily out of the rhythm of conscious functioning, but he clattered down the stairs on Pryke's heels, and actually overtook him at the door which let them out on to the street.

And having got there, he stopped, with his brain starting to work again, overwhelmed by the utter futility of what he was doing.

There was nothing sensational to be seen outside. The road presented the ordinary aspect of a minor thoroughfare in the Shepherd Market area at that time of day. There was an empty car parked on the other side of the road, a man walking by with a brief-bag, two women laden down with parcels puttering in the opposite direction, an errand-boy delivering goods from a tricycle. The commonplace affairs of the district were proceeding uninterrupted, the peace of the neighbourhood was unbroken by so much as a glimpse of any sinister figure with a smoking gun shooting off on the conventional getaway.

Teal's dizzy gaze turned back to his subordinate.

"Did you see him?" he rasped.

"Only his back," said Pryke helplessly. "But I haven't the faintest idea which way he went."

Teal strode across to the errand-boy.

"Did you see a man come rushing out of that building just now?" he barked, and the lad looked at him blankly.

"Wot sort of man, mister?"

"I don't know," said Teal, with a feeling that he was introducing himself as the most majestic lunatic in creation. "He'd have been running hell for leather—you must have noticed him—"

The boy shook his head.

"I ain't seen nobody running abaht, not till you come aht yerself, mister. Wot's the matter—'as 'e pinched something?"

Mr Teal did not enlighten him. Breathing heavily, he rejoined Junior Inspector Pryke.

"We'd better get back upstairs and see what's happened," he said shortly.

But he knew only too well what had happened. The murder of Johnny Anworth had been repeated, in a different guise, under his very nose—and that after he had pleaded so energetically for a chance to guard against it. He did not like to think what ecstatic sarabands of derision must have been dancing themselves silly under the smug exterior of Desmond Pryke. He clumped up the stairs and across the landing again in a dumb paroxysm of futile wrath, and went back into the flat.

And there he halted again, one step inside the room, with his eyes bulging out of their sockets and the last tattered remnants of his traditional pose of sleepiness falling off him like autumn leaves from a tree, staring at what he saw as if he felt that the final vestiges of sanity were reeling away from his overheated mind.

2

The body of Sunny Jim Fasson was no longer there. That was the brain-staggering fact which Chief Inspector Teal had to assimilate. It had simply ceased to exist. For all the immediate evidence which Teal's reddening gaze could pick up to the contrary, Sunny Jim Fasson might never have lived there, might never have been interviewed there, and might never have been shot there. The ultimate abysses of interplanetary space could not have been more innocent of any part of Sunny Jim Fasson than that shabby one room flatlet as Teal saw it then. There could hardly have been much less trace of Sunny Jim if he had never been born.

And instead of that, there was someone else sitting in the chair where the bullet had hit Sunny Jim—a man whose mere recollection was enough to raise Chief Inspector Teal's blood pressure to apoplectic heights, a man whose appearance on that spot, at that precise catastrophic moment, turned what might have been an ordinary baffling mystery into something that made Mr Teal's voice fail him absolutely for several seconds.

"Stand up, Saint," he got out at last, in a choking gurgle. "I want you!"

The man peeled himself nonchalantly up from the arm-chair, and managed to convey the impression that he was merely following a course which he had chosen for himself long ago, rather than that he was obeying an order. And Mr Teal glowered at him unblinkingly over every inch of that leisured rise.

To anyone unfamiliar with the dim beginnings and cumulative ramifications of the feud between those two (if anyone so benighted can be imagined to exist in the civilised world) Mr Teal's glower might justifiably have seemed to lack much of the godlike impartiality which ought to smooth the features of a conscientious detective. It was a glower that had no connection with any detached survey of a situation, any abstract weighing of clues and conundrums. It was, to describe it economically, the kind of glower on which eggs can be fried. It was as calorifically biased and unfriendly as a glower can be.

The Saint didn't seem to notice it. He came upright, a lean, wide-shouldered figure in a light grey suit which had a swashbuckling elegance that nothing Inspector Pryke wore would ever have, and met the detective's torrid glare with cool and quizzical blue eyes.

"Hullo, Claud," he murmured. "What are you doing here?"

The detective looked up at him dourly—Teal was not nearly so short as his increasing middle-aged girth made him appear, but he had to look up when the Saint stood beside him.

"I want to know what you're doing here," he retorted.

"I came to pay a call on Sunny Jim," said the Saint calmly. "But he doesn't seem to be here—or did you get here first and knock him off?"

There were times when Mr Teal could exercise an almost superhuman restraint.

"I'm hoping to find out who got here first," he said grimly. "Sunny Jim has been murdered."

23

The Saint raised one eyebrow.

"It sounds awfully exciting," he remarked, and his bantering eyes wandered over to Pryke. "Is this the bloke who did it?"

"This is Junior Inspector Pryke, of C Division," said Mr Teal formally, and the Saint registered ingenuous surprise.

"Is it really?" he murmured. "I didn't know they'd put trousers on the Women Police."

Chief Inspector Teal swallowed hastily, and it is a regrettable fact that a fraction of the inclement ferocity faded momentarily out of his glare. There was no lawful or official reason whatsoever for this tempering of his displeasure, but it was the very first time in his life that he had seen any excuse for the Saint's peculiar sense of humour. He masticated his gum silently for a couple of seconds that gave him time to recover the attitude of mountainous boredom which he was always praying for strength to maintain in the Saint's presence. But his relief was only temporary.

"I suppose you're going to tell me you came to see Fasson just to ask him what he thought about the weather," he said.

"Certainly not," said the Saint blandly. "I wouldn't try to deceive you, Claud. I blew in to see if he knew anything about some diamond bracelets that a bird called Peabody lost this afternoon. I might have pointed out to him that Peabody is very upset about losing those jools. I might have tried to show him the error of his ways, and done my best to persuade him that they ought to be sent back. Or something. But I can't say that I thought of shooting him."

"How did you know he was shot?" Teal cut in.

"My dear fathead, I don't. I merely said that I didn't think of shooting him. Was he shot?"

Teal hesitated for a moment, studying him with that deceptively bovine gaze.

"Yes, he was shot."

"When?"

"Just now."

The bantering blue eyes had an impish twinkle.

"You must have been doing some fast detecting," said the Saint. "Or did somebody tell you?"

Mr Teal frowned at him, shifting his gum from tooth to tooth till he got it lodged behind his wisdoms. His sluggish glance travelled once again over that keen sunburned face, handsome as Lucifer and lighted with an indescribable glimmer of devil-may-care mockery, and he wondered if there would ever be any peace for him so long as he was in the employment of the Law and that amazing buccaneer was on the other side.

For Simon Templar was the incalculable outlaw for whom the routines of criminal investigation had no precedents. He belonged to no water-tight classification, followed no rules but his own, fitted into no definite category in the official scheme of things. He was the Saint: a creation of his own, comparable to nothing but himself. From time to time, desperate creatures of that nebulously frontiered stratosphere commonly called "the Underworld" had gone forth vowing unprintable revenge, and had come back empty-handed—when they came back at all. Many times, Chief Inspector Claud Eustace Teal had thought that all his ambitions would be fulfilled if he could see the Saint safely locked away behind the bars of Larkstone Prison—and yet some of his most spectacular coups could never have been made without the Saint's assistance. And in spite of all the wrath that had been directed on him from these diametrically antagonistic quarters, the Saint had still gone on, a terror to the underworld and a thorn in the side of Scotland Yard, a gay crusader in modern dress who returned from his lawless raids with more booty than any adventurer had ever found before him.

And with all these memories freshened in his mind during that slothful survey, almost against his will, Chief Inspector Teal found himself impotent to believe that the High Fence could be merely another alias of the man before him. It was not psychologically possible. Whatever else could be said about him, the Saint was not a man who sat spinning webs and weaving complex but static mysteries. Everything that he did was active: he would go out to break up the web and take his illicit plunder from the man who wove it, but he wouldn't spin . . . And yet there was the evidence of Teal's own flabbergasted senses, there in that room, to be explained away, and Mr Teal had suffered too much at the Saint's hands to feel that there could ever be any comfortable certainty in the wide world when that incorrigible freebooter was around.

He clasped his pudgy hands behind his back and said, "Sunny Jim was shot in this room, less than five minutes ago. Somebody opened the door and shot him while I was talking to him. He was shot just in time to stop him telling me something I very much wanted to hear. And I want to know what you were doing at that time."

The Saint smiled rather mildly.

"Is that an invitation or a threat?" he inquired.

"It's whichever you like to make it," Teal answered grimly. "Sunny Jim didn't shoot himself, and I'm going to find out who did it."

"I'm sure you are, Claud," said the Saint cordially. "You always do find out these things, with that marvellous brain of yours . . . Have you thought of the High Fence?"

Teal nodded.

"I have."

"What do you know about the High Fence?" demanded Pryke suspiciously.

Simon took out a cigarette-case and looked at him equably.

"This and that. I've been looking for him for some time, you know."

"What do you want with the High Fence, Saint?" asked Mr Teal.

Simon Templar glanced with unwontedly passionless eyes at the chair where Sunny Jim had stopped talking, and smiled with his lips. He lighted a cigarette.

"The High Fence has killed two men," he said. "Wouldn't you like a chance to see him in the dock at the Old Bailey?"

"That isn't all of it," answered the detective stubbornly. "You know as well as I do that the High Fence is supposed to keep a lot of the stuff he buys together, and ship it out of the country in big loads. And they say he keeps a lot of cash in hand as well—for buying."

The glimmer of mockery in the Saint's eyes crisped up into an instant of undiluted wickedness.

"Teal, this is all news to me!"

"You're a liar," said the detective flatly.

He stared at the Saint with all the necessary symptoms of a return of his unfriendly glower, and added, "I know what your game is. You know the High Fence, but you don't know what he does with the stuff he's bought, or where he keeps his money. That's all you want to find out before you do anything about putting him in the dock at the Old Bailey on a charge of murder. And when that time comes, you'll buy a new car and pay some more cash into your bank balance. That's all the interest you have in these two men who've been killed."

"I can't get around to feeling that either of them is an irreparable loss," Simon admitted candidly. "But what's all this dramatic lecture leading to?"

"It's leading to this," said Teal relentlessly. "There's a law about what you're doing, and it's called being an accessory after the fact."

Simon aligned both eyebrows. The sheer unblushing impudence of his ingenuousness brought a premonitory tinge of violet into the detective's complexion even before he spoke.

"I suppose you know what you're talking about, Claud," he drawled. "But I don't. And if you want to make that speech again in a court of law, they'll want you to produce a certain amount of proof. It's an old legal custom." Only for the second time in that interview, Simon looked straight at him instead of smiling right through him. "There's a lot of laws about what you're doing, and they're called slander, and defamation of character, and—"

"I don't care what they're called!"

"But you've got to care," said the Saint reasonably. "After all, you're telling me that a bloke's been shot, and that I did it, or I know something about it. Well, let's begin at the beginning. Let's be sure the bloke's dead. Where's his body?"

In spite of certain superficial resemblances, it can be fairly positively stated that Chief Inspector Teal had never, even in some distant incarnation, been a balloon. But if he had been, and the point of a pin had been strategically applied to the most delicate part of his rotundity, it would have had practically the same effect as the Saint's innocently mooted question. Something that had been holding out his chest seemed to deflate, leaving behind it an expanding and exasperating void. He felt as if someone had unscrewed his navel and his stomach had fallen out.

The cigar which had slipped stupidly out of Sunny Jim's mouth when the bullet hit him was lying on the carpet in front of him, tainting the room with an acrid smell of singeing wool. Teal put his foot on it. It was his only concrete assurance that the whole fantastic affair hadn't been a grotesque hallucination—that the overworked brain which had struggled through so many of the Saint's shattering surprises hadn't finally weighed its anchor and gone wallowing off into senile monsoons of delirious delusion. His lips thinned out in an effort of self-control which touched the borders of homicidal fever.

"That's what I want to know," he said. "The body was here when I went out. When I came in again it had disappeared—and you were here instead. And I think you know something about it."

"My dear Claud," Simon protested, "what d'you think I am—a sort of amateur body-snatcher?"

"I think you're a—"

Simon raised his hand.

"Hush," he said, with a nervous glance at Inspector Pryke. "Not before the lady."

Teal gulped.

"I think—"

"The trouble is," said the Saint, "that you don't. Here you are shooting off your mouth about a body, and nobody knows whether it exists. You wonder whether I could have shot Sunny Jim, when you don't even know whether he's dead. You hint at pinching me for being an accessory after the fact, and you can't produce the fact that I'm supposed to be an accessory to."

"I can prove—"

"You can't. You can't prove anything, except your own daftness. You're doing that now. You ask me what's happened to Sunny Jim's body, with the idea that I must have done something with it. But if you can't produce this body, how d'you know it ever was a body? How d'you know it didn't get up and walk out while you were away? How d'you know any crime's been committed at all?" The Saint's lean forefinger shot out and tapped the detective peremptorily on the waistcoat, just above his watch-chain. "You're going to make a prize idiot of yourself again, Claud, if you aren't very careful, and one of these days I shall be very angry with you. I put up with the hell of a lot of persecution from you—"

"Will you stop that?" barked Mr Teal, jerking his tummy hysterically back from the prodding finger.

The Saint smiled.

"I am stopping it, dear old pumpkin," he pointed out. "I've just told you that my patience is all wore out. I'm not taking any more.

29

Now you go ahead and think out your move. Do you take a chance on running me in for murdering a bloke that nobody can prove was murdered, and stealing a corpse that nobody can prove is a corpse—or do you phone for your photographers and finger-print fakers and leave me out of it?"

Glowering at him in a supercharged silence that strained against his ribs, Mr Teal thought of all the things he would have liked to do, and realized that he could do none of them. He was tied up in a knot which there was no visible way of unravelling. He had seen similar knots wound round him too often to cherish any illusions on that score—had gorged his spleen too often on the maddeningly confident challenges of that debonaire picaroon to hope that any amount of thought could make this one more digestible.

It was air-tight and water-tight. It was as smooth as the Saint's languid tantalizing voice. It located the one unanswerable loophole in the situation and strolled through it with as much room to spare as an ant going through the Arc de Triomphe. It was exactly the sort of thing that the Saint could always be relied upon to do.

The knowledge soaked down into Mr Teal's interior like a dose of molten lead. The ancient duel was embarking upon the umpteenth round of a series which seemed capable of going on into eternity, and the prospect seemed as hopeless as it had always seemed. If Mr Teal had any formulated idea of hell, it was something exactly like that— an endless succession of insoluble riddles that he had to try to solve, while the Saint's impudent forefinger and the Assistant Commissioner's disparaging sniff worked in alternate relays to goad his thoughts away from the last relics of coherence. And there were moments when he wondered if he had already died without knowing, and was already paying for his long-forgotten sins.

"You can go, for the present," he said smoulderingly. "I'll find you again when I want you."

"I'm afraid you will," said the Saint sadly, and adjusted the brim of his hat to the correct piratical angle. "Well, I'll be seein' ya, Claud Eustace . . ." He turned his vague, unspeakably mischievous smile on to Junior Inspector Pryke, who had been standing sulkily mute since he was last noticed. "And you too, Sweet Pea," he said hopefully.

Chief Inspector Claud Eustace Teal watched his departure with malignant gloom. It was discouragingly reminiscent of too many other Saintly exits that Mr Teal had witnessed, and he had a very apathetic interest in the flashlight photography and finger-print dusting which he had to superintend during the next hour or two.

For those records were made only at the dictation of a system in which Mr Teal was too congenitally rut-sunk to question. There was a fire-escape within easy reach of the bathroom window which had more to tell than any number of photographs of an empty chair from which an unproven corpse had disappeared.

Sunny Jim Fasson had been shot at by somebody who had opened the door of the flatlet while Mr Teal was interrogating him, the same somebody who had found means of silencing Johnny Anworth on the verge of an identically similar squeak, after which Fasson had vanished off the face of the earth. And Teal had a seething conviction that the only living man who knew every secret of what had happened was walking free in the Saint's custom-built shoes.

The Assistant Commissioner was very polite.

"But it has possibly failed to occur to you," he commented, "that this is the sort of thing news editors pray for."

"If you remember, sir," Pryke put in smugly. "I was against the idea from the first."

"Quite," said the Commissioner. "Quite." He was a man who had won his appointment largely on the qualification of a distinguished career of pig-sticking and polo-playing with the Indian Army, and he was inclined to sympathize with the officer whom he regarded as a pukka sahib, like himself. "But you went with Mr Teal, and you may know why Templar was not at least arrested on suspicion."

"On suspicion of what?" demanded Teal wildly. "The worst you could prove is that he abetted Fasson's escape, and that means nothing, because Fasson hadn't even been arrested."

Pryke nibbled his thumb-nail.

"I believe that if we could account for the Saint, the rest of the mystery would be settled," he said.

"Mr Teal has been trying to account for the Saint for several years," the Assistant Commissioner reminded him acrimoniously.

What Mr Teal wanted to say would have reduced Scotland Yard to a small pool of steaming lava.

3

Simon Templar sauntered around the corners of a couple of blocks, and presently waited by the kerb while a big grey saloon cruised slowly up towards him. As it came level, he stepped neatly on to the running-board, opened the nearest door, and sank into the seat beside the driver. As if the upholstery on which he deposited his weight had had some direct connexion with the accelerator, the car picked up speed again and shot away into the traffic with its engine purring so smoothly that the leap of the speedometer needle seemed an absurd exaggeration.

With her small deft hands on the steering-wheel nosing a way through the traffic stream where no one else but the Saint himself would have seen a way visible, Patricia Holm took her eyes momentarily from the road to glance at him helplessly.

"What on earth," she inquired, "are we playing at?"

The Saint chuckled.

"Is the game puzzling you, old darling?"

"It's doing its best." She took his cigarette away from between his fingers while she thrust the murmuring grey car under the snout of a speeding lorry with the other hand. "You come down this way to see

Fasson about some diamonds. You and Hoppy go in to see him. After a while Hoppy comes out with a body, and a long time after that you come out yourself, looking as if you'd just heard the funniest story of your life. Naturally I'm beginning to wonder what we're playing at."

Simon took out his cigarette-case and replaced his stolen smoke.

"I suppose you aren't so wide of the mark, with the funny story angle," he admitted. "But I thought Hoppy would have put you on the trail."

He slewed round to cock an eyebrow at the passenger who rode in the back seat, but the passenger only gazed back at him with troubled blankness and said, "I dunno what de game is, neider, boss."

Hoppy Uniatz had never been really beautiful, even as a child, and the various contacts which his face had had with blunt instruments since then had not improved it. But it has sometimes been known for such faces to be lighted with a radiance of spirituality and intellect in which their battered irregularity of contour is easily forgotten.

The physiognomy of Mr Uniatz was illuminated by no such light. Reluctant as Simon Templar always was to disparage such a faithful friend, he could never honestly claim for Mr Uniatz any of those intellectual qualities which might have redeemed his other failings. A man of almost miraculous agility on the draw, of simple and unquestioning loyalties, of heroic appetite, and of a tank-like capacity for absorbing incredible quantities of every conceivable blend of alcohol—yes, Mr Uniatz possessed all those virtues. But a strenuous pursuit of most of the minor rackets of the Bowery had never left him time to develop the higher faculties of that curious organization of reactions which can only apologetically be called his brain. Simon Templar perceived that Mr Uniatz could not have enlightened anybody. He was in painful search of enlightenment himself.

Simon dropped an arm over the back of the seat and hauled up another hitherto invisible passenger, on whom Mr Uniatz had been thoughtlessly resting his feet.

"This is Sunny Jim, Pat," he explained.

"Hoppy did manage to tell me that much," said Patricia Holm with great patience. "But did you really have to bring him away?"

"Not really," said the Saint candidly, allowing the passenger to drop back again on to the floor. "But it struck me as being quite a good idea. You see, Sunny Jim is supposed to be dead."

"How do you know he isn't?"

Simon grinned.

"There might be some argument about it," he conceded. "At any rate, he's among the Saints."

"But what was it all about?"

The Saint lighted his cigarette and stretched himself out.

"Well, it was this way. Hoppy and I blew up the fire-escape, as arranged, and went in through the bathroom window. When we got inside, what should we hear but the voice of good old Claud Eustace Teal, holding converse with Sunny Jim. Apparently Claud was just on the point of getting a squeak out of him, and I was just getting down to the keyhole to take a look at the séance and hear what Sunny had to say, when a gun went off and broke up the party. As far as I've been able to make out, somebody opened the front door and took a pot at Sunny Jim at the crucial moment, and Teal went chasing the assassin down the stairs, along with a perfectly twee little policebody from Eton that he had with him."

Simon drew at his cigarette with a reminiscent smile, while the grey car whirled around Piccadilly Circus and plunged down the Haymarket.

"Anyway, Hoppy and I beetled in while they were away, and took a gander at Sunny Jim. And as a matter of fact, he isn't dead, though he's had the narrowest shave that any man ever had, and his head's going to ring carillons when he wakes up. He's been creased as neatly as I've ever seen it done—the bullet just parted his hair in a new place and knocked him out, but his skull hasn't any holes in it. That's when I had my brilliant idea."

"I was hoping we'd get to that," said the girl.

"But haven't you seen it already?" Simon demanded. "Look at what I've told you. Here's Sunny Jim preparing to squeal, and somebody tries to rub him out. Why? Squealers don't get bumped off, not in this country, just because they may have a little tit-bit to give away. Sunny Jim must have known something worth knowing, and there he was, sitting in his chair, out to the world, and nobody to get in our way. The bumper-offer can't be sure what's happened to him, and Claud Eustace is probably quite sure he's dead. But nobody knows . . . Isn't it all pretty obvious?"

"It's getting clearer."

"Of course it is! I tell Hoppy to grab the body and hustle it down the fire-escape, out to this car, and pick me up later. And I wait for Claud Eustace and his boy friend. We exchange the compliments of the season, and have lots of fun and games together. And then I walk out. As soon as the next editions are on the streets, the bumper-offer is going to know that his body disappeared while I was around, and he's going to work himself into seven different kinds of cold sweat wondering whether it is a body. He may guess that it isn't, and itch to bump me off for what I may have found out from it, but he can't do that because if I got killed he'd never know what had happened to the body and where it might turn up next. Doesn't that make you see the joke?"

Patricia nodded slowly.

"But who," she said, "was the bumper-offer?"

"Who else could it be," asked the Saint, "but our old friend that all the excitement and bubble is about—the High Fence?"

There were adequate grounds for the outbreak of official excitement and bubble which had been provoked by the man who was known only by that unusual name.

A fence, in the argot, is nothing to do with steeplechasing or an enclosure containing sheep. He is the receiver of stolen goods, the capitalist of crime, and incidentally the middle-man but for whose functioning larceny in most of its forms would soon die a natural death. He runs less risk than any of the actual stealers, and makes much bigger profits. And very often he takes his cut both ways, making his profit on the receipt of stolen goods and betraying the stealers to a friendly detective at the same time.

The fence is a member of an unchartered union, the only code of which is to pay as little for a purchase as the vendor can be persuaded to accept.

Seven or eight months ago, the invisible tentacles of the CID, which spread wider and more delicately than many of its critics would believe, touched on the rumour of a man who violated that rule. He bought nothing but metals and precious stones, and paid twice as much for them as any other receiver in London was offering. By contenting himself with a hundred per cent profit instead of three hundred per cent he could well afford to do it, but it is a curious fact that no other receiver before him has thought of such a scandalously unethical expedient. And through the strange subterranean channels in which such gossip circulates, the word went round that he was "good."

Because of the prices he paid, they called him the High Fence, but nobody knew anything more about him. He had no shop where he conducted his business. Anything that was offered to him for sale had to be sent through the post, to an accommodation address which was changed every week. The address was passed round the limited circle of his clients by word of mouth, and it was impossible to find out who first put it into circulation. Every client had always "heard about it" from another—the trail turned inevitably into a hopeless merry-go-round. Nor was the circle of initiates unrestricted. It was a jealously closed ring of talent which the High Fence picked for himself, and queer things were rumoured to have happened to those who had ventured to spread the good news among their friends without permission. To those who were tempted by circumstances to talk to the CID, even queerer things could happen—as we have shown.

The High Fence might never have encountered a serious setback, if there had not been one outlaw in England for whom queer happenings had no terrors, and to whom the scent of booty was the supreme perfume in the breath of life.

"I'm afraid Claud Eustace has a depressingly cynical idea of what I'm up to," said the Saint. "He thinks I know who the High Fence is—in which he's flattering me too much, and I wish he wasn't. And he thinks that all I'm wanting is to find out where this bird keeps his boodle and his cash, so that I can take it off him before he gets pinched."

"In which he's perfectly right."

The Saint sighed.

"I don't know where you get these ideas from," he said in a pained voice. "By the way, are you going anywhere in particular, or are we just sightseeing?"

"I'm waiting for you to tell me."

"Let's go to Abbot's Yard—it's about the only hide-out we have left that isn't in Teal's address-book. And I don't think Sunny Jim is going to be too keen on seeing callers for a while."

He relaxed at full length, with his eyes half closed against the smoke curling past them from his cigarette, while she circled Sloane Square and headed west along the King's Road. The soft waves of her fair golden head rippled in the gentle stir of air that came through the windows; her face was as calmly beautiful as if she had been driving them on nothing more innocuous than the commonplace sightseeing tour which he had mentioned. Perhaps she was only calm because even the most adventurous girl, after some years of partnership with such a man, must achieve permanent nonchalance or perish of nervous exhaustion, but one never knew . . . And in the back of the car, Mr Uniatz and Mr Fasson were both, in their respective ways, silently unconscious.

The car threaded its way more slowly through the clotted congestion of trucks, omnibuses, vans, and drays with which the King's Road is permanently constipated, and turned off abruptly into a narrow side street composed of cottage hovels with freshly painted and utterly dilapidated fronts in approximately equal proportions. It was one of those Chelsea backwaters which are undergoing a gloomy degradation from honest slumdom to synthetic Bohemianism, and the external symptoms of its decay gave it an air of almost pathetic indecision, like a suburban bank manager on a spree in the high spots, who is trying to make up his mind whether to be thoroughly folksy or very dignified, but who is quite certain that he is as sober and important as any of his co-revellers. But in spite of this uninviting aspect, it contained a comfortable studio which the Saint had found useful before, and Simon roused himself cheerfully to open the door beside him as the car stopped.

"I think it's a case for the wheel-chair and blanket," he said, after a judicial survey of Sunny Jim.

The transportation of an unconscious captive across a London pavement is not quite such an easy and automatic affair as the credulous reader of fiction may have been deluded to believe, but Simon Templar had had such problems to solve before. On one of the rare occasions on which Mr Uniatz did not find it necessary to delay the proceedings with unnecessary questions, he hopped intelligently out of the car and opened the door of the studio with a key which the Saint threw at him. After a brief absence, he returned with an invalid chair, Simon took the folded blanket from the seat, and between them they wrapped the limp figure of Sunny Jim Fasson tenderly up in it—so tenderly that there was not enough of him left protruding for any stray passerby to recognize. In this woolly cocoon they carried him to the chair, and in the chair wheeled him up the steps and into the house, with all the hushed solicitude of two expectant nephews handling a rich and moribund uncle. And, really, that was all about it.

"There is beer in the pantry," said the Saint, subsiding into a chair in the studio. "But don't let Hoppy see it, or I never shall. Hoppy, you get a sponge of cold water and see if you can bring the patient round."

"He does wake up, once," said Mr Uniatz reminiscently. "In de car. But I club him wit' de end of my Betsy and he goes to sleep again."

Simon gazed after him resignedly, and sipped the glass of Carlsberg which Patricia brought to him. A sense of tact and diplomacy could well be added to the other virtues in which Mr Uniatz was so unfortunately deficient. Hoping to extract information from a man by presenting oneself to him as his saviour and honorary guardian angel, one endeavours to calm the aching brain. One tends the wounds. One murmurs consolation and soothing comfort. One does not, intelligently, greet him on his first return to consciousness by clubbing him with the blunt end of a Betsy. It rather ruled out the potentialities of guile and cunning, but the Saint was equally prepared for the alternative.

He finished his cigarette at leisure while Mr Uniatz applied his belated ministrations, and presently an inaugural groan from the invalid chair brought him up to take over the management of the interview.

"Welcome, stranger," he said genially.

4

Sunny Jim Fasson did not seem happy. It is not over-stimulating for any man with less solid bone in his head than a Mr Uniatz to first have his skull grazed by a bullet, and then at the first sign of recovery from that ordeal to be slugged over the ear with a gun-butt, and certainly much of the sunshine from which Sunny Jim had once taken his nickname was missing from his countenance. With the damp traces of Hoppy's first-aid practice trickling down his nose and chin, he looked more like a picture of November Day than one of Hail, Smiling Morn.

It was perhaps discouraging that the first person he saw when he blinked open his eyes was Hoppy Uniatz. He stared at him hazily for a moment, while his memory worked painfully back to its last association with that homely face, and then, remembering all, he half rose from the chair and lashed out with his fist. That also was discouraging, for Mr Uniatz had won his scars in a vocation where the various arts of violence are systematized to the ultimate degree: he hopped aside from the blow with an agility that gave an unexpected meaning to his name, and in another split second he had caught Sunny Jim's wrist and twisted it firmly up behind his back.

He looked round at the Saint with a beam of justifiable pride, like a puppy that has performed its latest trick. If he had had a tail, he would have wagged it.

"Okay, boss?" he queried. "Or do I give him de heat?"

"That remains to be seen," said the Saint imperturbably. He picked up the sponge and weighed it meditatively in his hand. "Is your brain working again, Sunny, or would you like another refresher?"

Fasson glowered at him sullenly, with a hint of fear in his eyes.

"What do you want?" he snarled.

"Personally, I only want a little talk." Simon weighed the sponge again, and dropped it back in the basin. "But Hoppy seems to have other ideas. By the way, have you met Hoppy? This is Mr Uniatz, Jim—a one hundred per cent American from Poland."

"I know him," said Fasson viciously. "He hit me over the head with his gun."

"So he tells me," agreed the Saint, with some regret. "Otherwise this little chat of ours might have been much more amicable. But he's quite a tough guy in his way, is Hoppy, and he's got a kind of natural habit of hitting people with his gun—either with one end or the other. Do you know what he means when he talks about giving you the heat?"

Sunny Jim did not answer. Studying that suspicious surly face from which all the artificial sunshine had been removed, Simon realized that the friendly *conversazione* which he had had in mind at the beginning would have wanted a lot of organizing, even without Hoppy's intervening indiscretion.

"Well, he might mean one of two things, Sunny. He might mean taking you for a ride—ferrying you out to some nice secluded spot and dropping you in a ditch with a tummy-full of liver pills. Or he might mean just making himself sort of unpleasant—twisting your arm off, or burning your feet, or some jolly little romp like that. I never know, with Hoppy. He gets such fascinating ideas. Only the other day, he got hold of a fellow he didn't care for and tied him out on an iron bedstead and burnt candles under the springs—the bloke was awfully annoyed about it."

"Who are you?" rasped Fasson shakily.

The Saint smiled.

"Templar is the name, dear old bird. Simon Templar. Of course, there are all sorts of funny rumours about my having another name— people seem to think I'm some sort of desperado called . . . let me see, what is it?"

The fear in Sunny Jim's eyes brightened into a sudden spark of panic.

"I know who you are," he said. "You're the Saint!"

Simon raised his eyebrows innocently.

"The very name I was trying to remember. People think—"

"You're the High Fence!"

Simon shook his head.

"Oh, no. You're wrong about that."

"You're the swine who tried to shoot me just now."

"Wrong again, brother. When I try to shoot people, they don't usually have a chance to be rude to me afterwards. But don't let's talk about unpleasant things like that." The Saint flipped out his cigarette-case and put a smoke between his lips. "Let's be friendly as long as we can. I didn't shoot you, but I happened into your place just after the shooting. I sort of felt that you couldn't be feeling too happy about the way things were going, so I shifted you out of there. But I still think we ought to have a talk."

Fasson's shifty eyes travelled round the room, and came back to the Saint's face. He answered through his teeth.

"I can't tell you anything."

"Perhaps you haven't quite recovered yet," said the Saint persuasively. "After all, you were going to tell Chief Inspector Teal something. By the way, have you met Mr Uniatz? Only the other day—"

"I don't know anything!"

Hoppy Uniatz shuffled his feet. It is improbable that more than two consecutive words of the conversation which has just been recorded had percolated through the protective layers of ivory that encased his brain, but he had a nebulous idea that time was being wasted, and he could not see why.

"Do I give him de heat, boss?" he inquired hopefully.

Simon inhaled thoughtfully, and Mr Uniatz, taking silence for an answer, strengthened his grip. Fasson's face twisted and turned pale.

"Wait a minute!" he gasped shrilly. "You're breaking my arm!"

"That's too bad," said the Saint concernedly. "What does it feel like?"

"You can't do this to me!" shrieked Sunny Jim. "He'd kill me! You know what happened just now—"

"I know," said the Saint coolly. "But there are lots of different ways of dying. Hoppy knows no end of exciting ones, and I've tried to warn you about him. I don't really want to have to let him go ahead with what he's wanting to do, instead of just playing at it as he is now, but if you've absolutely made up your mind . . ."

Sunny Jim gulped. The sharp agony in his shoulder, where Hoppy Uniatz's powerful leverage was exerting itself, made the other unpleasant possibilities which the Saint had hinted at seem frightfully close at hand, but he could not find a shadow of pity or remorse in the clear blue eyes that were studying him with the dispassionate curiosity of an entomologist watching the wriggling of a captured insect.

"Do you want me to be murdered?" he sobbed.

"I shouldn't weep at your funeral," Simon confessed cold-bloodedly. "But I shouldn't look at things so pessimistically, if I were you. We could probably look after you for a bit, if you told us anything worth knowing—we might even get you out of the country and send you away for a holiday in the South of France until the excitement's all over. But you've got to spill what you know first, and I'm waiting for it to dawn on you that you'll either talk voluntarily or else we'll put you through the mangle and wring it out of you."

His voice was casual and almost kindly, but there was something so tireless and inflexible behind it that Sunny Jim shivered. He was no hot-house flower himself, but in the circles where he moved there were stories about the Saint, brought in by men who had met that amazing buccaneer to their misfortune—legends that told of a slim bantering outlaw whose smile was more deadly than any other man's anger, who faced death with a jest and sent men into eternity with his flippant farewell ringing in their ears . . . The pain in his shoulder sharpened under Hoppy's impatient hands, and he saw that the Saint's dark lawless face was quite impassive, with the trace of an old smile lingering absentmindedly on the reckless lips . . .

"Damn you!" he whimpered. "I'll talk . . . But you've got to let me go."

"Tell me something first."

Fasson's breath came in a grating sigh.

"The Kosy Korner—in Holborn—"

Simon blew a couple of smoke-rings, and nodded to Mr Uniatz.

"Okay, Hoppy," he said. "Give him a rest."

Hoppy Uniatz released his grip, and wiped his palms down his trousers. Insofar as his gargoyle features were capable of expressing such an emotion, he looked shocked. As one who had himself kept an iron jaw under everything that could be handed to him in the back rooms of more than one station house in his own country, the spectacle of a guy who came apart under a mere preliminary treatment filled him with the same half-incredulous disgust that an English gentleman feels on meeting a cad who is not interested in cricket.

"I guess dese Limeys can't take it, boss," he said, groping through genuine puzzlement to the only possible conclusion.

Sunny Jim glared at him in vengeful silence. His face was white with pain, and his shoulder really felt as if it had been dislocated. He rubbed it tenderly, while Simon recovered his beer and sat on the edge of the table.

"Well?" Simon prompted him gently.

"I don't know anything much. I've told you—"

"Have you traded with the High Fence before?"

"Yes." Sunny Jim sat hunched in his chair, shrugging his shoulder gingerly in an occasional effort to reassure himself that the joints were still articulating. The words dragged reluctantly through his mouth. "That's how I know. I wanted to know who the High Fence was. I sent him some stuff once, and waited outside the address to see who picked it up. I saw who took it. I started to tail him, but then I got picked up by a split, and I lost him while we were talking."

"But?"

"I saw him again the next day, by accident. In this restaurant."

"The Kosy Korner?"

Fasson nodded, and licked his lips.

"Can I have a drink?" he asked hoarsely.

The Saint made a sign to Hoppy, who abandoned his futile attempt to drain non-existent dregs out of the bottle from which Simon had refilled his glass, and left the room. The Saint's cool blue eyes did not leave Sunny Jim's face.

"And what happened there?"

Fasson got out of his chair and limped around the table, rubbing his head dazedly.

"This fellow shoved the packet in the pocket of an overcoat that was hanging on the rail—"

At that moment he was beside the empty bottle which Mr Uniatz had put down, and for once Simon Templar's understanding was a fraction of a second slow. He did not clearly comprehend what was happening until the neck of the bottle was clutched in Sunny Jim's fist, swinging up and spinning away from the hand with vicious speed.

With an instinct that was swifter than any reasoned understanding, he ducked his head and felt the cold graze of the glass stroking past his ear before it splintered on the wall behind him with an explosive smash, but that automatic movement of self-preservation lost him a vital second of time. He rolled off the table and leapt for the door, only to have it slammed in his face, and when he had wrenched it open again Sunny Jim's footsteps were clattering wildly down the second flight of stairs.

Sunny Jim Fasson tore out into the narrow street and started to run down towards the bright lights of the main thoroughfare. He didn't know exactly where he was going, but he knew that his one broad object was to remove himself as quickly as possible from the city where so many deadly things had begun to happen in one evening. Chance had given him one infinitesimal spark of knowledge that he should not have possessed, normal psychology had tempted him to use it in the purchase of his freedom when Chief Inspector Teal had called, but he had not thought of the retribution. Of what had happened since that brain-dulling bullet grazed across his head he preferred not to think, but he had a foggy idea that whichever way he turned in that perilous tangle would lead him into new dangers. He had had one warning that day. To be killed for squealing, to be tortured and perhaps killed for not squealing—he saw nothing but trouble in every prospect that was offered to him, except the one primitive remedy of frantic flight. He stumbled into the King's Road with his chest heaving, and hesitated on the corner in a moment's ghastly indecision . . . A motor-cycle with a particularly noisy exhaust had started up behind him, but he did not think to look round. It seemed to backfire twice in quick succession, and a tearing shattering agony beside which Hoppy Uniatz's third degree was a fleabite crashed into his back and sent him sprawling blindly forward into the gutter . . .

Simon Templar stood in the half-open doorway and saw the motor-cycle whip round the corner and vanish with its engine roaring. He was aware that Hoppy Uniatz was breathing heavily down his neck, making strange grunting noises in an ecstasy of impatience to get past him.

"Lemme go after him an' give him de woiks, boss," he was pleading. "I'll get him, sure."

The Saint's fingers were still curled over the butt of his own gun, which he had not had time to draw.

"You're too late, Hoppy," he said quietly. "He's got the works."

He stepped back into the hall and moved aside to let Mr Uniatz look out. A small crowd was gathering round the spread-eagled shape on the corner, and the wail of a police whistle drifted faintly over the rumble of untroubled traffic. Simon closed the door again.

"So ya had him on de spot," said Mr Uniatz, with proper admiration. "Chees, boss, you got it all on de top storey. Howja know he was gonna take a powder?"

"I didn't," said the Saint evenly, and went back up the stairs to Patricia.

He knew of nobody who would mourn the passing of Sunny Jim for long, and his own regret for the untimely accident was as sincere as anyone's.

"We'll be moving, kid," he said. "Sunny Jim has clocked out."

"Did you shoot him?"

He shook his head.

"That was the mistake Hoppy made. But I hadn't any reason to. There was a bloke waiting outside on a motor-bike, and he got him—it may have been the High Fence himself. I thought this address was our own secret, but somebody else seems to have got on to it. So we'll move on." He lighted another cigarette and trickled an airy feather of smoke through his lips, while Hoppy came plodding up to join them, and she saw that his blue eyes were as bright and cold as steel. "We've lost our insurance policy, old dear. But there may be something better than an insurance policy at the Kosy Korner, and I'm going to find out what it is if I eat there till I'm poisoned!"

5

Of the millions of people who read of the vanishing and double murder of Sunny Jim Fasson at their breakfast-tables the next morning—the ingredients of the case were sensational enough to give it a place on the front page of every newspaper that had a front page—a certain Mr Clive Enderby was not the least perturbed.

Nobody who saw him going to his office that morning would have thought it. Nobody who looked at him with a cynical eye would have suspected him of ever being perturbed about anything. Nobody would have suspected him of thinking about anything. Pottering down the steps of his old-fashioned apartment in Ladbroke Grove, he looked like a typical middle-aged British businessman.

He was rather thin and long-faced, a little stooped about the shoulders, a little flat about the feet, a little under-exercised about the stomach. These things were not positive characteristics, but rather vague and diffident tendencies: to have been positive about anything would have been bad form, a vulgar demonstration in which only temperamental foreigners (a subhuman species) indulged. He wore a respectable bowler hat, and although it was clear and warm, a dark overcoat and brown kid gloves, because the calendar had not yet announced the official advent of summer. He rode to Holborn Circus on a bus, ingesting his current opinions on every subject under the sun from the *Morning Post*. No one would have believed that under the crown of that respectable and unemphatic derby he held the key to a riddle that was working Scotland Yard into a lather of exasperation.

From Holborn Circus he walked to Hatton Garden. His office was on the third floor of a sombre building just off that most un-horticultural preserve, where the greatest jewel business in the world is conducted by nondescript men at street corners and over the tables of adjacent cafés and public houses. It consisted of no more than a couple of shabby unpretentious rooms, but a surprising volume of trade in precious stones passed through it. For three hours Mr Enderby was fully occupied, in his slow-moving way, poring over an accumulation of letters and cables from all parts of the world, and dictating stodgy replies to his unattractive secretary, who could have coped efficiently with two hundred and fifty words a minute, but in Mr Enderby's, employment had never been strained to a higher average than ten.

At a quarter past twelve he had a telephone call.

"Where are you lunching?" asked the voice.

Mr Enderby showed no surprise or puzzlement at being bluntly addressed with such a question by a caller who did not even announce his identity.

"I thought of going to the Kosy Korner again," he said primly.

He had a voice rather like an apologetic frog.

"That'll do," said the receiver, after a moment's thought, and a click terminated the conversation without further ceremony.

Mr Enderby put down the telephone and ponderously finished dictating the letter in which he had been interrupted. He got up, put on his bowler hat and his superfluous overcoat, and went out. On his way through Hatton Garden he stopped and bought two stones from an acquaintance on the pavement, wrapping them in bits of tissue-paper and tucking them away in his waistcoat pocket.

The Kosy Korner is one of those glorified tea-rooms run by impoverished dowagers of stupendous refinement with which the central areas of London are infested. At the time when Mr Enderby arrived there, it was already well filled with an assortment of business men, clerks, stenographers, and shop assistants, all apparently yearning after a spot of Kosiness to stimulate their digestion of that exquisite roast beef and boiled cabbage which has made English cooking famous among gourmets the world over. Mr Enderby filtered through the mob to a groaning coat-rack already laden with the outer garments of other customers, where he parked his bowler hat and overcoat. He sat in a vacant chair and ate his meal as if it were a necessary evil, a dull routine business of stoking his interior with the essential fuel for continued functioning, reading the *Morning Post* between mouthfuls and paying no attention to anyone else in the place. He washed the repast down with a cup of tea, folded his paper, paid his bill, pushed two coppers under the plate, and got up. He took down his hat from the rack and sorted out his overcoat. There was a small parcel in one side pocket, as he felt when he fished out his gloves, which had not been there when he hung up the coat, but even this did not make him register any surprise. He did not even take it out to see what it was.

Back in his office, Mr Enderby spoke to his secretary.

"I had a large order at lunch for some stones to go to America," he said. "They will have to catch the *Oceanic* tomorrow. Will you ring up the insurance company and make the usual arrangements?"

While she was at the telephone, he broke open the parcel from his overcoat pocket and spilled a small handful of diamonds on to his blotter. He looked at them for a moment, and then turned to the safe behind his desk. It was a comparatively new one of the very latest design, a huge gleaming hulk of steel which would have seemed more at home in a bank vault than in that dingy room. He set the two combinations, turned a key in the lock, and swung back the massive door. There was nothing on the shelves but a couple of cheap cardboard boxes. He took them out and tipped their contents on to the blotter also, submerging the first sprinkle of diamonds which he had put down. A solid heaped cone of glittering wealth, diamonds, emeralds, sapphires, and rubies, iridescent with all the colours of the rainbow, winked up at him.

"That will be all right, Mr Enderby," said his secretary. "They're sending a man round right away."

Mr Enderby nodded, and dragged his eyes away from the pile of jewels to glance at the cheap tin clock on the mantelpiece. He was not, as we have seen, very interested in food, but for more years than he could remember he had had a passionate interest in drink. And the hour had not yet struck when such Satanic temptations are officially removed from a nation which would otherwise be certain to spend all its afternoons in drunken debauchery.

"I must leave you to pack them up and attend to the formalities, Miss Weagle," he said. "I have—er—another appointment."

Miss Weagle's stoat-like face did not move a single impolite muscle, although she had listened to a similar ritual every working day for the past five years, and knew perfectly well where Mr Enderby's appointment would be kept. She was not even surprised that he should leave such a collection of gems in her care, for the casualness with which diamond traders handle huge fortunes in stones is only incredible to the layman.

"Very well, Mr Enderby. What is the value of the shipment?"

"Twenty-seven thousand six hundred and fifty pounds," replied Mr Enderby, after an almost imperceptible deliberation, and he knew his business so well that the most expert and laborious valuation could not have disputed his snap assessment by more than a five-pound note.

He put on his bowler hat and overcoat again, and paddled thirstily out to the streets, mumbling an apology to the red-faced walrus-moustached man whom he had to squeeze past at the top of the narrow stairs, and the walrus-moustached man gazed after him with thoughtful blue eyes which would have seemed incongruously keen and clear if Mr Enderby had noticed them.

The Saint went back across the landing as Mr Enderby's footsteps died away, and knocked on the door of the office.

"I'm from the insurance company," he said, when Miss Weagle had let him in.

"About the jewels?"

"Yes."

With his walrus moustache and air of disillusioned melancholy, he reminded Miss Weagle of her mother.

"You've been quick," she said, making conversation when she ought to have been making love.

"I was out on a job, and I had to ring up the office from just round the corner, so they told me to come along," Simon explained, wiping his whiskers on his sleeve. He had spent three hours putting on that ragged growth, and every hair was so carefully planted that its falsehood could not have been detected at much closer quarters than he was ever likely to get to with Miss Weagle. He glanced at the little heap of gems, which Miss Weagle had been packing into another cardboard box lined with cotton-wool, "Are these them?" he asked.

Miss Weagle admitted coyly that those were them. Simon surveyed them disinterestedly, scratching his chin.

"If you'll just finish packing them up, miss," he said, "I'll take 'em along now."

"Take them along?" she repeated in surprise.

"Yes, miss. It's a new rule. Everything of this kind that we cover has to be examined and sealed in our office, and sent off from there. It's on account of all these insurance frauds they've been having lately."

The illicit passion which Miss Weagle seemed to have been conceiving for him appeared to wane.

"Mr Enderby has been dealing with your firm for a long time," she began with some asperity.

"I know, miss, but the firm can't make one rule for one customer and another for another. It's just a formality as far as you're concerned, but them's my orders. I'm a new man in this district, and I can't afford to take a chance on my own responsibility. I'll give you a receipt for 'em, and they're covered from the moment they leave your hands."

He sat down at the desk and wrote out the receipt on a blank sheet of paper, licking his pencil between every word. The Saint was an incomparable artist in characterization at any time, but he had rarely practised his art under such a steady tension as he did then, for he had no means of knowing how soon the real insurance company's agent would arrive, or how long Mr Enderby's appointment would keep him. But he completed the performance without a trace of hurry, and watched Miss Weagle tucking a layer of tissue over the last row of jewels.

"The value is twenty-seven thousand six hundred and fifty pounds," she said coldly.

"I'll make a note of it, miss," said the Saint, and did so.

She finished packing the box, and he picked it up. He still had to get away with it.

"You doing anything particular next Saturday?" he asked, gazing at her with a hint of wistfulness.

"The idea?" said Miss Weagle haughtily.

"Do you like Greta Garbo?"

This was different.

"Oh," said Miss Weagle.

She wriggled. Simon had rarely witnessed such a revolting spectacle.

"Meet me at Piccadilly Circus at half-past one," he said.

"All right."

Simon stuffed the box into one of the pockets of his sober and unimaginative black suit, and went to the door. From the door, he blew a juicy kiss through the fringe of fungus which overhung his mouth, and departed with a wink that left her giggling kittenishly—and he was out of the building before she even looked at the receipt he had left behind, and discovered that his signature was undecipherable and there was no insurance company whatever mentioned on it . . .

It was not by any means the most brilliant and dashing robbery that the Saint had ever committed, but it had a pure outrageous perfection of coincidence that atoned for all its shortcomings in the way of gore. And he knew, without the slightest diminution of the scapegrace beatitude that was performing a hilarious massage over his insides, that nothing on earth could have been more scientifically calculated to fan up the flames of vengeance on every side of him than what he had just done.

What he may not have foreseen was the speed with which the inevitable vengeance would move towards him.

Still wearing his deep-sea moustache and melancholy exterior, he walked west to New Oxford Street and entered a business stationer's. He bought a roll of gummed paper tape, with which he made a secure parcel of Mr Enderby's brown cardboard box, and a penny label which he addressed to Joshua Pond, Esq., Poste Restante, Harwich. Then he went to the nearest post office and entrusted twenty-seven thousand six hundred and fifty pounds to the care of Her Majesty's mails.

Two hours later he crossed Piccadilly from the Green Park underground station, and a vision of slim fair-haired loveliness turned round from a shop window as he swung in towards her.

"Were you waiting for somebody?" he asked gravely. Her eyes, as blue as his own, smiled at him uncertainly.

"I was waiting for a bold bad brigand called the Saint, who doesn't know how to keep out of trouble. Have you seen him?"

"I believe I saw somebody like him sipping a glass of warm milk at a meeting of the World Federation for Encouraging Kindness to Cockroaches," he said solemnly. "Good-looking fellow with a halo. Is that the guy?"

"What else was he doing?" The Saint laughed.

"He was risking the ruin of his digestion with some of Ye Fine Olde Englishe Cookinge which is more deadly than bullets even if it doesn't taste much different," he said. "But it may have been worth it. There was a parcel shoved into a bloke's overcoat pocket some time when I was sweating through my second pound of waterlogged cabbage, just like Sunny Jim said it would be, and I trailed the happy recipient to his lair. I suppose I was rather lucky to be listening outside his door just when he was telling his secretary to get an insurance hound over to inspect the boodle—By the way, have you ever seen a woman with a face like a stoat and George Robey eyebrows wriggling seductively? This secretary—"

"Do you mean you—"

"That's just what I do mean, old darling. I toddled straight into the office when this bloke went out, and introduced myself as the insurance hound summoned as aforesaid in Chapter One. And I got out of Hatton Garden with a packet of boodle valued at twenty-seven thousand six hundred and fifty quid, which ought to keep the wolf from the door for another day or two." The glint of changeless mischief in his eyes was its own infinite elaboration of the theme. "But it'll bring a lot of other wolves around that'll want rather more getting rid of, and I expect we can look forward to fun and games."

She nodded.

"They've started," she said soberly. "There's a reception committee waiting for you."

He was quite still for a moment, but the edge of humour in his gaze was altered only to become keener and more subtly dangerous.

"How many?"

"One."

His brows sloped up in a hair-line of devil-may-care delight that she knew only too well—a contour of impenitent Saintliness that had made trouble-hunting its profession too long to be disturbed when the trouble came unasked.

"Not poor old Claud Eustace again?" he said.

"No. It's that new fellow—the Trenchard product. I've been waiting here three-quarters of an hour to catch you as you came along and tell you. Sam Outrell gave me the wire."

6

The Saint was unperturbed. He had removed the walrus moustache which had whiffled so realistically before Miss Weagle, and with it the rosy complexion and melancholy aspect on which it had bloomed with such lifelike aptness. The costume which he had worn on that occasion had also been put away, in the well-stocked wardrobe of another pied-à-terre which he rented under another of his multitudinous aliases for precisely those skilful changes of identity. He had left the plodding inconspicuous gait of his character in the same place. In a light grey suit which looked as if it had only that morning been unpacked from the tailor's box, and a soft hat canted impudently over one eye, he had a debonair and disreputable elegance which made the deputation of welcome settle into clammily hostile attention.

"I was waiting for you," said Junior Inspector Pryke damply.

"No one would have thought it," said the Saint, with a casual smile. "Do I look like your fairy godmother?" Pryke was not amused.

"Shall we go up to your rooms?" he suggested, and Simon's gaze rested on him blandly.

"What for, Desmond?" He leaned one elbow on the desk at his side, and brought the wooden-faced janitor into the party with a shift of his lazy smile. "You can't shock Sam Outrell—he knew me before you ever did. And Miss Holm is quite broadminded, too. By the way, have you met Miss Holm? Pat, this is Miss Desdemona Pryke, the Pride of the YWCA—"

"I'd rather see you alone, if you don't mind," said the detective.

He was beginning to go a trifle white about the mouth, and Simon's eyes marked the symptom with a wicked glitter of unhallowed mischief. It was a glitter that Mr Teal would have recognized only too easily, if he had been there to see it, but for once that long-suffering waist-line of the Law was not its victim.

"What for?" Simon repeated, with a puzzled politeness that was about as cosy and reliable as a tent on the edge of a drifting iceberg. "If you've got anything to say to me that this audience can't hear, I'm afraid you're shinning up the wrong leg. I'm not that sort of a girl."

"I know perfectly well what I want to say," retorted Pryke chalkily.

"Then I hope you'll say it," murmured the Saint properly. "Come along, now, Desmond—let's get it over with. Make a clean breast of it—as the bishop said to the actress. Unmask the Public School Soul. What's the matter?"

Pryke's hands clenched spasmodically at his sides.

"Do you know a man called Enderby?"

"Never heard of him," said the Saint unblushingly. "What does he do—bore the holes in spaghetti, or something?"

"At about ten minutes to three this afternoon," said Pryke, with his studiously smooth University accent burring jaggedly at the edges, "a man entered his office, falsely representing himself to be an agent of the Southshire Insurance Company, and took away about twenty-seven thousand pounds' worth of precious stones."

Simon raised his eyebrows.

THE SAINT GOES ON

"It sounds like a tough afternoon for Comrade Enderby," he remarked. "But why come and tell me? D'you mean you want me to try and help you recover these jools?"

The Antarctic effrontery of his innocence would have left nothing visible in a thermometer but a shrunken globule of congealed quicksilver. It was a demonstration of absolute vacuum in the space used by the normal citizen for storing his conscience that left its audience momentarily speechless. Taking his first ration of that brass-necked Saintliness which had greyed so many of the hairs in Chief Inspector Teal's dwindling crop, Desmond Pryke turned from white to pink, and then back to white again.

"I want to know what you were doing at that time," he said.

"Me?" Simon took out his cigarette-case. "I was at the Plaza, watching a Mickey Mouse. But what on earth has that got to do with poor old Enderby and his jools?"

Suddenly the detective's hand shot out and grabbed him by the wrist.

"*That's* what you've got to do with it. That scar on your forearm. Miss Weagle—Mr Enderby's secretary—saw it on this fake insurance agent's arm when he picked up the parcel of stones. It was part of the description she gave us!"

Simon looked down at his wrist in silence for a moment, the cigarette he had chosen poised forgotten in mid-air, gazing at the tail of the furrowed scar that showed beyond the edge of his cuff. It was a souvenir he carried from quite a different adventure, and he had usually remembered to keep it covered when he was disguised. He realized that he had under-estimated both the eyesight of Miss Weagle and the resourcefulness of Junior Inspector Pryke, but when he raised his eyes again they were still bantering and untroubled.

"Yes, I've got a scar there—but I expect lots of other people have, too. What else did this Weagle dame say in her description?"

"Nothing that couldn't be covered by a good disguise," said Pryke, with a new note of triumph in his voice. "Now are you coming along quietly?"

"Certainly not," said the Saint.

The detective's eyes narrowed.

"Do you know what happens if you resist a police officer?"

"Surely," said the Saint, supple and lazy. "The police officer gets a thick ear."

Pryke let go his wrist, and shoved his hands into his pockets.

"Do you want me to have you taken away by force?" he asked.

"I shouldn't want you to try anything so silly, Desmond," said the Saint. He put the cigarette between his lips and struck a match with a flick of his thumb-nail, without looking at it. "The squad hasn't been hatched yet that could take me away by force without a good deal of commotion, and you know it. You'd get more publicity than a Hollywood divorce—or is that what you're wanting?"

"I'm simply carrying out my orders—"

"Whose orders?"

"That's none of your business," Pryke got out through his teeth.

"I think it is," said the Saint mildly. "After all, I'm the blushing victim of this persecution. Besides, Desmond, I don't believe you. I think you're misguided. You're behind the times. How long have you been here waiting for me?"

"I'm not here to be cross-examined by you," spluttered the detective furiously.

"I'm not cross-examining you, Desmond. I'm trying to lead you into the paths of reason. But you don't have to answer that one if it hurts. How long has this petunia-blossom been here, Sam?"

The janitor glanced mechanically at the clock.

"Since about four o'clock, sir."

"Has it received any message—a telephone call, or anything like that?"

"No, sir."

"Nobody's come in and spoken to it?"

"No, sir."

"In fact, it's just been sitting around here all on its ownsome, like the last rose of summer—"

Junior Inspector Pryke thrust himself up between them, along the desk, till his chest was almost touching the Saint's. His hands were thrust into his pockets so savagely that the coat was stretched down in long creases from his shoulders.

"Will you be quiet?" he blazed quiveringly. "I've stood as much as I can—"

"As the bishop said to the actress."

"Are you coming along with me," fumed the detective, "or am I going to have you dragged out?"

Simon shook his head.

"You miss the idea, Desmond." He tapped the other firmly on the lower chest with his forefinger, and raised his eyebrows. "Hullo," he remarked, "your stomach hasn't got nearly so much bounce in it as dear old Teal's."

"Never mind my stomach!" Pryke almost screamed.

"I don't mind it," said the Saint generously. "I admit I haven't seen it in all its naked loveliness, but in its veiled state, at this distance, there seems to be nothing offensive about it."

The noise that Pryke made can only be likened to that of a kettle coming to the boil.

"I'll hear that another time," he said. "Simon Templar, I am taking you into custody—"

"But I'm trying to show you that that's exactly what you mustn't do, Desmond," said the Saint patiently. "It would be fatal. Here you are, a rising young officer on the threshold of your career, trying to pull a flivver that'll set you back four years' seniority. I can't let you do it. Why don't you curb the excessive zeal, Rosebud, and listen to reason? I can tell you exactly what's happened."

"I can tell you exactly what's going to happen—"

"It was like this," continued the Saint, as if the interruption had not merely fallen on deaf ears, but had failed miserably in its effort to occur at all. "This guy Enderby was robbed, as you say. Or he thought he was. Or, still more exactly, his secretary thought he was. A bloke calling himself an insurance agent blew into the office, and breezed out again with a parcel of jools. On account of various complications, the secretary was led to believe that this insurance agent was a fake, and the jools had been pinched. Filled with the same misguided zeal that's pulling the buttons of that horrible waistcoat of yours, Desmond, she called the police. Hearing of this, you came puffing round to see me, with your waistcoat bursting with pride and your brain addled with all the uncomplimentary fairy-tales that Claud Eustace Teal has told you about me."

"Who said so?"

"I did. It's a sort of clairvoyant gift of mine. But you must listen to the rest of it. You come blowing round here, and wait for me from four o'clock onwards. Pepped up with the idea of scoring a solo triumph, you haven't said anything to anyone about your scheme. Consequently, you don't know what's happened since you left headquarters. Which is this. Shortly after the secretary female called for the police, Comrade Enderby himself returned to the office, the shemozzle was explained to him, he explained the shemozzle, and the long and the short of it was that the insurance agent was found to be perfectly genuine, the whole misunderstanding was cleared up, the whole false alarm exposed, and it was discovered that there was nothing to arrest anybody for—least of all me."

"What makes you think that?"

Simon took in a lungful of tobacco smoke, and inhaled through his nose with a slight smile. What made him think that? It was obvious. It was the fundamental formula on which fifty per cent of his reputation had been built up.

A man was robbed. Ninety-eight times out of a hundred, the fact was never published at all. But if ever, through some misguided agent, or during a spasm of temporary but understandable insanity on the part of the victim himself, the fact happened to be published, that same victim, as soon as he discovered the accident or came to his senses, was the first and most energetic on the field to explain away the problem with which Scotland Yard had been faced—for the simple reason that there would be things much harder to explain away if the robber were ever detected.

And the bereavement of Mr Enderby was so perfectly on all fours with the formula that, with the horns of the dilemma touched in, it would have looked like a purple cow. There was no answer to it. So Mr Enderby had been robbed of some jewels? Well, could he give a description of the jewels, so that if they were recovered . . . How did the Saint know? He smiled, with unusual tolerance.

"Just the same old clairvoyant gift—working overtime for your special benefit, Desmond. But I'll back it for anything you like to bet—even including that perfectly repulsive shirt you're wearing. If you only got wise to yourself, you'd find that nobody wanted me arrested any more, and it'd save both of us no end of trouble. Now, why don't you get on the phone to Headquarters, and bring yourself up to date? Let me do it for you, and then you can save your two-pence to buy yourself a bar of milk chocolate on the way home . . ."

He picked up the telephone on the porter's desk, and pushed his forefinger persuasively into the initial "V" of the Victoria exchange. It was all ancient history to the Saint, an old game which had become almost stereotyped from many playings, even if with this new victim it had the semblance of a new twist to it. It hadn't seriously occurred to him that the routine could be very different.

And then something hard and compact jabbed into his chest, and his eyes shifted over with genuine surprise from the telephone dial. There was a nickel-plated little automatic in Junior Inspector Pryke's hand—the sort of footling lady-like weapon, Simon couldn't help reflecting, which a man with that taste in clothes must inevitably have affected, but none the less capable of unpleasant damage at contact range. His gaze roamed up to the detective's flaming eyes with a flicker of pained protest that for once was wholly spontaneous and tinged with a glitter of urgent curiosity.

"Put that telephone down," said Pryke sizzlingly.

Simon put the telephone down. There was something in the other's rabid glare which told him that disobedience might easily make Pryke do something foolish—of which the Saint had no desire to suffer the physical effects.

"My dear old daffodil," he murmured, "have you stopped to think that that dinky little pop-gun—"

"Never mind what I think," rasped the detective, whose range of repartee seemed to make up in venom what it lacked in variety. "If there's any truth in what you're saying, we can verify it when we get you to the station. But you aren't going to run away until it has been verified. Come along!"

His finger was twitching over the trigger, and the Saint sighed.

He felt rather sorry for Junior Inspector Pryke. While he disliked the man's face, and his voice, and his clothes, and almost everything else about him, he had not actually plumbed such implacable depths of hatred as to wish him to turn himself into a horrible example which would be held up for the disgusted inspection of students of the Police College for the next decade.

But it seemed as if this was the only ambition Desmond Pryke had to fulfil, and he had left no stone unturned in his efforts to achieve it. From permitting himself to be lured into an argument on comparative gastrometry to that final howler of pulling a gun to enforce an ordinary arrest, Junior Inspector Pryke had run doggedly through the complete catalogue of Things A Young Policeman Should Not Do, but it was not Simon Templar's fault.

The Saint shrugged.

"Okay, Desmond," he murmured. "If that's the way you feel about it, I can't stop you. I've done my best. But don't come round asking me for a pension when they drum you out of the Force."

He put on his hat, and pulled the brim out to the perfect piratical tilt. There was not a shadow of misgiving in the smile that he gave Patricia, and he saw no reason for there to be a shadow.

"Be seein' ya, keed," he said. "Don't worry—I'll be back for dinner. But I'm afraid Desdemona is going to have a pain in her little tum-tum before then."

He sauntered out unhurriedly into Stratton Street, and himself hailed the nearest taxi. Pryke put away his gun and climbed in after him. The cab turned into Piccadilly with a burden of internal silence that was almost broken by the exuberance of its own one-sided rancour.

Simon's nostrils detected a curious sweet scent in the air he was breathing. Ever the genial optimist, he tried to thaw out the polar obmutescence with a fresh turn of pleasant gossip.

"That perfume you're using, Desmond," he said. "I don't think I've come across it before. What's it called—*Pansy's Promise*? Or is it *Quelques Tantes*?"

"You wait till we get to the station," said the detective, with sweltering monotony. "Perhaps you won't feel so funny then."

"Perhaps I won't," Simon agreed languidly. "And perhaps you won't look so funny."

He yawned. The cab, with all its windows tightly closed, was warm and stuffy, and the conversational limitations of Inspector Pryke were also conducive to slumber.

The Saint closed his eyes. He felt limp and bored and his brain was starting to wander in a most remarkable and disjointed manner. It was all rather voluptuous and dreamy, like sinking away in some Elysian hop-joint . . . Suddenly he felt faintly sick.

He sat up, with a tremendous effort. A message was trying to get through to his brain, but it seemed to be muffled in layer after layer of cotton-wool. His chest was labouring, and he could feel his heart pounding at crazy speed. The face of Junior Inspector Pryke stared back at him through a kind of violet haze. Pryke's chest was heaving also, and his mouth was open: it crossed the Saint's mind that he looked like an agitated fish . . . Then everything within his blurring vision whirled round like a top, and the blood roared in his ears like a thousand waterfalls. The message that had been trying to break through to him flashed in at last, and he made a convulsive lunge towards the window behind the driver's impassive back, but he never reached it. It seemed as if the bottom fell out of the world, and he went plunging down through fold after fold of numbing silence, down and down through cold green clouds of that curious perfume into an infinity of utter nothingness . . .

7

There was a decanter and three sherry-glasses on the table, and one of the glasses was untouched. They had been set out there more than an hour ago, and the decanter was nearly empty.

Patricia Holm wandered restlessly about the living-room. Her face was quiet and untroubled, but she couldn't relax and sit down. The dark had come down, and the view of the Green Park from the tall windows was hidden by a grey-blue veil in which the yellow specks of the street lamps shone brighter than the stars, and the lights of cars travelling up and down the Mall gleamed like flocks of dawdling comets. She drew the curtains, for something to do, and stole her thirty-seventh glance at the clock. It was a couple of minutes after nine.

"What's happened to him?" she said.

Mr Uniatz shook his head. He stretched out a spade-shaped hand for the decanter, and completed his solo conquest of its contents.

"I dunno," he said feebly. "Maybe he couldn't shake de diddo. Dey come dat way, sometimes."

"He's been arrested before," she said. "It's never kept him as long as this. If anything had gone wrong, he ought to have got word through to us somehow."

Mr Uniatz chewed desperately at his poisonous cigar. He wanted to be helpful. As we have already explained, he was not naturally hot on the higher flights of the intellect, but on such an occasion as this he was not the man to shirk his obligations. The deep creases in his rudimentary forehead bore their own witness to the torture he was enduring from these unaccustomed stresses on his brain.

"Maybe he's on his way, right now," he hazarded encouragingly.

Patricia threw herself into a chair. It was another restless movement, rather than an attempt to rest.

"That's not enough, Hoppy." She was thinking aloud, mechanically, more for the anaesthetic effect of actual speech than with any hope of coaxing something useful out of her companion. "If anything's gone wrong, we've got to be ready for it. We've got to pick up our own cue. He'd expect us to find the answer. Suppose he isn't on his way—what has he done?"

"He's got de ice," said Mr Uniatz, vaguely.

"I don't know whether he's got it now. Probably he parked it somewhere on his way here. That's what he'd have done if he was expecting trouble. Sometimes he simply puts things in the mail—sends them to a hotel or a poste restante somewhere, and picks them up later on when it's all clear. Usually they aren't even addressed to his own name."

Hoppy frowned.

"But if dey ain't addressed to his own name," he said, "how does he pick dem up?"

"Well, when he goes to pick them up, he gives the name that they were addressed to," explained Patricia kindly.

Mr Uniatz nodded. He had always been lost in admiration of the Saint's intellectual gifts, and this solution was only one more justification of his faith. Obviously a guy who could work out things like that in his own head had got what it takes.

"But this time we don't know where he's sent them, or what name he addressed them to," she said.

The tentative expression of pleased complacency faded away from Hoppy's face, and the flutings of honest effort crowded themselves once more into the restricted space between his eyebrows and his hair. He was too loyal to give way to the feeling that this was an unnecessary complication, invented simply to make things more difficult for him, but he wished people wouldn't ask him to tackle problems like that. Reaching again for the decanter and finding it empty, he glowered at it plaintively, like a trusted friend who had done him a gratuitous injury.

"So what?" he said, passing the buck with an air of profound reluctance.

"I must know what's happened to him," said Patricia steadily.

She got up and lighted a cigarette. Twice more she paced out the length of the room with her supple boyish stride, and then with a sudden resolution she slipped into the chair by the telephone, and dialled Teal's private number.

He was at home. In a few moments his drowsy voice came over the wire.

"Who's that?"

"This is Patricia Holm." Her voice was as cool and careless as the Saint's own. "Haven't you finished with Simon yet? We're waiting for him to join us for dinner, and I'm getting hungry and Hoppy is getting away with all the sherry."

"I don't know what you mean," he answered suspiciously.

"You ought to know, Claud."

He didn't seem to know. She explained. He was silent for so long that she thought she had been cut off, and then his suspicious perplexity came through again in the same lethargic monotone.

"I'll ring you again in a few minutes," he said.

She sat on at the table, smoking her cigarette without enjoyment, playing a noiseless tattoo with her fingertips on the smooth green Bakelite of the instrument. Over on the other side of the room, Hoppy Uniatz discovered the untouched glass which had been reserved for the Saint, and drew it cautiously towards him.

In five minutes the telephone bell rang.

"They don't know anything about it at Scotland Yard or Market Street," Teal informed her. "And it's the first I've heard of it myself. Is this another of your family jokes, or what?"

"I'm not joking," said Patricia, and there was a sudden chill in her eyes which would have made the statement superfluous if Teal could have seen her. "Pryke took him away about half past five. It was a perfectly ridiculous charge, but he wouldn't listen to reason. It couldn't possibly have kept the Saint as long as this."

The wire was silent again for a second or two. She could visualize the detective sucking his chewing-gum more plainly than television could have shown him.

"I'll come round and see you," he said.

He was there inside the quarter-hour, with his round harvest-moon face stodgy and disinterested under his shabby pot hat, chewing the same tasteless cud of chicle and listening to the story again. The repetition added nothing to the sum of his knowledge, except that there was no joke involved. When he had heard it through and asked his questions, he called Scotland Yard and Market Street police station again, only to have his inquiries answered by the same blank negatives. Junior Inspector Pryke, apparently, had left Market Street at about a quarter to four, without saying where he was going, and nothing had been heard of him since. Certainly he had not reported in with an arrest anywhere in the Metropolitan area.

Only one thing required no explanation, and he knew that Patricia Holm knew it, by this time, as well as he knew it himself—although her recital had carefully told him, nothing more than Simon Templar himself would have done.

"The Saint was after the High Fence," he said bluntly. "He robbed Enderby this afternoon. I know it, and you know it, even if it is quite true that Enderby got on to us shortly after the alarm and swore it was all a mistake. Therefore it's obvious that Enderby is something to do with the High Fence. Maybe we can't prove it, but the High Fence knows his own men. It doesn't take much more to work out what happened."

"I think you're jumping to a lot of conclusions," said Patricia, with Saintly sweetness, and did not deceive him for an instant.

"Perhaps I am," he said stolidly. "But I know what I'd have done if I'd been the High Fence. I'd have heard what had happened as soon as Scotland Yard did, and I'd have watched this place. I'd have seen Pryke come in, and even that mightn't have stopped me . . . They left here in a taxi, did they? Well, you ought to be able to work it out as well as I can."

"You mean de High Fence puts de arm on him?" asked Mr Uniatz, translating innuendo into an idiom that he could understand.

Teal looked round at him with heavy-lidded eyes in which the perpetual boredom was as flimsy a sham as anyone was likely to see it.

"If you know the answers, I expect you'll go to work on them," he said, with a stony significance of which he would have been the first to disclaim all knowledge. "I've got my own job to do. If one of you keeps in touch with this address, I'll let you know if I find out anything."

He left a roomful of equally stony silence behind him, and went out to take a taxi to Scotland Yard.

73

The High Fence had got the Saint and Junior Inspector Pryke—he had no doubts about that. He knew, although he could never prove it, that his analysis of the situation had been as mathematically accurate as any jig-saw he would ever put together could hope to be. And it was easier to put together than most problems. He would have been happier if his own course of action had been no less clearly indicated, and it disturbed him more than he would have cared to admit to realize that he was far more concerned about the fate of the Saint than he was about the fate of his own smug subordinate.

This secondary concern, however, was settled shortly after ten o'clock, when a police constable observed a pair of feet protruding from a bush on the edge of Wimbledon Common, and used the feet to haul out the body of a man. In the first flush of instinctive optimism, the policeman thought that the body was dead, and pictured himself (with photograph and biographical note) in the headlines of a sensational murder mystery, but closer investigation showed it to be alive, and with medical assistance it was quite easily resuscitated into a healthily profane Junior Inspector of unmistakable Trenchard parentage.

"So the High Fence didn't kill you," said Mr Teal malignantly, when a police car had brought the salvage to Scotland Yard.

"I thought you'd be pleased," retorted Pryke pettishly.

He had a sick headache from the gas which had been pumped into the cab, and he was on the defensive for trouble. Mr Teal did not disappoint him.

"Who told you to arrest the Saint?" he inquired mucilaginously, when Pryke had given his account of the affair.

"I didn't know I had to be told. I heard of the robbery at Enderby's, and there were grounds for believing that the Saint had a hand in it—"

"You know that Enderby has denied that there ever was a robbery, and said it was entirely a misunderstanding?"

"Has he? That's what the Saint told me, but I didn't believe him. I knew nothing about it. I went out as soon as I received the first information, and waited for him at his flat."

"And you had to use a gun to arrest him."

Pryke flushed. He had thought it wiser to say nothing about that.

"He refused to come with me," he said sulkily. "I had to do something, and I didn't want to make a scene."

"It would have made the biggest scene you're ever likely to be in, if you had got him to the station and that gun had been mentioned in the police court," Teal said caustically. "As it is, you'll be on the carpet first thing in the morning. Or will you tell the Assistant Commissioner that all this was my idea, too?"

Pryke scowled, and said nothing.

"Anyhow," Teal wound up, "the Saint has got to be found now. After your performance, he's technically an escaped prisoner. Since it was your arrest, you'd better do something about it."

"What do you suggest?" asked Pryke, with treacherous humility.

Teal, having no answer, glared at him. Everything that could be prescribed for such an emergency had been done already—every alarm issued, every feeler put out, every net spread. If he could have thought of anything more, Chief Inspector Teal would have done it himself. But there was nothing to guide him: even what had been done was a mere firing of routine shots in the dark. The taxi had disappeared, and no one had even noticed its number. Beyond any doubt, the man who had ordered its movements was the same man who had killed Johnny Anworth and Sunny Jim Fasson—who, unless something were done quickly, would be just as likely to kill Simon Templar. A man knew too much, and he died: the logical sequence was quite clearly established, but Teal found no pleasure in following it to its conclusion.

"Since you're so damned independent of orders and regulations," he said, with excessive violence, "you might pay some attention to this man Enderby. I know he swears that the whole thing was a mistake, but I've heard of plenty of those mistakes before. There's no evidence and nothing we can charge him with, but if those stones that were stolen weren't stolen property already, I'll eat my hat. And if Enderby isn't hand in glove with the High Fence, even if he isn't the High Fence himself, I'll eat yours as well."

Pryke shook his head.

"I don't know that I agree. Fasson was shot as he was running out of Abbot's Yard, and when we made a house-to-house inquiry we found out that Templar had a place there under one of his aliases—"

"Well, what about it? I've never believed that the Saint didn't have something to do with it. I don't believe he killed Fasson, but I do believe that he got the body away from the flat where Fasson was shot, and that Fasson wasn't dead. I believe that he made Fasson talk, and that Fasson wasn't really killed until either the Saint let him go, or he ran away. I think Fasson told him something that made him go after Enderby, and—"

Pryke shook his head again, with an increase of confidence and patronizing self-satisfaction that made Teal stop short with his gorge rising under the leaven of undutiful thoughts of murder.

"I think you're wrong," he said.

"Oh, I am, am I?" said Mr Teal malevolently. "Well, what's the right answer?"

The smug shaking of Junior Inspector Pryke's head continued until Teal could have kicked him.

"I have a theory of my own," he said, "which I'd like to work on— unless you've got something definite that you want me to do."

"You go ahead and work on it," replied Teal blisteringly. "When I want something definite done, I shan't ask you. In another minute you'll be telling me that the Assistant Commissioner is the High Fence."

The other stood up, smoothing down the points of his waistcoat. In spite of the situation for which he was responsible, his uncrushable superciliousness was reviving outwardly untouched, but Teal saw that underneath it he was hot and simmering.

"That wouldn't be so wild as some of your guesses," he said mysteriously. "I'd like to get the Saint—if anyone can be made a Chief Inspector for failing to catch him, they'd have to make a Superintendent of anyone who did it."

"Make you a Superintendent?" jeered Teal. "With a name like yours?"

"It's a very good name," said his junior tartly. "There was a Pryke at the Battle of Hastings."

"I'll bet he was a damn good cook," snarled Mr Teal.

8

For Simon Templar there was an indefinite period of trackless oblivion, from which he was roused now and again to dream curious dim dreams. Once the movement of the cab stopped, and he heard voices; then a door slammed, and he sank back into the dark before his impression had more than touched the fringe of consciousness. Once he seemed to be carried over a gravel path: he heard the scrunch of stones, and felt the grip of the hands that were holding him up, but there was no power of movement in his limbs. It was too much trouble to open his eyes, and he fell asleep again almost immediately. Between those momentary stirrings of awareness, which were so dull and nebulous that they did not even stimulate a desire to amplify them, stretched a colourless void of languorous insensibility in which time had no landmarks.

Then there was the feeling of a hard chair under him, a constriction of cords about his wrists and ankles, and a needle that stabbed his forearm. His eyelids felt weighted down almost beyond his power to lift, but when he dragged them up once he could see nothing. He wondered vaguely whether the room was in darkness, or whether he was blind but he was too apathetic to dwell earnestly on a choice between the alternatives. There was a man who talked softly out of the blackness, in a voice that sounded hazily familiar, asking him a lot of questions. He had an idea that he answered them, without conscious volition and equally without opposition from his will. Afterwards, he could never remember what he said.

Presently the interval of half-consciousness seemed to merge back without a borderline into the limitless background of sleep.

When he woke up again his head ached slightly with a kind of empty dizziness, and his stomach felt as if it had been turned inside out and spun round on a flywheel till it was raw and tender. It was an effort to open his eyes, but not such a hopeless and unimportant feat as it had seemed before. Once open, he had more difficulty at first in focusing them. He had an impression of bare grey boards, and his own feet tied together with strands of new rope. The atmosphere was warm and close, and smelt nauseatingly of paint and oil. There was a thrumming vibration under him, coupled with a separate and distinct swaying movement: after a while he picked an irregular splash and gurgle of water out of the background of sound, and induced his eyes to co-ordinate on a dark circular window framed in tarnished brass.

"So you're waking up for a last look round, are you?" growled a voice somewhere to his left.

Simon nodded. Shifting his gaze gingerly about, he made out more details. There was an unshaded electric bulb socketed into the low ceiling which gave a harsh but sufficient light. He was in the cabin of a boat—a small craft, by the look and motion of it, either a canal tug or a scrap-heap motor cruiser. From the rows of orderly lights that drifted past the port-holes on both sides of the cabin, he deduced that they were running down the Thames.

The man who had spoken sat on an old canvas sack spread out on the bare springs of a bunk. He was a thick-set prognathous individual with thin reddish hair and a twisted mouth, most un-nautically clad in a striped suit, a check cap, and canary-yellow shoes.

"Where are we off to?" Simon asked.

The man chuckled.

"You're going to have a look at some fishes. I don't know whether they'll like you, but they'll be able to go on lookin' at you till they get used to it."

"Is that the High Fence's joke?" inquired Simon sardonically.

"It's the High Fence you're talkin' to."

The Saint regarded him contemptuously.

"Your name is Quincey. I believe I could give you a list of all your convictions. Let me see. Two for robbery with violence, one for carrying firearms without a licence, one for attempted—"

"All right," said Quincey good-humouredly. "I know 'em all myself. But the High Fence and me are like *that*." He locked his thick fingers together symbolically. "We're more or less the same thing. He wouldn't be able to do much without me."

"He mightn't have been able to get Sunny Jim murdered," Simon agreed thoughtfully.

"Yes, I did that. It was pretty neat. I was supposed to be waitin' for both of you, but when Fasson came out an' ran down to King's Road, I was frightened of losin' him, so I had to go without you. Yes, I was ridin' the motor-bike. They can't prove it, but I don't mind tellin' you, because you'll never tell anyone else. I killed Sunny Jim—the rat! An' now I'm goin' to feed the great Simon Templar to the fishes. I know a lot of fellers who'd give their right hands to be in my place."

Simon acknowledged the truth of that. The list of men who would have paid drastically for the privilege of using him for ground-bait in the deepest and hungriest stretch of water at their disposal could have been conveniently added up in round dozens. But his brain was still far from clear, and for the moment he could not see the High Fence's object in sending him to that attractive fate so quickly.

"If you feed me to the fishes, you feed them twenty-seven thousand six hundred and fifty pounds' worth of stones as well—did you know that, brother?" he asked.

Quincey grinned.

"Oh, no, we don't. We know where those are. They're at the Harwich Post Office, addressed to Mr Joshua Pond. You told us all about that. The High Fence has gone to Harwich to be Mr Pond."

The Saint's eyes hardened into chips of flint. For an instant of actual physical paralysis, he felt exactly as if he had been kicked in the middle. The terse, accurate, effortless, unhesitating throwing back at him of an arrangement which he had not even told Patricia, as if his brain had been flung open and the very words read out of it, had a staggering calamitousness like nothing he had ever experienced before. It had an unearthly, inescapable completeness that blasted the foundations from under any thought of bluff, and left him staring at something that looked like a supernatural intervention of Doom itself.

His memory struggled muzzily back over the features of his broken dream. The taxi—he had taken it off the kerb right outside his door, without a thought. Ordinarily he would never have done such a thing, but the very positive presence of trouble in the shape of Junior Inspector Pryke had given him a temporary blind spot to the fact that trouble in another shape could still be waiting for him—and might logically be expected to wait in much the same place.

The sickly sweet perfume which he had accused Pryke of using. Pryke's agitated face, gulping like a fish, and the labour of his own breathing. Gas, of course—pumped into the closed cab by some mechanism under the control of the driver, and quick enough in its action to put them out before they were sufficiently alarmed to break a window. Then the scrunch of gravel, and the grip of hands carrying him. He had been taken somewhere. Probably Pryke had been dumped out somewhere on the route. Unlike Mr Teal, Simon hoped he had not been killed—he would have looked forward to experimenting with further variations on that form of badinage to which Desmond was so alluringly sensitive.

The prick of the needle, and the soft voice that asked him questions out of the darkness. Questions that he couldn't remember, that dragged equally forgotten answers out of a drugged subconsciousness that was too stupefied to lie . . . Understanding came to him out of that fuddled recollection with stunning clarity. There was nothing supernatural about it—only unexpected erudition and refinement. So much neater and surer than the old-fashioned and conventional systems of torture, which, even when they unlocked a man's mouth, gave no guarantee that he spoke the truth . . . He could even identify the drug that must have been used.

"Scopolamine?" he said, without any indication on his face of the shocks he had taken to reach that conclusion.

Quincey scratched the back of his ear.

"I think that's the name. The High Fence thought of it. That's what we are—scientific."

Simon glanced steadily at the opposite port-hole. Something like a solid black screen cut off the procession of embankment lights, briefly, and slid by. It told him that they had not yet passed under all the bridges, but he found it impossible to identify their whereabouts any more particularly. Seen from the unfamiliar viewpoint of the water, the passing lights formed themselves into no patterns which he could positively recognize, and an occasional glimpse of a neon sign, high up on a building, was no more illuminating, except on the superlative merits of Bovril or Guinness. Somewhere below London Bridge, down past the Pool, probably, he would be dropped quietly over the side. There was a queer quiet inevitability about it, a dispassionate scientific precision, which seemed an incongruous end for such a stormy and impetuous life.

"May I have a cigarette?" he asked.

Quincey hesitated for a moment, and then took out a packet of Player's. He put one between the Saint's lips and lighted it for him, and then returned watchfully to his seat on the bunk.

"Thanks," said the Saint.

His wrists were bound together in front of him, so that he was able to use one hand on the cigarette. He was also able to make an inconspicuous test of the efficiency of the knotting; it was well done, and the new cord would swell up tighter as soon as it got wet.

He got a view of his wrist-watch, and saw that it was a quarter-past ten.

"What day is this?" he said.

"The same day as it's been all the time," answered Quincey. "You didn't think we'd keep you under for a week, did you? The sooner you're out of the way, the better. You've given us too much trouble already."

So it was less than five hours since he had gone to sleep in the taxi. Simon got a perspective on his dream. At that rate, there was a sound chance that the High Fence couldn't have got him to wherever he had been taken, drugged and questioned him, and caught a train out of London in time to reach Harwich before the post office closed. Therefore he might not be able to collect the package from the poste restante before morning. And if the Saint escaped . . .

Simon realized that he was building some beautiful castles in the air. A dog thrown into the river with a brick tied round its neck would have more or less the same chance of escape as he was offered.

And yet . . . there was a dim preposterous hope struggling in his mind that a miracle might happen—or had happened. Where had he felt the stab of that hypnotic needle? He felt sure that it had been in his right forearm, and there was a vague sort of ache in the same place to confirm the uncertain memory. In that case, was there any reason why his left forearm must have been touched? It was a wildly fantastic hope, an improbable possibility. And yet . . . such unlikely things had happened before, and their not wholly improbable possibility was part of the inspiration behind the more unconventional items of his armoury. It might seem incredible that anyone who knew anything of him could fail to credit him with having something up his sleeve in any emergency, and yet . . . Smoking his cigarette in long tranquil inhalations, he contrived to press his left forearm unobtrusively against his thigh, and what he felt put the dawn of a grim and farfetched buoyancy into his heart.

Quincey got up and pressed his face against one of the portholes.

"It's about time for you to be goin'," he said unemotionally.

He hauled out a heavy iron weight from under the bunk, and bent a short length of rope to a ring set in it. The other end of the rope he knotted to the cords that bound the Saint's ankles. Then he tore a strip of canvas from the sack which he had been sitting on, and stood waiting with it.

"Finish that cigarette," he said.

Simon drew a last leisured puff, and dropped it on the floor. He looked Quincey in the eyes.

"I hope you'll ask for fish for your last breakfast, on the day they hang you for this," he said.

"I'll do that for you," said Quincey, knotting the canvas across his mouth in a rough but effective gag. "When they hang me. Stand up."

He pulled the Saint across his shoulder in a fireman's lift, picking up the weight in his left hand, and moved slowly across to the narrow steep companion which led up from the cabin. Mounting the steps awkwardly under his burden, he lifted the hatch with his head and climbed up till he could roll the Saint off on to the deck.

The craft was a small and shabby single-cabin motor boat. A man muffled up in a dark overcoat, with a peaked cap pulled down over his eyes until it almost met the top of his turned-up collar, who was apparently the only other member of the crew, stood at the wheel beside the hatch, but he did not look round. Simon wondered if it was Mr Enderby. The numbers of the gang who actually worked in direct contact with the High Fence would certainly be kept down to the irreducible minimum consistent with adequate functioning, and it might well be that by this time he knew all of them. It was not a racket which called for a large staff given the original idea and the ingenious leader. His one regret was that he had not been able to make the acquaintance of that elusive quantity: it seemed a ridiculously commonplace problem to take out unanswered into eternity, after solving so many mysteries.

Quincey stepped out over him, picked up the weight again, and rolled him like a barrel towards the stern. As he turned over, the Saint saw the rusty deck of a tramp moored in midstream swing by over his head, punctured with an occasional yellow-lighted port. Over on the Surrey side, a freighter was discharging cargo in a floodlit splash of garish flarelight. He heard the rattle and clank of the tackle, the chuffing of steam winches, the intermittent rise of voices across the water. A tug hooted mournfully, feeling its way across the stream.

He lay on the very edge of the deck, with the wake churning and hissing under his side. Quincey bent over him.

"So long, Saint," he said, without vindictiveness, and pushed outwards.

9

Simon stocked his lungs to the last cubic millimetre of their capacity, and tensed his muscles involuntarily as he went down. He had a last flash of Quincey's tough freckled face peering after him, and then the black waters closed over his head.

The iron weight jerked at his ankles, and he went rolling over and upright into the cold crushing darkness.

Even as he struck the water he was wrenching his wrists round to seize the uttermost fraction of slack from the cords that bound them. The horror of that helpless plunging down to death, roped hand and foot and ballasted with fifty pounds of iron, was a nightmare that he remembered for the rest of his life, but it is a curious fact that while it lasted his mind was uncannily insulated from it. Perhaps he knew that to have let himself realize it fully, to have allowed his thoughts to dwell for any length of time on the stark hopelessness of his position, would have led inevitably to panic.

His mind held with a terrible intensity of concentration on nothing but the essentials of what he had to do. With his hands twisted round till the cords cut into his flesh, he could get the fingers of his right hands a little way up his left sleeve, and under their tips he could feel the carved shape of something that lay just above his left wrist. That was the one slender link that he had with life, the unconventional item of his armoury which the search that must have been made of his clothes had miraculously overlooked: the thin sharp ivory-hilted knife which he carried in a sheath strapped to his forearm, which had saved him from certain death before and might save him once again. Somehow, slowly, clumsily, with infinite patience and agonizing caution, he had to work it out and get it in his hand—moving it in split shavings of an inch, lest it should come loose too quickly and slip out of his grasp to lose itself in the black mud of the river bed, and yet not taking so long to shift it that his fingers would go numb and out of control from the cutting off of the circulation by the tightening ropes. His flesh crawled in the grip of that frightful restraint, and his forehead prickled as if the sweat was trying to break out on it even under the cold clutch of the water that was pressing in at his eardrums. He could feel his heart thudding hollowly in the aching tension of his chest, and a deadly blackness seemed to be swelling up in his brain and trying to overwhelm him in a burst of merciful unconsciousness: every nerve in his body shrieked its protest against the inhuman discipline, cried out for release, for action, for the frantic futile struggle that would anaesthetize the anguish just as surely as it would hasten on the end— for any relief and outlet, however suicidal, that would liberate them from the frightful tyranny of his will.

Perhaps it lasted for three minutes, from beginning to end, that nightmare eternity in which he was anchored to the bottom of the Thames, juggling finickily for life itself. If he had not been a trained underwater swimmer, he could never have survived it at all. There was a time when the impulse to let out his precious breath in a sob of sheer despair was almost more than flesh and blood could resist, but his self-control was like iron.

He won out, somehow. Trickling the air from his lungs in jealously niggard rations that were just sufficient to ease the strain on his chest, he worked the hilt of the knife up with his finger and thumb until he could get another finger on it . . . and another . . . and another . . . until the full haft was clutched in a hand which by that time had practically gone dead. But he was just able to hold it. He forced himself down, bending his knees and reaching forward, until his numbed fingers could feel the taut roughness of the rope by which he was held down to the weight. And then, giving way for the first time in that ghastly ordeal, he slashed at it wildly—slashed again and again, even when his knife met no resistance and he felt himself leaping up through the reluctant waters to the blessed air above . . .

For a long while he lay floating on the stream, with only his face above the surface, balancing himself with slight movements of his legs and arms, sawing in an ecstasy of leisure through the other ropes on his wrists and ankles, and drinking in the unforgettable glory of the night. Afterwards, he could never remember those moments clearly: they were a space out of his life that was cut off from everything in the past and everything in the future, when he thought of inconsequential things with an incomparably vivid rapture, and saw commonplace things with an exquisite sensuous delight that could not have been put into words. He couldn't even recollect how long it lasted, that voluptuous realization of the act of living; he only knew that at the end of it he saw the black bulk of a ship looming up towards him with a tiny white crest at her bows, and had to start swimming to save himself from being run down. Somehow the swim brought him close to the north bank of the river, and he cruised idly upstream until he found a flight of stone steps leading up into a narrow alley between two buildings. The alley led into a narrow dingy street, and somewhere along the street he found a taxi which, in an unlikely spot like that, could only have been planted there for his especial service by a guardian angel with a most commendable sense of responsibility.

The driver peered at him keenly in the light of the melancholy street lamp under which the cab was parked.

"You're wet," he said at last, with the same pride of discovery that must have throbbed in Charles Darwin's breast when he gave the fruit of his researches to the world.

"You know, George, I believe you've hit it," said the Saint, in a whisper of admiring awe in which the old unconquerable mockery was beginning to lift itself again. "I thought something was wrong, but I couldn't make out what it was. Do you think I can have been in some water?"

The driver frowned at him suspiciously. "Are you drunk?" he asked, with disarming frankness, and the Saint shook his head.

"Not yet—but I have a feeling that with very little encouragement I could be. I want to go to Cornwall House, Piccadilly, and I'll pay for any damage I do to your lovely cushions."

Probably it was the tone and manner of what the chauffeur would have described as a toff which dissolved suspicion away into a tolerant appreciation of aristocratic eccentricity, and induced him to accept the fare. At any rate, he accepted it, and even went so far as to oblige Simon with a cigarette.

Lounging back in a corner with the smoke sinking luxuriously into his lungs, the Saint felt his spirits rising with the speed of an irresponsible rocket. The ordeal he had been through, the shadow of death and the strange supreme joy of life after it, slipped back into the annals of memory. To the High Fence, he was dead: he had been dropped off a boat into the lower waters of the Thames with a lump of iron tied to his feet—swallowed up in the bottom ooze and slime of the river, where any secret might well be safe. Both as a proven interferer and a potentially greater menace, he had been removed. But before being drowned, he had given up his secret. He had told exactly what he had done with the parcel of precious stones of which Mr Clive Enderby had been bereaved—and the High Fence was going to Harwich to take the name of Joshua Pond in vain . . . And Simon Templar had an increasingly blissful idea that he was going to be there to witness the performance.

As the cab drew up before Cornwall House he saw a girl and a man coming out, and decanted himself on to the pavement before the taxi had properly reached a standstill.

"Are you looking for some fun, souls?" he murmured. "Because if so, I could use you."

Patricia Holm stared at him for a moment in breathless silence, and then, with an incoherent little cry, she threw herself into his arms . . .

Mr Uniatz swallowed, and touched the Saint with stubby fingers, as if he were something fragile.

"Howja get wet, boss?" he asked.

Simon grinned, and indicated the interested taxi-driver with a movement of his head.

"George here thinks I must have been in some water," he said. "Give him a quid for the inspiration, will you?—I only had a fiver on me when I went out, but they pinched it."

He led Patricia back into the building with a damp arm round her shoulders, while Hoppy paid off the taxi and rejoined them in the foyer. They rode up in the lift in an enforced silence, but Patricia was shaking him by the arm as soon as the door of the apartment had closed behind them.

"Where have you been, boy? What's happened?"

"Were you worried?"

"You know that."

He kissed her.

"I guess you must have been. Where were you off to?"

"We were going to call on Enderby." She was still holding herself in the curve of his arm, wet as he was. "It was the only line we had—what you told me outside here, before Pryke took you off."

"I could of made him talk, boss," said Mr Uniatz, in a tone of pardonable disappointment. "After I'd got t'ru wit' him—"

The Saint smiled.

"I suppose he'd've been lucky to be able to talk. Well, the scheme might still be a good one . . ." He toyed with the idea for a thoughtful moment, and then he shook his head. "But—no we don't need it now. And there may be something much more useful for you to do. Get me a drink, Pat, if Hoppy's left anything, and I'll tell you."

Half an hour in his sodden clothes had left him chilled and shivery, but a steep tot of whisky would soon put that right. He lay submerged in a hot bath, with the glass balanced on the edge, and told them the story of his adventures through the open door. It was a tale that made Patricia bite her lips towards the end, but for him it was all in the past. When he came through into the living-room again, cheerful and glowing from the massage of a rough towel, with his hair sleekly brushed again and a woolly bath-robe slung round him, lighting a cigarette with steady hands and the old irrepressible laughter on his lips, it was difficult to imagine that barely an hour ago he had fought one of his most terrific fights with death.

"So here we are," he said, with the blue lights crisp and dancing in his eyes. "We don't know who the High Fence is, but we know where he's going, and we know the password he's going to give. It's rather quiet and logical, but we've got him. Just because he's made that one natural mistake. If I were swinging at the bottom of the Pool, as he thinks I am, there wouldn't be a snag in his life. He'd just go to Harwich and recover his boodle, and that would be the end of a spot of very satisfactorily settled bother. But he's going to have a surprise."

"Can we come with you?" said Patricia.

The Saint shook his head.

"I'd like you to. But I can't be everywhere at once, and I shall want someone in London. You mayn't have realized it, but we still have our own bills to pay. The swine knocked a fiver off me when they took me for that ride, and I want it back. Teal's going to achieve his ambition and lag the High Fence, and that parcel of jools that's going to give the High Fence away is evidence now, but we've got our Old Age Pensions to think about. Anyone who wants to amuse himself by pumping me up with gas and dope and heaving me into the river has got to pay for his fun. And that's where you two come in."

He told them of what was in his mind, in terse sparkling sentences, while he dressed. His brain was working at high pressure by that time, throwing ideas together with his own incomparable audacity, building a plan out of a situation that had not yet come to pass, leaving them almost out of breath behind the whirlwind pace of his imagination. And yet, despite the breakneck pace at which he had swept his strategy together, he had no misgivings about it afterwards—not even while he drove his great thundering car recklessly through the night to Harwich, or when he stood outside the post office in the early morning waiting for the doors to open.

It should be all right . . . About some things he had a feeling of sublime confidence, a sense of joyous inevitability, that amounted to actual foreknowledge, and he had the same feeling that morning. These things were ordained: they were the reward of adventure, the deserved corollaries of battle, murder, and—a slight smile touched his lips—the shadow of sudden death. But with all this assurance of foreknowledge, there was still a ghostly pulse of nervous excitement flickering through his spinal cells when the doors opened to let him in—a tingle of deep delight in the infinitely varied twists of the game which he loved beyond anything else in life.

He went up to the counter and propped his elbows on the flat of the telegraph section. He wanted to send a cable to Umpopo in British Bechuanaland, but before he sent it he wanted to know all about the comparative merits of the various word rates. He was prepared, according to the inducements offered, to consider the relative attractions of Night Letters, Week-end Letters, or Deferreds, and he wanted to know everything there was to know about each. Naturally, this took time. The official behind the grille, although he claimed a sketchy familiarity with the whereabouts of British Bechuanaland, had never heard of Umpopo, which is not surprising, because the Saint had never heard of it either before he set out to invent a difficult place to want to send a cable to. But with that indomitable zeal which is the most striking characteristic of post-office officials, he applied himself diligently to the necessary research, while Simon Templar lighted another cigarette and waited patiently for results.

He was wearing a brown tweed cap of a pattern which would never ordinarily have appealed to him, and a pair of tortoise-shell glasses and a black military moustache completed the job of disguising him sufficiently to be overlooked on a casual glance even by anyone who knew him. As the last man on earth whom the High Fence would be expecting to meet, he was as well hidden as if he had been buried under the floor . . . The official behind the counter, meanwhile, was getting buried deeper and deeper under a growing mound of reference books.

"I can't seem to find anything about Umpopo," he complained peevishly, from behind his unhelpful barricade. "Are you sure there is a telegraph office there?"

"Oh, yes," said the Saint blandly. "At least," he added, "there's one at Mbungi, which is only half a mile away."

The clerk went back through his books in a silence too frightful to describe, and the Saint put his cigarette back between his lips, and then suddenly remained very still.

Another early customer had entered the office. Simon heard his footsteps crossing the floor and passing behind him, but he did not look round at once. The footsteps travelled along to the poste restante section, a couple of yards away, and stopped there.

"Have you anything for Pond?"

The soft voice came clearly to Simon's ears, and he lifted his eyes sidelong. The man was leaning on the counter, like himself, so that his back was half turned, but the Saint's heart stopped beating for a moment.

"What is the first name?" asked the clerk, clearing out the contents of one of the pigeon-holes behind him.

"Joshua."

Rather slowly and dreamily, the Saint hitched himself up off his elbow and straightened up. Behind his heaped breakwater of reference books, the steaming telegraph official was muttering something profane and plaintive, but the Saint never heard it. He saw the cardboard box which he had posted pushed over to its claimant, and moved along the counter without a sound. His hand fell on the man's shoulder.

"Would you like to see a good-looking ghost?" he drawled, with a throb of uncontrollable beatitude in his voice.

The man spun round with a kind of gasp that was almost a sob. It was Junior Inspector Desmond Pryke.

10

The writer, whose positively Spartan economy of verbiage must often have been noted and admired by every cultured student, recoils instinctively from the temptation to embellish the scene with a well-chosen anthology of those apt descriptive adjectives with which his vocabulary is so richly stocked. The pallor of flabbergasted faces, the glinting of wild eyes, the beading of cold perspirations, the trembling of hands, the tingling of spines, the sinking of stomachs, the coming and going of breath in little short pants—all those facile clichés which might lure less ruggedly disciplined scribes into the pitfall of endeavouring to make every facet of the situation transparent to the most nitwitted reader—none of these things, on this occasion at least, have sufficient enticement to seduce him. His readers, he assures himself, are not nitwits: they are highly gifted and intelligent citizens of phenomenal perspicacity and acceleration on the uptake. The situation, he feels, stated even in the baldest terms, could hide none of its facets from them.

It hid none of them from Simon Templar, or from Junior Inspector Pryke. But Simon Templar was the first to speak again.

"What are you doing here, Desmond?" he asked gently.

Pryke licked his lips, without answering. And then the question was repeated, but Simon Templar did not repeat it.

Chief Inspector Teal stepped out from behind a screen which cut off the Savings Bank section of the counter, and repeated it. His hands were in the pockets of his unnecessary raincoat, and his movement had the same suggestion of weary and reluctant effort that his movements always had, but there was something in the set of his rounded plump jaw and the narrowness of his sleepy-lidded eyes which explained beyond any need of words that he had watched the whole brief incident from beginning to end, and had missed none of the reactions which a police officer on legitimate business need not have shown.

"Yes—what are you doing?" he said.

Pryke's head jerked round again, and his face went another shade greyer. For a further interval of thrumming seconds he seemed to be struggling to find his voice, and the Saint smiled.

"I told you the High Fence would be here to collect his boodle, Claud," he said, and looked at Pryke again. "Quincey told me," he said.

"I don't know what you're talking about." Pryke had got some kind of control over his throat, but there was a quiver in his breathing which made odd little breaks in the sentence. "I heard that there were some stolen jewels here—"

"Who from?" Teal asked quietly.

"From a man I found on the theory I was working on. You told me I could—"

"What was his name?"

"That's a long story," said Pryke hoarsely. "I met him . . ."

Probably he knew that the game was over—that the bluff was hopeless except as a play for time. The attack was too overwhelming. Watching him with smiling lips and bleak blue eyes, the Saint knew that there wasn't a man living who could have warded it off—whose brain, under the shock, could yet have moved fast enough to concoct a story, instantaneously and without reflection, that would have stood the light of remorseless investigation which must have been directed into it.

"I met him last night," said Pryke. "I suppose you have some reason—"

Simon nodded.

"We have," he said gently. "We came here to play the grand old parliamentary game of Sitting on the Fence, and it looks as if you are what might be called the sittee."

"You're crazy," said Pryke harshly.

His hand was sliding towards his hip, in a casual movement that should have been merely the conventional search for a cigarette-case, and Simon saw it a fraction of a second late.

He saw the flash of the nickel-plated gun, and the shot blasted his eardrums as he flung himself aside. Pryke swerved frantically, hesitated an instant, and turned his automatic on the broad target of Chief Inspector Teal, but before he could touch the trigger again the Saint's legs had swung round in a flailing scissor-sweep that found its marks faultlessly on knee-joint and ankle-bone. Pryke cursed and went down, clean and flat as a dead fish, with a smack that squeezed half the breath out of his body, and the Saint rolled over and held him in an ankle lock while the local men who had been posted outside poured in through the doors.

And that was approximately that.

The Saint continued to lie prostrate on the floor after Pryke had been handcuffed and taken away, letting the profound contentment of the day sink into his soul and make itself gorgeously at home. Misunderstanding his stillness, Mr Teal bent over him with a shadow of alarm on his pink face.

"Are you hurt?" he asked gruffly, and the Saint chuckled.

"Only in my pride." He reached out and retrieved his cigarette, which had parted company with him during the scuffle, and blew the dust off it before replacing it in his mouth. "I'm getting a worm's-eye view of life—you might call it an act of penance. If I'd had to make a list of all the people who I didn't think would ever turn out to be the High Fence, your Queen of the May would have been first on the roll. Well, I suppose Life has these surprises . . . But it all fits in. Being on duty at Market Street, he wouldn't have had any trouble in poisoning Johnny Anworth's horseradish, but I'm not quite sure how he got Sunny Jim—"

"I am," said Teal grimly. "He was standing a little behind me when I was talking to Fasson—between me and the door. He could have shot Fasson from his pocket and slammed the door before I could look round, without taking a tremendous risk . . . After all, there was no reason for anyone to suspect him. He put it over on all of us." Teal fingered a slip of chewing-gum out of his pocket and unwrapped it sourly, for he also had his pride. "I suppose it was you who took Sunny Jim away," he said suddenly.

Simon grinned.

"Teal! Will you always think these unkind thoughts about me?"

The detective sighed. He picked up the evidential package from the counter, opened it, glanced at the gleaming layers of gems, and stuffed it firmly into his pocket. No one knew better than himself what unkind thoughts he would always have to think. But in this case at least the Saint had done him a service, and the accounts seemed to be all square—which was an almost epoch-making denouement. "What are you getting out of this?" he inquired suspiciously.

The Saint rose to his feet with a smile, and brushed his clothes.

"Virtue," he said piously, "is its own reward. Shall we go and look for some breakfast, or must you get on with your job?"

Mr Teal shook his head.

"I must get back to London—there are one or two things to clear up. Pryke's flat will have to be searched. There's still a lot of stolen property to be recovered, and I shouldn't be surprised to find it there— he must have felt so confident of never being suspected that he wouldn't bother about a secret headquarters. Then we shall have to pull in Quincey and Enderby, but I don't expect they'll give us much trouble now." The detective buttoned his coat, and his drowsy eyes went over the Saint's smiling face with the perpetual haze of unassuageable doubt still lingering in them. "I suppose I shall be seeing you again," he said.

"I suppose you will," said the Saint, and watched Teal's stolid portly figure lumbering out into the street before he turned into the nearest telephone booth. He agreed with Mr Teal that Pryke had probably been confident enough to use his own apartment as his headquarters. But Patricia Holm and Hoppy Uniatz were already in London, whereas Mr Teal had to get there, and Simon Templar had his own unorthodox interpretation of the rewards of Virtue.

THE ELUSIVE ELLSHAW

1

The visitors who came to see the Saint uninvited were not only members of the CID. In several years of spectacular outlawry, Simon Templar had acquired a reputation which was known wherever newspapers were read.

"There must be something about me that excites the storytelling instinct in people," he complained once to Patricia Holm, who should have known better than anyone how seriously to take his complaint. "Four out of every five have it, and their best friends won't tell 'em."

Most of the legends that circulated about him were fabulously garbled, but the fundamental principles were fairly accurate. As a result, he had an ever-growing public which seemed to regard him as something between a benevolent if slightly weak-minded uncle and a miracle-working odd-job man. They ranged from burglars who thought that his skill might be enlisted in their enterprises for a percentage of the proceeds, to majestic dowagers who thought that he might be instrumental in tracing a long-lost Pekinese; from shop girls in search of romance to confidence men in search of a likely buyer of a gold brick. Sometimes they were interesting, sometimes they were pathetic;

mostly they were merely tiresome. But on rare occasions they brought the Saint in touch with those queer happenings and dark corners in other people's lives from which many of his adventures began, and for that reason there were very few of them whom he refused to see.

There was one lady in particular whom he always forced himself to remember whenever he was tempted to dodge one of these callers, for she was quite definitely the least probable herald of adventure who ever crossed his path. He was, as a matter of fact, just ready to go out one morning when Sam Outrell telephoned up to announce her.

"Your Jersey 'as come back from the cleaners, sir," was his cryptic postscript to the information.

Sam Outrell had been raised on a farm, many years before he came to be head porter in the apartment building on Piccadilly where the Saint lived, and incidentally one of Simon's loyalest watch-dogs, and the subterfuges by which he managed to convey a rough description of visitors who were standing at his elbow were often most abstrusely bucolic. Simon could still remember the occasion when he had been suffering tireless persecution from a stout Society dame who was trying to manufacture divorce evidence against her doddering spouse, on which Sam had told him that "Your silk purse has turned up, sir," and had explained later that he meant to convey that "The old sow's 'ere."

"I'll have a look at it," said the Saint, after a brief hesitation.

Viewing Mrs Florence Ellshaw for the first time, when he opened the door to her, Simon could not deny that Sam Outrell had an excuse for his veiled vulgarity. She was certainly very bovine in build, with stringy mouse-coloured hair and a remarkable torso—the Saint didn't dislike her, but he did not feel that Life would have been incomplete if she had never discovered his address.

"It's about me 'usband, sir," said Mrs Ellshaw, putting the matter in what must have looked to her like a nutshell.

"What is about your husband?" asked the Saint politely.

"I seen 'im," declared Mrs Ellshaw emphatically. "I seen 'im last night, plain as I can see you, I did, 'im wot left me a year ago wivout a word, after all I done for 'im, me that never gave 'im a cross word even when 'e came 'ome late an' left all 'is money at the local, as large as life 'e was, an' me workin' me fingers to the bone to feed 'is children, six of 'em wot wouldn't 'ave a rag to their backs if it weren't for me brother Bert as 'as a job in a garridge, with three of his own 'im to look after and his wife an invalid, she often cries all night, it's pitiful—"

Simon perceived that to let Mrs Ellshaw tell her story in her own way would have required a lifetime's devotion.

"What do you want me to do?" he interrupted.

"Well, sir, I seen 'im last night, after 'im leaving me wivout a word, 'e might 'ave bin dead for all I was to know, after all I done for 'im, as I says to 'im only the day before 'e went, I says 'Ellshaw,' I says, 'I'm the best wife you're ever likely to 'ave, an' I defy you to say anythink else,' I says, an' me workin' me fingers to the bone, with varicose veins as 'urts me somethink terrible sometimes, I 'as to go an' sit down for an hour, this was in Duchess Place—"

"What was in Duchess Place?" asked the Saint weakly.

"Why, where I sore 'im," said Mrs Ellshaw, "'im wot left me wivout a word—"

"After all you done for him—"

"An' me doing for gentlemen around 'ere all these months to feed 'is children, wiv me pore legs achin' an' 'e turns an' runs away when 'e sees me as if I 'adn't bin the best wife a man ever 'ad, an' never a cross word between us all these years."

The Saint found it hard to believe that Mrs Ellshaw had reached an intentional full stop, and concluded that she had merely paused for breath. He took a mean advantage of her momentary incapacity.

"Didn't you run after him?" he put in.

"That I did, sir, wiv me pore legs near to bursting after me being on them all day, an' 'e runs into an 'ouse an' slams the door, an' I gets there after 'im an' rings the bell an' nobody answers, though I waits there 'arf an hour if I waited a minnit, ringin' the bell, an' me sufferin' with palpitations wot always come over me if I run, the doctor tole me I mustn't run about, an' nobody answers till I says to meself, 'All right, Ellshaw,' I says, 'I'll be smarter'n you are,' I says, an' I goes back to the 'ouse this morning, not 'arf an hour ago it wasn't, an' rings the bell again like it might be a tradesman delivering something, an' 'e opens the door, an' when 'e seen me 'e gets all angry, as if I 'adn't bin the best wife ever a man 'ad—"

"And never a cross word between you all these years—"

"'Yer daft cow,' 'e says, 'can't yer see yer spoilin' everythin'?' 'Never you mind wot I'm spoiling,' I says, 'even if it is some scarlet 'ussy yer livin' with in that 'ouse, you gigolo,' I says, 'leaving me wivout a word after all I done for you,' I says, and 'e says to me, ''Ere's some money, if that's wot yer after, an' you can 'ave some more any time you want it, so now will you be quiet an' get out of 'ere or else you'll lose me job, that's wot you'll do, if anybody sees you 'ere,' 'e says, an' 'e shoves some money into me 'and an' slams the door again, so I come straight round 'ere to see you, sir."

"What for?" asked the Saint feebly.

He felt that he was only inviting a fresh cataract of unpunctuated confidences, but he could think of no other question that seemed so entirely apt.

Mrs Ellshaw, however, did not launch out into another long-distance paragraph. She thrust one of her beefy paws into the fleshy canyon that ran down from her breastbone into the kindly concealment of her clothing, and dragged out what looked at first like a crumpled roll of white paper.

"That's wot for," she said, thrusting the catch towards him.

Simon took it and flattened it out. It was three new five-pound notes clumsily crushed together, and for the first time in that interview he was genuinely interested.

"Is that what he gave you?"

"That's wot he gave me, exactly as 'e put it in me 'and, an' there's somethink dirty about it, you mark my words."

"What sort of job was your husband in before he—er—left you?" Simon inquired.

"'E never 'ad no regular job," said Mrs Ellshaw candidly. "Sometimes 'e made a book—you know, sir, that street betting wot's supposed to be illegal. Sometimes 'e used to go to race meetings, but I don't know wot 'e did there, but I know 'e never 'ad fifteen pounds in 'is life that 'e came by honestly, that I know, and I wouldn't let 'im be dishonest, it ain't worth it, with so many coppers about, and 'im a married man wiv six children—"

"What's the address where you saw him?"

"It's in Duchess Place, sir, wot's more like a mews, and the 'ouse is number six, sir, that's wot it is, it's next door to two young gennelmen as I do for, such nice gennelmen they are too, always askin' about me legs—"

The Saint stood up. He was interested, but he had no intention of resuming a study of Mrs Ellshaw's varicose veins.

"I don't know whether I can do anything for you, but I'll see what I can find out—you might like to let me change these fivers for you," he added. "Pound notes will be easier for you to manage, and these may help me."

He put the three banknotes away in a drawer, and saw the last of Mrs Ellshaw with some relief. Her troubles were not so utterly commonplace as he had expected them to turn out when she started talking, and some of the brightest episodes in his career had had the most unpromising beginnings, but there was nothing in the recital he had just listened to which struck him as giving it any special urgency. Even when the whole story was an open book to him, the Saint could not feel that he was to blame for failing to foresee the consequences of Mrs Ellshaw's visit.

He was occupied at that time with quite a different proposition—the Saint was nearly always occupied with something or other, for his ideas of good living were put together on a shamelessly plutocratic scale, and all his expenses were paid out of the proceeds of his raids on those whom he knew as the Ungodly. In this case it was a man of no permanent importance who claimed to be the owner of a mining concession in Brazil. There were always one or two men of that kind on the Saint's visiting list—they were the providential pot-boilers of his profession, and he would have considered it a crime to let them pass him by, but only a very limited number of them have been found worthy of commemoration in these chronicles. He walked home from the conclusion of this casual episode at two o'clock in the morning, and might have died before dawn if Sam Outrell had been less conscientious.

"The men have been to fix your extension telephone," was the message passed on to him by the night porter, and the Saint, who had not ordered an extension telephone at all, was silently thoughtful in the lift that whisked him up to his floor.

He walked down the corridor, as soundless as a prowling cat on the thick carpet, past the entrance of his own suite to another door at the very end of the passage. There was a key on his chain to unlock it, and he stepped out on to the fire-escape and lighted a cigarette under the stars.

From the handrail of the grating where he stood, it was an easy swing to his bathroom window, which was open. He passed across the sill like a shadow and went from room to room with a gun in his hand, searching the darkness with supersensitive faculties for anything that might be waiting to catch him unawares. Everything was quiet, but he touched pieces of furniture, and knew that they had been moved. The drawers of his desk were open, and his foot rustled against a sheaf of papers carelessly thrown down on the floor. Without touching a light switch he knew that the place had been effectively ransacked, but he came to the hall without finding a trace of any more actively unfriendly welcome.

It was not until he switched on the hall light that he saw what his fate ought to have been.

There was a cheap fibre attaché-case standing close to the entrance— if he had moved another step to one side he would have kicked it. Two thin insulated wires ran from it to the door and terminated in a pair of bright metal contacts like a burglar alarm, one of them screwed to the frame and the other to the door itself. If he had entered in the normal way, they would have completed the circuit directly the door began to open, and he had no doubt what the sequel would have been.

An ingenious mixture of an electrical detonator, a couple of pounds of gelignite, and an assortment of old scrap-iron was indicated inside that shabby case, but the Saint did not attempt to make certain of it, because it was not beyond the bounds of possibility that some such eccentric entrance as he had made could have been foreseen, and a second detonator provided to act on anyone who opened the valise to investigate it. He disconnected the wires, and drove out to Hammersmith Bridge with the souvenir, very cautiously, as soon as he could fetch his car from the garage, and lowered his potential decease on a string to the bottom of the Thames.

So far as he could tell, only the three five-pound notes which he had put away in his desk had been taken. It was this fact which made him realize that the search of his rooms had not been a merely mechanical preliminary to the planting of a booby-trap by one of the many persons who had reason to desire his funeral. But it was not until the next morning that he realized how very important the disappearance of Mr Ellshaw must be, when he learned how Mrs Ellshaw had left her troublesome veins behind her for all time.

2

The body was taken out of the Thames just below London Bridge by the river police. There were no marks of violence beyond a slight bruise on the forehead which might have been caused by contact with the piers of one of the upper bridges. Death was due to drowning.

"It's as obvious as any suicide can be," said Chief Inspector Claud Eustace Teal. "Apparently the woman's husband left her about a year ago, and she had to work like a slave to keep the children. Her neighbours say she was very excited the night before, talking incoherently about having seen her husband and him having refused to recognize her. If that was true, it provides a motive; if it wasn't, it covers 'unsound mind.'"

The Saint lounged back in his chair and crossed his feet on a sheaf of reports on Mr Teal's sacred desk.

"As a matter of fact, it was true," he said. "But it doesn't provide a motive—it destroys it."

If anybody else had made such a statement Mr Teal would have jeered at him, more or less politely according to the intruder's social standing, but he had been sitting at that desk for too many years to jeer spontaneously at anything the Saint said. He shuffled his chewing-gum to the back of his mouth and gazed across the Saint's vandal shoes with sporously clouded eyes.

"How do you know?"

"Because she came to see me yesterday morning with the same story, and I'd promised to see what I could do for her."

"You think it was murder?" asked Teal, with cherubic impassivity.

Simon shrugged.

"I'd promised to look into it," he repeated. "In fact, she had a date to come and see me again on Friday evening and hear if I'd managed to find out anything. If she had enough faith in me to bring me her troubles in the first place, I don't see her diving into the river before she knew the verdict."

Teal brought his spearmint back into action, and worked on it for a few seconds in silence. He looked as if he were on the point of falling asleep.

"Did she say anything to make you think she might be murdered?"

"Nothing that I understood. But I feel kind of responsible. She was killed after she'd been to see me, and it's always on the cards that she was killed because of it. There was something fishy about her story, anyhow, and people in fishy rackets will do plenty to keep me out of 'em . . . I was nearly murdered myself last night."

"Nearly?" said Mr Teal.

He seemed disappointed.

"I'm afraid so," said the Saint cheerfully. "Give me something to drink and find out for yourself whether I'm a ghost."

"Do you think it was because of something Mrs Ellshaw told you?"

"I'm damned if I know, Claud. But somebody put down all the makings of a Guy Fawkes picnic in Cornwall House last night, and I shouldn't be talking to you now if I hadn't been born careful as well as lucky—there's something about the way I insist on keeping on living which must be frightfully discouraging to a lot of blokes, but I wouldn't believe for a moment that you were one of them."

Chief Inspector Teal chewed his way through another silence. He knew that the Saint had called on him to extract information, not to give it. Simon Templar gave nothing away, where Scotland Yard was at the receiving end. A Commissioner's post-mortem on the remains of a recent sensational case in which the Saint had played a leading and eventually helpful part had been held not long ago: it had, however, included some unanswerable questions about the fate of a large quantity of stolen property which the police had expected to recover when they laid the High Fence by the heels, and Mr Teal was still smarting from some of the things which had been said. He had been wielding his unavailing bludgeon in the endless duel between Scotland Yard and that amazing outlaw too long to believe that the Saint would ever consult him with no other motive than a Boy Scout ambition to do him a good turn. Every assistance that Simon Templar had ever given the Metropolitan Police had had its own particular string tied to it, but in Teal's job he had to take the strings with the favours. The favours had helped to put paid to the accounts of many elusive felons; the strings accounted for many of the silver threads among Mr Teal's dwindling fleece of gold, and seemed likely to account for many more.

"If you think Mrs Ellshaw was murdered, that's your affair," he said at last. "We haven't any reason to suspect it—yet. Or do you want to give us any?"

Simon thought for a moment, and said, "Do you know anything about the missing husband?"

"As a matter of fact, we did use to know him. He was about the worst card-sharp we ever had on our records. He used to work the race trains, usually—he always picked on someone who'd had too much to drink, and even then he was so clumsy that he'd have been lagged a dozen times if the mugs he found hadn't been too drunk to remember what he looked like. Does that fit in with your theory?" Teal asked, with the disarming casualness of a gambolling buffalo.

The Saint smiled.

"I have no theory, Claud. That's what I'm looking for. When I've got one, we might have another chat."

There was nothing more to be got out of him, and the detective saw him go with an exasperated frown creasing down over his sleepy blue eyes.

As a matter of fact, the Saint had been perfectly straightforward—chiefly because he had nothing to conceal. He had no theory, but he was certainly looking for one. The only thing he had kept back was the address where Mrs Ellshaw had seen her mysterious husband. It was the only information he had from which to start his inquiries, and Mr Teal remembered that he had forgotten to ask for it five minutes after the Saint had left.

It was not much consolation for him to realize that the Saint would never have given him the information even if he had asked for it. Simon Templar's idea of criminal investigation never included any premature intrusions by the Department provided by London's ratepayers for the purpose, and he had his own methods of which that admirable body had never approved.

He went out of Scotland Yard and walked round to Parliament Square with a strange sensation going through him as if a couple of dozen fleas in hobnailed boots were playing hopscotch up and down his spine. The sensation was purely psychic, for his nerves were as cold as ice, as he knew by the steadiness of his hand when he stopped to light a cigarette at the corner of Whitehall, but he recognized the feeling. It was the supernatural, almost clairvoyant tingle that rippled through his consciousness when intuition leapt ahead of logic—an uncanny positive prescience for which logic could only trump up weak and fumbling reasons. He knew that Adventure had opened her arms to him again—that something had happened, or was happening, that was bound to bring him once more into the perilous twisted trails in which he was most at home—that because a garrulous charwoman had taken it into her head to bring him her troubles, there must be fun and games and boodle waiting for him again under the shadow of sudden death. That was his life, and it seemed as if it always would be.

He had nothing much to go on, but that could be rectified. The Saint had a superb simplicity of outlook in these matters. A taxi came cruising by, and stopped when he put up his hand.

"Take me to Duchess Place," he said. "It's just at the back of Curzon Street. Know it?"

The driver said that he knew it. Simon relaxed in a corner and propped up his feet on the spare seat diagonally opposite, while the cab turned up Birdcage Walk and wriggled through the Green Park towards Hyde Park Corner. Once he roused himself to test the mechanism of the automatic in his hip-pocket; once again to loosen the thin-bladed knife in its sheath under his left sleeve. Neither of those weapons was part of the conventional outfit which anyone so impeccably dressed as he was would have been expected to wear, but for many years the Saint had placed caution so far before convention that convention was out of sight.

He paid off his taxi at the corner of Duchess Place and walked up towards number six. It was one of a row of those dingy unimaginative brick houses, with rusty iron railings and shabbily painted windows, which would be instantly ranked as cheap tenement cottages by any stranger who had not heard of the magic properties of the word "Mayfair." Simon went up the steps and rang the tarnished brass bell without hesitation—he hadn't the faintest notion how he would continue when the door was opened, if it was opened, but he had gone into and emerged from a great deal of trouble with the same blithe willingness to let circumstances provide for him.

The door opened in a few moments, and circumstances proceeded to provide for him so completely and surprisingly that he was ready for some unpleasantness.

The man who looked out of the door was rather small and wiry, with thin grey hair and a sallow bird-like Cockney face on which the reddish tint of his nose stood out so unexpectedly that it looked at first sight like one of those ageless carnival novelties which give so much harmless pleasure to adult infants engaged in the laborious business of having a good time. With his threadbare and baggy trousers, and his pink shirt fastened together with a stud at the neck but virginally innocent of collar or tie, he looked like the very last sort of man who ought to be answering a doorbell in that expensive slum.

"I want to see Mr Ellshaw," said the Saint, with sublime directness, and knew at once that he was talking to the man he wanted.

His first surprise was when this was admitted.

"I'm Ellshaw," said the man at once. "You're Mr Templar, ain't yer?"

The Saint drew at his cigarette with a certain added thoughtfulness. He never forgot a face, and he was sure that this little bird with the carmine beak could not have slipped out of his mind very easily if their paths had ever crossed before. But he acknowledged the identification with outwardly unaltered amiability.

"How did you know that, Archibald?"

"I was just comin' round to see yer, guv'nor." The little man opened the door wider, and stepped back invitingly. "Would yer like ter step inside fer a minute?—I've got somefink to tell yer."

The Saint stepped inside. He put his hands in his pockets as he crossed the threshold, and one of them rested on the butt of his gun.

Ellshaw led him through the uncarpeted hall to the nearest door, which brought them into the front ground-floor room. There was hardly any furniture in it—a piece of cheap hair carpet, a painted deal table carrying a bottle and glasses and the scars of cigarette-ends, and a couple of ancient arm-chairs with soiled chintz covers would have formed a practically complete inventory. There were grimy lace curtains nailed up on the windows at the street end, and a door communicating with the back room at the other. From the oak parquet floor, the tinted ceiling and tasteful electric-light fittings, it was obvious that the room had once been lived in by someone of a definite class, but everything in it at that moment spoke loudly of the shoddiest stock of the second-hand sale-room.

"Sit down, guv'nor," said Ellshaw, moving over to the chair nearer the window and leaving Simon no choice about the other. "'Ow abaht a drink?"

"No, thanks," said the Saint, with a faint smile. "What is it you were so anxious to tell me?"

Ellshaw settled himself in his chair and lighted a drooping fag.

"Well, guv'nor, it's abaht me ole woman. I left 'er a year ago. Between you an' I, she 'ad a lot of bad points, not that I want to speak evil of the dead—oh, yes, I know 'ow she committed suicide," he said, answering the slight lift of the Saint's eyebrows. "I sore it in the pypers this mornin'. But she 'ad 'er faults. She couldn't never keep 'er mouf shut. Wot could I do? The rozzers was lookin' for me on account of some bloke that 'ad a grudge against me an' tried ter frame me up, an' I knew if she'd knowed where I'd gorn she couldn't 'ave 'elped blabbin' it all over the plyce."

Simon was beginning to understand that he was listening to a speech in which the little Cockney had been carefully rehearsed—there was an artificial fluency about the way the sentences rattled off the other's tongue which gave him his first subtle warning. But he lay back in his chair and crossed his legs without any sign of the urgent questions that were racing through his mind.

"What was the matter?" he asked.

"Well, guv'nor, between you an' I, seein' as you understands these things, I used ter do a bit of work on the rice trains. Nothink dishonest, see—just a little gamble wiv the cards sometimes. Well, one dye a toff got narsty an' said I was cheatin', an' we 'ad a sort of mix-up, and my pal wot I was workin' wiv, 'e gets up an' slugs this toff wiv a cosh an' kills 'im. It wasn't my fault, but the flatties think I done it, an' they want me for murder."

"That's interesting," said the Saint gently. "I was talking to Chief Inspector Teal only a little while ago about you, and he didn't tell me you were wanted."

Ellshaw was only disconcerted for a moment.

"I don't spect 'e would've told yer, knowin' wot you are, guv'nor— if you'll ixcuse me syin' so. But that's Gawd's troof as sure as I'm sittin' 'ere, an' I wanted to come an' see yer—"

Simon was watching his eyes, and saw them wavering to some point behind his shoulder. He saw Ellshaw's face twitch into a sudden tension, and remembered the communicating door behind him in the same instant. With a lightning command of perfectly supple muscles he threw himself sideways over the arm of the chair, and felt something swish past his head and thud solidly into the upholstery, beating out a puff of grey dust.

In a flash he was on his feet again, in time to see the back of a man ducking through the door. His gun was out in his hand, and his brain was weighing out pros and cons with cool deliberation even while his finger tightened on the trigger. The cons had it—it was no use shooting unless he aimed to hit his target, and at that embryonic stage of the developments a hospital capture would be more of a liability than an asset. He dropped the automatic back in his pocket and jumped for the door empty-handed. It slammed in his face as he reached it, and a bottle wildly thrown from behind smashed itself on the wall a foot from his head. Calmly ignoring the latter interruption, Simon stepped back and put his heel on the lock with his weight behind it. The door, which had never been built to withstand that kind of treatment, surrendered unconditionally, and he went through into a chamber barely furnished as a bedroom. There was nobody under the bed or in the wardrobe, but there was another door at the side, and this also was locked. Simon treated it exactly as he had treated the first, and found himself back in the hall—just at the moment when the front door banged.

Ellshaw himself had vanished from the front room when he reached it, and the Saint leaned against the wreckage of the communicating door and lighted a fresh cigarette with a slow philosophical grin for his own ridiculous easiness.

As soon as they learned that the bomb had failed to take effect, of course, they were expecting him to follow up the clue which Mrs Ellshaw must have given him. Probably she had been followed from Duchess Place the previous morning, and it would not have been difficult for them to find out whom she went to see. The rest was inevitable, and the only puzzle in his mind was why the attempt had not been made to do something more conclusive than stunning him with a rubber truncheon while he sat in that chair with his back to the door.

But who were "they"? He searched the house from attic to basement in the hope of finding an answer, but he went through nothing more enlightening than a succession of empty rooms. Inquiries about the property at neighbouring estate agents might lead on to a clue, but there was none on the premises. The two ground-floor rooms were the only ones furnished—apparently Ellshaw had been living there for some time, but there was no evidence to show whether this was with or without the consent and knowledge of the landlord.

Simon went out into the street rather circumspectly, but no second attack was made on him. He walked back to Cornwall House to let

Patricia Holm know what was happening, and found a message waiting for him.

"Claud Eustace Teal rang up—he wants you to get in touch with him at once," she said, and gazed at him accusingly. "Are you in trouble again, old idiot?"

He ruffled her fair hair.

"After a fashion I am, darling," he confessed. "But it isn't with Claud—not yet. What the racket is I don't know, but they've tried to get me twice in the last twelve hours, which is good going."

"Who are they?"

"That's the question I've been asking myself all day. They're just 'person or persons unknown' at present, but I feel that we shall get to know each other better before long. And that ought to be amusing. Let's see what Claud Eustace is worrying about."

He picked up the telephone and dialled Scotland Yard. Instructions must have been left with the switchboard operator, for he had scarcely given his name when he heard Teal's sleepy voice.

"Were you serious about getting a bomb last night, Templar?"

"Mr Templar to you, Claud," said the Saint genially. "All the same, I was serious."

"Can you describe the bomb again?"

"It was built into a small fibre attaché-case—I didn't take it apart to inspect the works, but it was built to fire electrically when the door was opened."

"You haven't got it there, I suppose?"

Simon smiled.

"Sure—I wouldn't feel comfortable without it. I keep it on the stove and practise tap-dancing on it. Where's your imagination?"

Teal did not answer at once.

"A bomb that sounds like exactly the same thing was found in Lord Ripwell's house at Shepperton today," he said at last. "I'd like to come round and see you, if you can wait a few minutes for me."

3

The detective arrived in less than a quarter of an hour, but not before Simon had sent out for a packet of spearmint for him. Teal glanced at the pink oblong of waxed paper sitting up sedately in the middle of the table, and reached out for it with a perfectly straight face.

"Ripwell—isn't he the shipping millionaire?" said the Saint.

Teal nodded.

"It's very nearly a miracle that he isn't 'the late' shipping millionaire," he said.

Simon lighted a cigarette.

"Did you come here to tell me about it or to ask me questions?"

"You might as well know what happened," said the detective, unwrapping a wafer of his only vice with slothful care. "Ripwell intended to go down to his river house this evening for a long week-end, but during the morning he found that he wanted a reference book which he had left down there on his last visit. He sent his chauffeur down for it, but when the man got there he found that he'd forgotten to take the key. Rather than go back, he managed to get in through a window, and when he came to let himself out again he found the bomb.

It was fixed just inside the front door, and would have been bound to get the first person who opened it, which would probably have been Ripwell himself—apparently he doesn't care much about servants when he uses the cottage. That's about all there is to tell you, except that the description I have of the bomb from the local constabulary sounded very much like the one you spoke of to me, and there may be some reason to think that they were both planted by the same person."

"And even on the same day," said the Saint.

"That's quite possible. Ripwell's secretary went down to the house the day before for some papers, and everything was quite in order then."

The Saint blew three perfect smoke-rings and let them drift up to the ceiling.

"It all sounds very exciting," he murmured.

"It sounds as if you may have been right about Mrs Ellshaw, if all you told me was true," said Teal grimly. "By the way, where was it she saw her husband?"

Simon laughed softly.

"Claud, that 'by the way' of yours is almost a classic. But I wouldn't dream of keeping a secret from you. She saw him at number six, Duchess Place, just round a couple of corners from here. I know he was there, because I saw him myself a little while ago. But you won't find him if you go round now."

"How do you know that?"

"Because he's pulled his freight—he and another guy who tried to blip me over the head."

Teal chewed out his gum into a preoccupied assortment of patterns, gazing at him stolidly.

"Is that all you mean to tell me?"

Simon cocked an abstracted eyebrow at him.

"Meaning?"

"If an attempt was made to murder you, there must be a reason for it. You may have made yourself dangerous to this man, or this gang, in some way, and they want to get rid of you. Why not let us give you a hand for once?"

Pride would not let Mr Teal say any more, but Simon saw the blunt sincerity in the globular pink face, and knew that the detective was not merely putting on a routine blarney.

"Are you getting sentimental in your old age, Claud?" he protested, in a strain of mockery that was kinder than usual.

"I'm only doing my job." Teal made the admission grudgingly, as if he was afraid of betraying an official secret. "I know you sometimes get on to things before we hear of them, and I thought you might like to work in with us for a change."

Simon looked at him soberly. He understood the implications of everything that Teal had left unsaid, the unmentioned vials of acid comment which must have been decanted on that round lethargic head as a result of their last contest, and he sympathized. There had never been any malice behind the ebullitions of Teal-baiting which enlivened so many chapters of his scapegrace career.

He hooked one leg over the arm of his chair.

"I'd like to help you—if you helped me," he said seriously "But I've damned little to offer."

He hesitated for a moment, and then ran briefly over the events which had made up the entertainment in Duchess Place.

"I don't suppose that's much more use to you than it is to me," he ended up. "My part of it hangs together, but I don't know what it hangs on. Mrs Ellshaw was killed because she'd seen her husband, and I was offered the pineapple because I knew she'd seen him. The only thing I don't quite understand is why they didn't try to kill me when they had me in Duchess Place, but maybe they didn't want to hurry it. Anyway, one gathers that Ellshaw is a kind of unhealthy guy to see—I wonder if Ripwell saw him?"

"I haven't seen Ripwell myself yet," said Teal. "He's gone down to Shepperton to look at things for himself, and I shall have to go down tonight and have a talk with him. But I thought I'd better see you first."

The Saint fixed him with clear and speculative blue eyes for a few seconds, and then he drawled, "I could run you down in the car."

Somehow or other, that was what happened; Mr Teal was never quite sure why. He assured himself that he had never contemplated such a possibility when he set out to interview the Saint. In any case on which he was engaged, he insisted to this sympathetic internal Yes-man, the last thing he wanted was to have Simon Templar messing about and getting in his way. He winced to think of the remarks the Assistant Commissioner would make if he knew about it. He told himself that his only reason for accepting the Saint's offer was to have both his witnesses at hand for an easier comparison of clues, and he allowed himself to be hurled down to Shepperton in the Saint's hundred-mile-an-hour road menace with his qualms considerably soothed by the adequacy of this ingenious excuse.

They found his lordship pottering unconcernedly in his garden—a tall spare vigorous man with white hair and a white moustache. He had an unassuming manner and a friendly smile that were leagues apart from the conventional idea of a big business man.

"Chief Inspector Teal? I'm pleased to meet you. About that bomb, I suppose—a ridiculous affair. Some poor devil as mad as a hatter about capitalists or something, I expect. Well, it didn't do me any harm. Is this your assistant?"

His pleasant grey eyes were glancing over the Saint; Teal performed the necessary introduction with some trepidation.

"This is Mr Templar, your lordship. I only brought him with me because—"

"Templar?" The grey eyes twinkled. "Not the great Simon Templar, surely?"

"Yes, sir," said Teal uncomfortably. "This is the Saint. But—"

He stopped, with his mouth open and his eyes starting to protrude, blinking speechlessly at one of the most astounding spectacles of his life. Lord Ripwell had got hold of the Saint's hand, and was pumping it up and down and beaming all over his face with spontaneous warmth that was quite different from the cheerful courtesy with which he had greeted Mr Teal himself.

"The Saint? Bless my soul! What a coincidence! I think I've read about everything you've ever done, but I never thought I should meet you. So you really do exist. That's splendid. My dear fellow—"

Mr Teal cleared his throat hoarsely.

"I was trying to explain to your lordship that—"

"Remember the way you put it over on Rayt Marius twice running?" chortled his lordship, continuing to pump the Saint's hand. "I think that was about the best thing you've ever done. And the way you got Hugo Campard, with that South American revolution? I never had any use for that man—knew him too well myself."

"I brought him down," said Mr Teal, somewhat hysterically, "because he had the same—"

"And the way you blew up Francis Lemuel?" burbled Lord Ripwell. "Now, that was a really good job of bombing. You'll have to let me into the secret of how you did that before you leave here. I say, I'll bet Chief Inspector Teal would like to know. Wouldn't he? You must have led him a beautiful dance."

Mr Teal felt that he was gazing at something that Could Not Possibly Happen. The earth was reeling across his eyes like a fantastic roundabout. He would have been incapable of further agonies of dizzy incredulity if Lord Ripwell had suddenly gone down on all fours behind a bush and tried to growl like a bear.

The effort which he had to exert to get a grip on the situation must have cost him two years of life.

"I brought the Saint down, your lordship, because he seemed to have some kind of knowledge of the matter, and I thought—"

"Quite," drivelled his lordship. "Quite. Quite right. Now I know that everything's in good hands. If anybody knows how to solve the mystery, it's Mr Templar. He's got more brains than the whole of Scotland Yard put together. I say, Templar, you showed them how to do their own job in that Jill Trelawney case, didn't you? And you had them guessing properly when Renway—that Treasury fellow—you know—"

Chief Inspector Teal suppressed an almost uncontrollable shudder. Lord Ripwell was actually digging Simon Templar in the ribs.

It was some time before Mr Teal was able to take command again, and even then it was a much less positive sort of command than he had intended to maintain.

"Have you ever come across a man named Ellshaw?" he asked, when he could persuade Lord Ripwell to pay any attention to him.

"Ellshaw? Ellshaw? Never heard of him. No. What is he?"

"He is a rather bad card-sharper, your lordship."

"I don't play cards. No. I don't know him. Why?"

"There is some reason to believe that he may be connected with these bombing attempts. Did you ever by any chance meet his wife— Mrs Florence Ellshaw? She was a sort of charwoman."

Ripwell shook his head.

"I don't think I've ever employed any sort of charwoman." He looked up and raised his voice. "Hey, Martin, have we ever had a charwoman called Mrs Ellshaw?"

"No, sir," answered the youngish man who was coming across the lawn from the house, as he joined them. "At least, not in my time."

Ripwell introduced them.

"This is Mr Irelock—my secretary. He's been looking after me for five years, and he knows as much as I do."

"I'm sure that we've never employed anyone of that name," said Martin Irelock. To describe him in a sentence, he looked like a grown-up and rather serious-minded Kewpie with hornrimmed glasses fixed across the bridge of his nose as firmly as if they had grown there. "Do you think he has something to do with this business, Inspector?"

"It's just a theory, but it's the only one we have at present," said Mr Teal.

He summarized Simon Templar's knowledge of the mystery for them. Lord Ripwell was interested in this. He slapped the Saint on the back.

"Damn good," he applauded. "But why ever didn't you shoot the man when you had the chance? Then everything would have been cleared up."

"Claud Eustace doesn't like me shooting people," said the Saint mildly, at which Lord Ripwell guffawed in a manner which removed the last shadow of doubt from Teal's mind that at least one member of the peerage was in an advanced and malignant stage of senile decay.

Teal almost strangled himself.

"Apparently both the bombs were planted on the same day," he said, trying to lead the conversation back into the correct vein with all the official dignity of which he was capable. "I understand that your secretary—"

"That's right," agreed Irelock. "I had to come down here the day before yesterday, and there was no bomb here then."

"What time did you leave?"

"Just after six—I caught the six-twenty back to town."

"So the bomb must have been placed here at some time between six o'clock on Wednesday and the time the chauffeur found it this morning." Teal's baby-blue eyes, throttled down again to a somewhat strained drowsiness, were scanning the house and garden. The grounds were only about three-quarters of an acre in extent, bordered by the road on one side and the river on another, and separated from its neighbours by well-grown cypress hedges on the other two boundaries. In such a comparatively quiet situation, it might not be difficult to hear of anyone who had been seen loitering about the vicinity. "The local police may have learnt something more by this time, of course," he said.

"We'll get the Inspector to come round after dinner," said Ripwell affably. "You'll stay, of course."

Teal chewed for a while, pursing his lips.

"I'd rather take your lordship back to London with me," he said, and Ripwell frowned puzzledly.

"What on earth for?"

"Both the bombing attempts failed, but these people seem pretty determined. They made a second attempt to get Templar a few hours after the first. There's every chance that they may make a second attempt to get you, and it's easier to look after a man in London."

If it is possible for a man to snort good-humouredly, Lord Ripwell achieved the feat.

"Stuff and nonsense, Inspector," he said. "I came down here for a rest and some fresh air, and I'm not going to run away just because of a thing like this. I don't expect we'll hear any more about it, but if we do, I'm in good hands. Anybody who tries to kill me while the Saint's here will be biting off a bit more than he can chew—eh? What d'you say, Templar?"

"I was trying to explain to your lordship," said Teal thickly, "that I only brought Templar down to compare his story with yours. He has no official standing whatever, and as far as I am concerned he can go home—"

"Eh? What? Go home?" said Lord Ripwell, who had suddenly become very obtuse or very determined. "Don't be silly. I'm sure he doesn't want to go home. He likes this sort of thing. It isn't troubling him at all. And I want to talk to him about some of his exploits—I've wanted to for years. I like him. Wish my son was half the man he is." His lordship gurgled, with what Mr Teal, from his prejudiced viewpoint, considered to be positively doddering glee. "You don't want to go home, do you, Templar?"

Simon tapped out a cigarette on his case, and smiled. It was certainly rather a gorgeous situation. His gaze flickered wickedly over Claud Eustace Teal's reddening face.

"All the excitement seems to go on round Lord Ripwell and me," he murmured. "With both of us here together under the same roof, we could look forward to a gay week-end. I think it would be a grand idea to stay."

4

"Well, what d'you make of it, Templar?" asked Ripwell, when they were scattered about the living-room around a bottle of excellent dry sherry.

Simon shrugged.

"Up to the present, nothing at all. All of you know as much as I do. There seems to be some kind of move afoot to discourage people from seeing Ellshaw, but I've taken a gander at him myself, and I didn't notice anything about him that anyone would be crazy to see. All the same, there must be something big behind it—you don't get three murders planned for the same day because somebody wants to keep the name of his tailor secret."

"Do you think you could ever have known Ellshaw under another name, your lordship?" asked Teal. "Can you think of anyone who might have a bad enough grievance against you to want to blow you up?"

"I haven't an enemy in the world," said Lord Ripwell, and, looking at his clean pleasant face and friendly eyes, the statement was easy to believe.

The Saint grinned slowly, and reached out to refill his glass.

"I have plenty," he remarked. "But if you haven't any, it disposes of that motive. Anyway, it's my experience that your enemies won't take nearly as many risks to kill you as the blokes who just think you might stand in their way. Revenge may be sweet, but boodle buys a hell of a lot more cigars."

"Are we to consider ourselves in a state of siege?" inquired Irelock somewhat ironically.

"Not unless it amuses you," answered the Saint coolly. "But I don't think anyone in this gathering who wants to live to a great age ought to be too casual about standing in front of windows or wandering around the garden after dark. The Ellshaw-hiding outfit keeps moving pretty quickly, by the looks of things, and they have enterprising ideas."

Ripwell looked almost hopeful.

"I suppose you've got a gun, Inspector?"

Mr Teal moved his head in a slow negative gesture, with his jaws working phlegmatically.

"No, I'm not armed," he said tolerantly, and his gaze shifted deliberately on to the Saint, as if estimating the degree of certainty with which he could pick out one man who was.

"I think we have a revolver somewhere," said Irelock.

"By George, so we have!" exclaimed Ripwell. "See if you can find it, Martin."

"There isn't any ammunition," said Irelock cynically.

His lordship's face fell momentarily. Then he recovered buoyantly.

"We'll have to get some—I've got a licence for it. Never thought I should want it, but this is absolutely the time. Where can I get some cartridges? What d'you say, Inspector? With all this business going on, I'm entitled to have a gun in self-defence, what?"

Mr Teal had the typical English police officer's distaste for firearms, but he had no authority to show his disapproval.

"Certainly, if you have a licence, you're entitled to it," he replied unenthusiastically. "The local police may be able to lend you a few rounds of ammunition."

There was another arrival before dinner in the shape of Lord Ripwell's son, the Honourable Kenneth Nulland, who drove up in a very small and very noisy sports car. Irelock went out to meet him and brought him in—he was a young man with fair wavy hair and a face rather like a bright young cod, and he was very agitated. He shook hands limply.

"Haven't you solved the mystery yet? It's no good asking me to help you. I think it was the jolly old Communists, or the Fascists, or something. Anyhow, I hope they don't try anything more while I'm here—I can only just stay to dinner."

"I thought you were coming down for the week-end," said his father slowly.

"Sorry, Pop. Old Jumbo Ferris rang up and asked me to go to a party—he's having a jolly old beano down at his place in Hampshire."

"Did you have to accept? Cicely's coming over tomorrow."

Nulland shook his head. He grabbed a drink and hung himself over a chair, rather like a languid eel in plus fours.

"Sorry, Pop. But she won't miss me."

"I don't blame her," said Ripwell, with devastating candour. He turned to Teal and the Saint. "Cicely Holland's a sort of protégée of mine. Works in my office. Daughter of a pal of mine when I was young. Never made any money, but he was a pal till he died. Damned fine girl. I wish Kenneth was fit to marry her. She won't look at him as he is, and I wouldn't either."

Kenneth Nulland grinned weakly.

"Pop thinks I'm a jolly old prodigal son," he explained.

The explanation was scarcely necessary. Simon sensed the bitter disappointment behind Lord Ripwell's vigorous frankness, and, for his own comfort, led the conversation away into a less personal channel. But while he went on casually talking he studied Lord Ripwell's heir-presumptive more closely, and realized that Nulland was simultaneously studying him. The youngster was a mass of undisciplined nerves under his flaccid posturing, and the inane clichés which made up ninety per cent of his dialogue came pattering out so noisily at the slightest lull in the general talk that Simon wondered why he was so afraid of silence.

Teal noticed it too.

"What do you think?" he asked the Saint.

They were alone together for a moment after dinner—Lord Ripwell was telephoning the local Inspector, and Nulland had taken Martin Irelock out to admire some new gadget he had had fitted to his car.

"He's frightened," said the Saint carefully. "But I don't know that it would take much to frighten him. Maybe he doesn't want to be blown up."

Mr Teal sucked at his after-dinner ration of spearmint. He was letting himself become temporarily resigned to the irregularity of his position. After all, there was nothing else that he could do about it. The house was Lord Ripwell's, and the case was more or less Lord Ripwell's: if Lord Ripwell wanted the Saint to stay with him, that was Lord Ripwell's business and nobody else's. Even the Assistant Commissioner, Teal tried to tell himself with more confidence than he actually felt, could have found no flaw in the transparent logic of the argument. Therefore, proceeded Chief Inspector Teal, brilliantly scoring all the points in this pleasant imaginary debate with the spectre of his superior officer, since the Saint had to be accepted, it was simply an obvious stroke of masterly and unscrupulous cunning to pick his brains for any help they could be induced to yield.

"That fellow has something on his mind," said the detective, astutely pursuing this Machiavellian plan.

"If you could call it a mind," said the Saint, docilely surrendering the fruits of his cerebration.

Teal screwed up a scrap of pink paper in his pudgy fingers.

"I suppose he'd come into all Ripwell's money, if a bomb went off as it was meant to."

"Don't forget he'd come into all Mrs Ellshaw's money as well—and mine," said the Saint, with the utmost kindness. "And I'll bet he'd need it all. There's a beautiful motive in that, waiting for some bright detective to dig it out, Claud. I expect Ripwell gives him a perfectly miserly allowance, don't you? Ripwell strikes one as that sort of man."

Mr Teal's mouth tightened—he was an amiable man in most ways, but he had a train of memories behind him which were apt to start a quite unreasonably truculent inflammation in his stout bosom when the Saint smiled at him so compassionately and said things which made him feel that his legs were being playfully lengthened. He might even have responded with fatal rudeness, if he had had time to compose a sufficiently crushing retort, but Lord Ripwell joined them again before this devastating gem of repartee was polished to his mordant satisfaction.

"Inspector Oldwood will be over in ten minutes," said his lordship. "He's bringing some ammunition for my gun—I wish I knew where the damned thing was." He went to the French window that opened on to the garden at the side, and peered out. "Hey, Martin!"

It was nearly dark outside, and the air had turned cool directly the sun went down. Simon Templar, lighting one of Lord Ripwell's cigars by the mantelpiece, wondered if that seasonable evening chill was enough to account for the way Kenneth Nulland seemed to be shivering when he came in behind the secretary.

"Martin, where *is* that damned revolver? I haven't seen it for months."

"I think it's in the loft," said Irelock. "Shall I have a look for it tomorrow?"

"Tomorrow?" repeated Ripwell, screwing up his face like a disappointed schoolboy. "Eh? What? I want it now. Suppose this gang comes back tonight? Nonsense. What's the matter with looking for it now?"

"Right-ho," said Irelock peaceably. "I'll look for it now."

"Right-jolly-old-ho," echoed Nulland, peeling himself off the edge of the table in his undulating boneless way. "And I must be tootling along. Cheerio, Pop. Sorry I can't stay longer, but jolly old Jumbo Ferris is always complaining about me being late for his parties. Toodle-oo, Martin—"

Mr Teal cleared his throat.

"Just a minute, Mr Nulland," he said. "There are one or two small questions you might be able to help us with before you go."

The young man's restless eyes travelled about the room.

"What are they? I don't know anything."

"Have you ever met a man named—"

"*Look!*"

It was Irelock's voice, sharp and unnatural. Wheeling round to look at him, the Saint saw that his face was tense and startled, his weak eyes in their tortoise-shell frames staring rigidly at the window.

"What is it?" snapped Teal.

"A man looked in—just now—with a mask on his face. I saw him—"

Teal put his gum away in the side of his mouth and waded towards the casement with surprising speed for a man of his flabby dimensions, but Simon was even quicker. His hand dropped on the detective's shoulder.

"Wait for it, Claud! You may be just ballast at Scotland Yard, but you're the light of my life—and I'd hate you to go out too soon. Switch off those lights, somebody!"

It was Lord Ripwell who carried out the order, and the Saint's voice went on speaking in the dark.

"Okay, souls. Now you can get on with it. But try to remember what I told you about standing in front of lighted windows—and watch your step outside. Will someone show me the way to the back door?"

"I will," barked Ripwell eagerly.

He grabbed Simon by the arm and hustled him into the hall. Irelock called out, "Shall Ken and I take the front?"

"Do that," said the Saint, and slipped out his automatic as he followed Ripwell into the kitchen.

"I wish I knew where that damned revolver of mine was," said his lordship plaintively, as he shot back the bolt of the trades door.

The Saint smiled.

"Since you haven't got it, you'd better let me go first. And put down that cigar—it's a swell target."

He slipped out into the cool darkness, thumbing down the safety catch of his gun with an absurd feeling of unreality. The night was moonless, and the sky was a film of deep grey, only a shade lighter than the dull black of the earth and the trees. A stir of the air that was too soft even to be called a breeze brought the mingled scents of the river and damp grasses to his nostrils: everything was so suddenly quiet and peacefully commonplace after the boisterous confusion of their dispersal that he almost put his gun away again and laughed at himself. Such things did not happen. And yet—he would have liked to know why Kenneth Nulland was afraid, and what his reaction to the name of Ellshaw would have been . . .

Crack!

The shot crashed out from the front of the house, and a shout followed it. He heard the roar of an engine, and all the feeling of unreality vanished. As he raced up the strip of turf under the shadow of the wall he heard a shrill cry for help, in what sounded like Kenneth Nulland's voice.

Crack!

A tongue of flame split the blackness ahead, and he heard Lord Ripwell gasp at his heels. He whipped up his gun and fired at the flash—there was no danger of mistaken identity there, for on the analysis they had held a short while ago he was the only one of the party who was armed. Therefore the other gun belonged to one of the raiding party—however many of them there were. It spoke again, and the thunder of his second shot rang out on the reverberations of the first, but it was blind shooting with a hundred chances to one against a hit.

Someone ran over the grass and plunged through the cupressus hedge into the road, and the car's engine roared louder. Simon tore recklessly in pursuit, and came out into the gravelled lane as the flaring headlights leapt towards him. A man lurched out of the darkness and struck at him, catching him on the shoulder, and the Saint spun round and caught the striking wrist. The forefinger of his other hand took up the resistance of the trigger.

"Are you ready to die?" he said softly.

"Oh, Lord!" ejaculated Martin Irelock.

Simon let him go, and turned round again as the red tail light of the car whirled round the near corner.

"Hell!" He dropped the gun in his pocket. "Maybe I can catch them with my car."

He ran over the drive and leapt into the seat of the Hirondel. There was not a sound when he pressed the starter button, and he slid his hand along under the dash and felt wires trailing loose. It would take precious minutes to get out a light and re-connect them, and by that time the chase would be hopeless. With a sigh he opened the door and stepped down again, and then a match flared some distance away, and he heard Teal's voice.

"Give me a hand, someone."

He went back to the corner of the house, and saw that the man who lay on the ground, with Teal bending over him, was Lord Ripwell.

5

The match flickered out, and Teal struck another. Ripwell's eyes were open, and he was breathing painfully.

"Don't bother about me . . . I'm not hurt. Just a scratch. I'll . . . be all right. Did you get . . . any . . . of those villains?"

"I'm afraid not," said the Saint grimly.

They picked him up and carried him into the house. The bullet had passed through his chest just below the right shoulder—there was an ugly exit wound which had smashed his shoulder-blade, but the internal injuries were probably clean.

"I forgot to . . . put down . . . the cigar," he said with a twisted mouth, when they had settled him on his bed.

The Saint understood. Ripwell had been running just behind him and a little to one side when the first shot that he saw was fired. Simon realized now that he had heard him gasp when the bullet struck, but in the excitement of the moment he had not recognized the sound.

"Where's the nearest doctor?" asked Teal, turning to Irelock.

It was only then, when they were all gathered in the same room, that Simon realized that they were still one short of their number.

"Where's Ke—"

He started the question without thinking, and could have bitten his tongue the next moment, but he broke off too late. Ripwell struggled up on his elbow and stared from face to face, finishing the name for him in his clear commanding voice.

"Kenneth! Where's Kenneth?"

There was an answer in Irelock's pale strained features, at least enough answer for the Saint to read, even before the secretary began to stammer, "He's . . . he's gone . . ."

"Gone to see if he can catch Inspector Oldwood on his way here, hasn't he?" Simon caught him up in an instant, with cold blue eyes cutting off the truth with a flash of steel. "We'd better go and grab this doctor, and we may meet them."

He dragged Irelock out of the room and ran him down the stairs. In the hall he faced him, taking out a cigarette and straightening it between steady brown fingers.

"What has happened to Kenneth?" he asked.

"They got him." Irelock was trembling slightly, and his grown-up Kewpie face looked older and tensely hard. "We opened the front door, and somebody fired at us. Got me in the arm—only a graze." He pulled up his sleeve to show a raw straight furrow scored at an angle across his wrist. "I ran out and got hit in the stomach—not with a bullet this time, but it almost laid me out. I heard Ken yell for help, and then I heard people running away. I ran after them, and then I caught you. You remember. But they must have got Ken."

Simon flicked his thumb over his lighter, and drew his cigarette red in the flame.

"I only heard one shot before they started potting at me. Have you got a torch?"

They went out and searched the garden with an electric flashlight which Irelock produced from the kitchen. Inspector Oldwood arrived and challenged them while they were doing it, but relaxed when he recognized Ripwell's secretary. He had come from the opposite direction to that which the escaping car had taken, and he had seen no one on the road near the cottage. Certainly he had not seen Nulland.

One or two startled villagers and a handful of young people from adjacent bungalows, attracted by the noise and the shooting, were revealed at the gate in the fringe of the torchlight, and Oldwood pressed them into the search while Irelock went back into the house to telephone for a doctor. There was not a great deal of ground to cover, and two of the holiday bungalow party had torches. In twenty minutes the last of the searchers had drifted back to the front drive.

"Perhaps he went for help," said Oldwood, who had not had time to learn more than the vaguest rudiments of the story.

"I don't think so," said the Saint.

He noticed something else, in the reflected glow of the hovering ovals of torchlight, and swept his own light over the drive again. The Hirondel showed up its gleaming lines of burnished metal, exactly where he had left it when he first drove in, but it was the only car there. Of Kenneth Nulland's noisy little roadster there was no trace but the tyre tracks in the gravel.

Simon whistled softly.

"In his own car, too, by God! That's hot stuff—or is it?"

He saw something else, which had been overlooked in the first search—a small dark shadow on the ground close to the place where Nulland's car had stood—and went over to it. It was a red silk handkerchief, and when he picked it up he felt that it was wet and sticky.

"We'd better see how badly Ripwell's hurt," he said.

The doctor had arrived while the search was going on, stopping his car outside the gates, but he was still busy upstairs when Teal came down and joined them.

"He ought to pull through," was Teal's unofficial report. "He's stopped a nasty packet, but the doctor says his constitution is as sound as a bell. What's this about Nulland?"

"What's this about, anyhow?" asked Oldwood more comprehensively.

He was a red-faced grizzled man who looked more like a rather hard-bitten farmer than anything else, with an air of quiet self-contained confidence which was not to be flustered even by such sensational events as he had walked into. When his knowledge had been brought up to date he was still quiet and deliberate, stuffing his pipe with square unhurried fingers.

"I haven't anything for you," he said at the end. "I haven't been able to trace any suspicious characters hanging around here yet, but I'm still making inquiries."

"I wonder whether Nulland was kidnapped, or if he ran away," said Teal stolidly.

"The evidence doesn't show that he ran away," said the Saint.

He produced the silk handkerchief which he had picked up in the drive. There was an embroidered "K" in one corner, and the wet stickiness on it was blood.

Teal studied the relic and passed it over to the local man, who put it away in an envelope.

"What are the roads like around here, Oldwood? We can try to stop that car."

"They can't have gone Chertsey way," said Oldwood, striking a match. "Because that's the way I came from. They may have gone almost anywhere else. There's a road to Staines, another to Sunbury, and another to Walton—and half a dozen different routes they could take from any of those places."

"Added to which," murmured the Saint, "there must be at least fifty other baby sports cars exactly like his wandering about Surrey tonight."

"It'll have to be tried," said Teal doggedly. "Do you know the number, Mr Irelock?"

The secretary hadn't noticed it. Apparently Nulland changed his cars at an average rate of about once a month, except when one of his frequent accidents compelled an even quicker change, and it was almost beyond anyone's power to keep track of the numbers. The instructions that Teal telephoned out were hardly more than a hopeless routine, and all of them knew it.

He had just finished when the doctor came downstairs to confirm the preliminary bulletin.

"He's fairly comfortable now, but he'll want looking after for the next couple of days—I don't think there's any need to move him to the hospital. I'll send a nurse along tonight if I can get hold of one—otherwise I'll bring her over with me tomorrow morning."

"I suppose you didn't find a bullet," said Teal.

The doctor shook his head.

"It went right through him. From the look of the wound I should say it must have been fired from a fairly large-calibre gun."

"That reminds me," said Oldwood, searching his jacket pockets, "I brought over those cartridges that he asked for. You may as well have them, but I don't know that they're much use now."

"They may be useful," said Irelock. "We'd better keep some sort of guard while all this is going on."

"I'll send a man over as soon as I get back to the station," said Oldwood, and stood up. "You might give me a lift, Doctor, if it isn't taking you out of your way. There's nothing more we can do tonight."

Irelock saw them out, and then went back up the stairs to look in on Ripwell, and the Saint lighted another cigarette and stretched out his legs under the table. There was a train of thought shunting about in the half-intuitive sidings of his mind, backing and puffing tentatively, feeling its way breathlessly over a maze of lines with only one dim signal to guide it, but something about the way it was moving sent that weird sixth-sense tingle coursing again over his thoracic vertebræ. Teal trudged about over a minute area of carpet with his jaw oscillating rhythmically, and his sleepy eyes kept returning to the inscrutable immobility of the Saint's brown face.

"Well, what do you make of it now?" he said at last.

Simon came far enough out of his trance to put his smouldering cigarette back between his lips.

"I think it was magnificently staged," he said.

"How do you mean—magnificently? To try something like this only an hour or two after we get here, and make a success of it—"

"I like the organization," said the Saint dreamily. "Think it over, Claud. A bloke pushes his face against the window, and there's a first-class scare. The gathering breaks up and goes dashing out in the dark through three separate doors. There are five of us milling around in all directions, and yet it only takes a few seconds to sort out the right people and make a job of it. The bullet that hit Ripwell may have been meant for either him or me, but we were the two who got the bombs to begin with. Young Nulland is snatched off—a member of the same family—but nobody seems to have tried to grab Irelock when he was knocked out. And nobody tries to damage that beautiful stomach of yours."

"That may only be because they didn't have time."

"Or else because you don't know enough to be dangerous."

Mr Teal scowled.

"Nulland's car was only a two-seater, wasn't it?" He stared at the curtained windows, working at the problem in his own slow methodical way. "We ought to have tried the river . . . These people are clever."

"How many have you counted up to?"

"Ellshaw's the only one we know personally, but you saw another man in Duchess Place when you went there. I don't know how many more there are, but Ellshaw couldn't do it all alone. I know that man, and I'd swear he wasn't a killer."

The door opened and Irelock returned, bringing a bottle and glasses on a tray.

"What are the four motives that might make anyone a killer?" asked the Saint.

Teal's heavy lids settled more wearily over his eyes.

"Revenge? Nobody whom he's attacking ever seems to have met him before, except his wife. Jealousy?"

"Of what?"

"The fear of being found out?" suggested Irelock.

"We haven't anything against him," answered the detective. "And I don't know how to believe that he's done anything before that would be big enough to give him such a guilty conscience. He's the type that makes the usual whine about persecution when he's caught, but he always goes quietly."

Simon nodded.

"So that only leaves the best motive of all. Money. Big money."

"Extortion?" queried Teal sceptically.

"It has been done," said the Saint mildly. "But it doesn't meet all the facts this time. What's he going to extort from Mrs Ellshaw and me? And how can we know anything that might spoil the racket before Nulland's even been kidnapped—much less before anyone's put in the bill for ransom? And how the hell could you get a ransom out of Lord Ripwell if he was dead? Don't forget that he was on the bumping-off list before tonight."

Chief Inspector Teal breathed audibly.

"Well, if you've got a theory of your own, I'd like to hear it. All you've done yet is to make it more complicated."

"On the contrary," said the Saint, with that intangible intuitive train of thought still shuffling through the untracked subconscious labyrinths of his imagination. "I think it's getting simpler."

"You've got a theory?" Irelock pressed him eagerly.

The Saint smiled.

"For the first time since all the excitement started, I've got more than a theory," he answered softly. "I've got a fact."

"What is it?" demanded Teal, too quickly, and the Saint grinned gently, and got up with a swing of his long legs.

"You'd like to know, wouldn't you? Well, how do you know you don't?"

Mr. Teal swallowed the last faint scrap of flavour out of his gum, and blinked at him.

"How do I know—"

"How do you know you don't? Because you do." Simon Templar flattened the stump of his cigarette in an ash-tray, and laughed at him soundlessly. He put his hand on Teal's cushy shoulder. "It's all there waiting for you, Claud, if you figure it out. Think back a bit, and work on it. Who's supposed to be the detective here—you or me?"

"Do you mean you know who's responsible?" asked Irelock.

The Saint turned his head.

"Not yet. Not positively. I've just got a few ideas walking around in my mind. One or two of 'em have got together for a chat, and when they've all met up I think they're going to tell me something. I'd like to see how his lordship's getting on."

He went upstairs and let himself quietly into the bedroom. Ripwell was smoking a cigar and reading a book, and he looked up with a steady smile that overcame the pallor of his face.

"Looks as if I'm pretty hard to kill, what? You were splendid—wish we'd caught one of those blighters. Why the devil didn't I have that damned revolver? I might have bagged one myself."

"Inspector Oldwood brought over some ammunition for you," said the Saint. "I'll see that you have it before we turn in. It's a comforting thing to have under your pillow."

"Damned comforting," agreed his lordship. "I don't mind telling you I'm glad to have you in the house—you won't be leaving yet, will you?"

"Not for a while."

Lord Ripwell grunted cheerfully.

"That's good. They got Kenneth, didn't they? Oh, yes, I know—I dragged it out of Martin just now. Decent of you to try and keep it from me, but I'd rather know. I can stand a good deal. Wish Kenneth could. Still, an experience like that may wake him up a bit. What d'you think they'll do to him?"

"I don't know. But somehow I don't think it'll be anything . . . fatal."

Ripwell nodded.

"Neither do I. If they'd wanted to . . . do that . . . they needn't have taken him away. I'm glad you think so too, though. I wouldn't like to feel I was hoodwinking myself. Somebody'd better ring up that chap Ferris and tell him Ken won't be coming down."

"Do you know the number?"

"Never did know it. Ring up his flat in London and see if you can get it from there. The least we can do is to save Kenneth from getting in trouble for being late again. You'll find a directory under that table. Address in Duchess Place somewhere, I think."

"*What?*"

The question was slapped out of the Saint with such spontaneous startlement that Ripwell dropped his cigar and scorched the sheet.

"Eh? What? What's the matter?"

"Did you say Duchess Place?"

Ripwell picked up his cigar and dusted off the debris of ash from the bedclothes.

"I think that's right. Kenneth has talked about it. Why?"

Simon did not answer. He sprang up and dived under the extension telephone table by the bedside for the directory. He could hear Mrs Florence Ellshaw's unmusical voice rasping in his ear as clearly as if her ghost had been standing beside him, repeating the fragments of her long-winded and meandering story:

"*. . . in Duchess' Place, sir . . . number six . . . next door to two young gennelmen as I do for, such nice young gennelmen . . .*"

"Does he share this flat with another fellow?" Simon jerked out, whipping over the pages.

Lord Ripwell raised his eyebrows foggily.

"I believe he does. Don't know who it is, though. How did you know?"

The Saint didn't answer that one, either. He had found his place in the directory and ran down the list of Ferrises until he came to one whose address was in Duchess Place—at number eight, Duchess Place. And he was staring at the entry with a queer short-winded feeling sinking into his solar plexus and an electric buck-and-wing careering over his ganglions in a style that eclipsed everything else of its kind hitherto. It was several seconds before he spoke at all.

"Holy smoke," he breathed. "Jolly Old Jumbo!"

6

"What's the matter?" repeated Lord Ripwell, with pardonable blankness.

"Nothing," said the Saint absently. "It's just some more of the pieces falling into place. Wait a minute."

He jumped up and began to pace quickly up and down the room, slamming the directory shut and chucking it back under the table. The train of thought was moving faster, dashing hectically up and down over its maze of sidings faster than he was covering the floor. His tanned keen face was cut into bronze lines of intense thought, with his sea-blue eyes blazing vividly against the sunburned background. He wheeled round with his fist smashing impetuously into his palm.

"It's getting together . . . To kill Mrs Ellshaw just because she'd come to see me wasn't such a good motive. I was flattering myself a bit. But she'd always have to talk—to someone. Suppose it was the two young gennelmen that she did for? That's the sort of coincidence that happens. When Ellshaw had to disappear, who could have foreseen that his wife might go to work for someone who knew the bloke who . . . Wait for it again . . . Yes, they knew Kenneth. And Kenneth never said whether he'd heard of Ellshaw—never had a chance to . . . My God, I'd forgotten that piece of organization!"

Ripwell's pleasant face was hardening uncertainly.

"What are you driving at? If you're suggesting that Kenneth is a murderer—"

"Murderer?" The Saint came up with a start, half dazed, out of the trance in which he had been letting his thoughts race on aloud, without making any effort to dictate their destination. "I never said that. But—God, am I getting this untied?"

"I don't know what you mean," persisted Ripwell hoarsely.

Simon swung back to the bed and dropped his hands on the old man's shoulders.

"Don't worry," he said gently. "I'm sorry—I didn't mean to scare you. Even now. I'm not quite sure what I do mean. But I'll look after things. And I'll be right back."

He pressed Ripwell quietly back on the pillows and went out quickly, making for the stairs with an exuberant stride that almost bowled Martin Irelock off the landing.

"What's the excitement?" demanded the secretary.

"I've got some more ideas." Simon kept hold of the arm which he had clutched to save Irelock from taking the worst of the spill. "Are you busy?"

"No—I was just making sure that your room's all right."

"Then come downstairs again. I want to talk to you."

He did not release the arm until they were downstairs in the living-room. The French casement was ajar, the half-drawn curtains stirring in the draught. Simon took out his cigarette-case.

"Where's Teal?"

"I don't know. Oldwood's man just arrived—I expect he's showing him round."

The Saint put a cigarette between his lips and took a match from the ash-stand, stroking it alight with his thumb-nail.

"I've remembered something that may interest you," he said. "An interesting scientific fact. If you have a sample of fresh blood, it's possible to analyse its type and get an exact mathematical ratio of probabilities that it came from some particular person."

Irelock blinked.

"Is it really? That's interesting."

"I said it was interesting. How does it appeal to you?"

The secretary picked up the whisky decanter mechanically, and poured splashes into the three glasses on the tray. All the splashes did not go into the glasses.

"I don't know—why should it appeal to me particularly?"

"Because," answered the Saint deliberately, "I've an idea that if I asked Teal to have the blood on Ken's handkerchief analysed, and then we took a sample of your blood from that graze on your arm, we'd find that the odds were that it was your blood!"

"What do you—"

"What do I mean? I'm always hearing that question. I mean that I told you and Teal just now that I'd got a fact, and this is it. There was only one shot fired in the front of the house. It scratched your wrist—low down. This handkerchief was in Kenneth's breast pocket. I noticed it. While it's possible that you may have gone out of the door with your hands shoulder high, it's damned unlikely, and therefore I didn't quite see how a bullet that passed you about the level of your hips could have hit Ken in the chest, unless the warrior who fired it was lying at your feet—which again is unlikely."

Irelock's knuckles showed white where he gripped his glass, and for a second or two he made no reply. Then, with an imperceptible shrug, he looked back at the Saint, tight-lipped.

"All right," he said, with a nod of grim resignation. "You've seen through it. I'm afraid I should make a rotten criminal. It was my blood."

"How come?"

Irelock grimaced ruefully.

"Teal suspected it."

"You mean to tell me that Ken ran away?"

"Yes."

Simon drew smoke from his cigarette and trickled it through his nostrils.

"Go on."

"That's about all I know. I don't know why. I could see a silhouette of the car against the headlights when they were switched on, and there was only one man in it. I found the handkerchief while I was pretending to help you to look for him, and I wiped it on my arm and dropped it back on the drive. I suppose it was a silly thing to do, but the only thing I could think of was how to try and cover him up—to make it look as if he hadn't run away."

There was no doubt that he was speaking the truth, but Simon drove on at him relentlessly.

"Why should you think he wanted covering up?"

"Why else should he want to run away? Besides, you must have seen that there was something on his mind all the evening—I saw you looking at him. I don't know what it was. But he's always been wild. I've tried to help him. Lord Ripwell would probably have disinherited him more than once if I hadn't been able to get him out of some of his scrapes."

"Such as?"

"Oh, the usual wild things that a fellow like that does. He gambles. And he drinks too much."

"Gets obstreperous when he's tight, does he?"

"Yes. You wouldn't think it of him, but he does. When he's drunk he'd pick a fight with anybody, but when he's sober he'd run away from a mouse."

"Could he have killed anyone when he was drunk?"

Irelock stared at him with horror.

"Good Lord!—you don't think that?"

"I don't know what I think," said the Saint impatiently. "I'm just trying to sort things out. Ripwell hasn't disinherited him yet, has he? Well, who'd make the biggest profit out of Ripwell's death? . . . But even that hasn't anything to do with the rest of it. There are two mysteries tangled up, and I'm trying to make them tie. The hell with it!"

He picked up a glass and subsided with it into a chair, frowning savagely. Odd loose ends out of the tangle kept on linking up and matching, tantalizing him with a deceptive hope that the rest of the pattern was just about to follow on and fall neatly into place, but at the climax there was always one clashing colour, some shape or other that did not fit. Somewhere in the web there must be a thin tortuous thread that would hold it all together, but the thread was always dancing just beyond his grasp.

"If . . . if you're not quite sure," Irelock was saying hesitantly, "have you got to say anything to Teal? I mean, unless Lord Ripwell . . . unless everybody's got to know that Kenneth funked . . ."

He broke off at the sound of a footstep on the path outside, but his bright eyes continued the appeal. Simon moved his head non-committally, but he had no immediate intention of making Chief Inspector Teal a free gift of the wear and tear on his own valuable grey matter.

"I've posted the constable outside, under the bedroom window," said the detective, and looked at the glass which Irelock was offering him. "No, thank you—fat men didn't ought to drink. It's bad for the heart. The doctor hasn't been able to get hold of a nurse yet, so we'd better take it in turns to sit up."

Irelock nodded, and took the first sip at his highball.

"I don't mind taking the—"

His voice wrenched into a ghastly retching sound, and they stared at him in momentary paralysis. And then, as Simon started to his feet, he lurched forward and knocked the glass spinning out of the Saint's hand with a convulsive sweep of his arm.

"For God's sake!" he gasped. "Don't drink . . . Poison!"

7

Simon sprang forward and caught him before Teal's lumbering movement in the same direction had more than started, but Irelock flung him off with demented energy and went staggering to the window. They heard him vomiting painfully outside.

"Get on the phone for a doctor," snapped the Saint, as he dashed after him.

Irelock reeled into his arms in the darkness.

"Get me back," he panted huskily. "Maybe . . . all right . . . Get . . . mustard and water—"

Simon brought him back into the room and laid him, down on the sofa—he was curiously black about the eyes and the perspiration was streaming off him. Teal came in with the emetic almost at once, having gone out and found it on his own initiative, and there was a further period of unpleasantness . . .

"All right—thanks."

Irelock lay back at last with a groan. His breathing was still laboured, but the spasmic twitching of his limbs was reduced to a faint trembling.

"I'm feeling . . . better . . . Think we . . . got rid of it . . . in time . . .
That would have been . . . another mystery . . . for you!"

To Simon Templar there was no mystery. His glance flashed from
the whisky decanter to the still open French door through which
Teal had come in, and he looked up to find Mr Teal's somnolent eyes
following the same route. His gaze crystallized thoughtfully.

"While you were outside posting your cop under the window,
Claud Eustace! Is that organization and is that nerve, or what is it?"

He took up the untouched glass which Mr Teal had declined, and
moistened his mouth from it, holding the liquid only for a moment.
There was a distinctive sweet oily taste in it which might have passed
unnoticed under the sharper bite of the spirit unless he had been
looking for it, and he retained a definition of the savour in his memory
after he had spat out the sip.

Teal's eyes were wide open.

"Then they still can't be far away," he said.

The Saint's lips stirred in an infinitesimal reckless smile.

"One day you'll be a detective after all, Claud," he murmured.
Teal was starting to move ponderously towards the window, but Simon
passed him with his long easy stride and stopped him. "But I'm afraid
you'll never be a night hunter. Let me go out."

"What can you do?" asked Teal suspiciously.

"I can't arrest him," Simon admitted. "But I can be a good dog
and bring you the bone. We missed a trick last time—crashing out like
a mob of blasted red-faced fox-hunting squires after a poacher. You
wouldn't catch anyone but a damn fool that way, on a dark night like
this. But I know the game. I'll go out and be as invisible as a worm,
and if anyone steps inside these grounds again I'll get him. And I think
somebody will be coming!"

The detective hesitated. His memories of the Assistant
Commissioner floated bogeyly across his imagination; the memory of

all the deceptions he had suffered from the Saint narrowed his eyes. But he knew as well as anyone what amazing things Simon Templar could do in the dark, and he knew his own limitations.

"If you do catch anyone, will you promise to bring him in?"

"He's yours," said the Saint tersely, but he made a mental reservation about the exact time at which that transfer of property would come into effect.

He went out alone, dissolving noiselessly into the night like a wandering shadow. From the blackness outside the window he watched Teal using the telephone, and presently saw the lights of a car drive up and stop outside the gate. The doctor walked up the short drive and was challenged on his way by the police guard, and Simon took that opportunity of introducing himself.

"This is a funny business, sir, isn't it?" said the constable, when the doctor had gone on into the house.

He was a middle-aged beefy man who kept shaking himself down uncomfortably in his plain clothes, as if he had been wearing a uniform too long to feel thoroughly at home in any other garb. He would probably continue to wear a uniform for the rest of his life, but it was no less probable that he was quite contented with the prospect.

Simon strolled back with him to his post, and gave him a cigarette. He did not expect the man he was waiting for to enter the grounds for a little while.

"Kidnapped 'is lordship's son, too, didn't they?" said the policeman. "Now, why should they want to do that?"

The question was put more or less in rhetorical appeal to some unspecified oracle, rather than as one demanding a direct answer, and the Saint did not immediately attempt to answer it.

"I suppose you know Lord Ripwell fairly well," he said, striking a match.

"Well, so-and-so," said the constable, puffing. "Must be about five year now, sir—ever since 'e bought the house."

"I shouldn't think he'd be an easy man to extort money from."

"I wouldn't like to be the man to try it. Mind you, 'is lordship's known to be a generous gentleman—do anything for a fellow oo's out of luck, if he's asked properly. But not the kind you could force anything out of. No, sir. Why, I remember in my time what 'appened to a chap oo tried to blackmail 'im."

The stillness of the Saint's eyes could not be seen in the dark.

"Somebody tried to blackmail him once, did they?" he said quietly.

"Yes, sir. It wasn't nothing much they 'ad to blackmail 'im with, but you can see for yourself 'is lordship must've been quite a lad in 'is time, and some people are that narrow-minded they don't expect a man to be even 'uman." There was a sympathetic note in the constable's voice which hinted that he himself could modestly claim, in his own time, to have been Quite A Lad. "Anyway, all 'is lordship did was to get the Inspector up and 'ave him listen to some of this talk. And then, when he could 'ave 'ad the fellow sent to prison, he wouldn't even prosecute 'im."

"No?"

"Wouldn't even make a charge. 'I don't want to be vindictive,' he says. 'The silly ass 'as had a good fright,' he says, 'and now you let him go. You can see he's just some down-and-out idiot oo thought 'e could make some easy money.' And in the end I believe 'e gave the chap 'is fare back to London."

"Who was this fellow?" Simon asked.

"I dunno. Said 'is name was Smith, like most of 'em do when they're first caught. We never had no chance to find out oo he really was, on account of 'is lordship not prosecuting 'im, but 'e did look pretty down and out. Seedy little chap with a great red nose on 'im like a stop light."

The doctor came out and returned to his car—Simon heard his parting conversation with Teal at the door, and gathered that Martin Irelock was in no danger. The hum of the car died away, and Simon gave the talkative guard another cigarette and faded back into the dark to resume his own prowling.

His brain was becoming congested with new things to think about. So an attempt had been made to extort money from Ripwell. He was confirmed in his own estimate of the prospects of the hopeful extorter, but apparently the aspirant himself had required to be convinced by experience. There was something about the anecdote as he felt it which gave him a distinct impression of a trial balloon. Someone had wanted first-hand knowledge of Lord Ripwell's reaction to such an attempt, and the constable's brief description of the aspiring blackmailer had one prominent feature in common with the elusive Mr Ellshaw. Curiously enough, in spite of the increased congestion of ideas, the Saint felt that the mystery was gradually becoming less mysterious . . .

He moved round the house as soundlessly as a hunting cat. As Chief Inspector Teal knew and admitted, queer things, almost incredible things, happened to Simon Templar when he got out in the dark—things which would never have been believed by the uninitiated observer who had only seen him in his sophisticated moods. He could leave his immaculately dressed, languidly bantering sophistication behind him in a room, and go out to become an integral part of the wild. He could go out and move through the night with the supple smoothness of a panther, without rustling a blade of grass under his feet, merging himself into minute scraps of shadow like a jungle animal, feeling his way uncannily between invisible obstructions, using strange faculties of scent and hearing with such weird certainty that those who knew him best, when they thought about it, sometimes wondered if the roots of all his amazing outlawry might not be found threading down into the deeps of this queer primitive instinct.

No living man could have seen or heard him as he passed on his silent tour, summarizing the square lights of windows in the black cube of the house. Lord Ripwell's lighted window, under which the police guard stood, was on one side. A bulb burned faintly in the hall, at the front, facing closely on to the road. The dully luminous colour of curtains on the other side marked the living-room which he had left not long ago. At the back of the house, where the Thames margined the grounds, he could see one red-shaded lamp in an upstairs window— presumably that was Irelock's room, for he had gathered that the only domestic servant employed at the cottage was a daily woman who had gone home immediately after dinner. Chief Inspector Teal must have been keeping watch downstairs with a dwindling supply of spearmint, and Simon wondered whether he had been jarred far enough out of his principles to take over Lord Ripwell's revolver and the ammunition, to wait with him for the sudden death that would surely stalk through that place again before morning.

He came down to the water's edge and sat with his back to a tree, as motionless as if he had been one of its own roots. Surely, he knew, the death would come, but whether it would successfully claim a victim depended largely upon him. There was a smooth speed about every move of the case which appealed to him: it was cut and thrust, parry and riposte—a series of lightning adjustments and counter-moves which he could appreciate for its intrinsic qualities even while he was still fumbling for the connecting link that held it all together. The poison which had found its way into the whisky less than an hour ago belonged to the same scheme of things. He could recall its peculiar sweet oily taste on his tongue, and he thought he knew what it was. The symptoms which Martin Irelock had shown corroborated it. Very few men would have known that it was poisonous at all. How should an illiterate little race-train rat like Ellshaw have known it?

A mosquito zoomed into his ear with a vicious ping, and one of his thighs began to itch, but still he did not move. At other times in his life he had lain out like that, immobile as a carved outcrop of rock, combing the dark with keyed-up senses as delicate as those of any savage, when the first man whose nerves had cracked under the unearthly strain would have paid for the microscopic easing of a cramped muscle with his life. That utter relaxation of every expectant sinew, the supersensitive isolation of every faculty from all disturbances except those which he was waiting for, had become so automatic that he used no conscious effort to achieve it. And in that way, without even turning his head, he became aware of the black ghost of a canoe that was drifting soundlessly down the stream towards the place where he sat.

Still he did not move. A nightingale started to tune up in the branches over his head, and a frail wisp of cloud floated idly across the hazy stars which were the only light in the darkness. The canoe was only a dim black brush-stroke on the grey gloom, but he saw that there was only one man in it, and saw the ripple of tarnished-silver water as the unknown dipped his paddle and turned the craft in towards the bank. It seemed unlikely that any ordinary man would be cruising down the river at that hour alone, revelling in a dreamy romance with himself, and the Saint had an idea that the man who was coming towards him was not altogether ordinary. Unless a dead man creeping down the Thames in a canoe at midnight could be called ordinary.

The canoe slid under the bank, momentarily out of sight, but the Saint's ears carried on the picture of what was happening. He heard the soft rustle of grasses as the side scraped the shore, the plip-plop of tiny drops of water as the wet paddle was lifted inboard, the faint grate of the wood as it was laid down. He sat on under his tree without a stir in his graven stillness, building sound upon sound into a construction of every movement that was as vividly clear to him as if he had watched it in broad daylight. He heard the scuff of a leather shoe-sole on the wood, quite different from the dull grate of the paddle; the rustle of creased clothing; the whisper of turf pressed underfoot. Then a soundless pause. He sensed that the man who had disembarked was probing the night clumsily, looking for some sign or signal, hesitating over his next move. Then he heard the frush of trodden grass again, and a sifflation of suppressed breathing that would have been quite inaudible to any hearing less uncannily acute than his.

A shadow loomed up against the stygian tarnish of the water, half the height of a man, and remained still. The prowler was sitting on the bank, waiting for something which Simon could not divine. There was a longer and more complicated rustling, a tentative scratch and an astonishingly loud sizzle of flame, and the man's head and shoulders leapt up out of the dark for an instant in startlingly crisp silhouette against the glow of a match cupped in his hands.

The Saint moved for the first time. He rolled up silently and smoothly on to his feet, straightening his knees gradually until he came upright. The pulsing of his heart had settled down to a steady acceleration that did nothing to disturb the feline flow of any of his movements. It was only a level beat of excitement in his veins, a throbbing eagerness to complete his acquaintance with that elusive man around whose fanatical seclusion centred so much violence and sudden death.

Simon came up behind him very quietly. The man never knew he was coming, had no warning of danger before two sets of steel fingers closed on his throat. And then it was too late for him to do anything useful. He was not very strong, and he was almost paralysed with the heart-stopping horror of that silent attack out of the dark. The cry that burst involuntarily from his lungs was crushed by the choking grip of his neck before it could come to sound in his mouth, and a heavy knee settled snugly into the small of his back and pinned him helplessly to the ground in spite of all his frantic struggles. It was all over very quickly.

The Saint felt him go limp, and cautiously relaxed the pressure of his hands. Then he slipped his arms under the man's unconscious body and lifted him up. The whole encounter had made very little noise, and Simon was no less attentive to silence than he had been before, while he carried the man down the bank and laid him out in the canoe. A couple of deft sweeps of the paddle sent the craft skimming out into the stream, but the Saint kept it moving until a bend in the river hid the lights of the house before he struck a match and inspected the face of his capture.

It was Ellshaw.

8

"Now you are going to talk, brother," said the Saint. He sat facing his trophy over another flickering match, giving the other every facility to recognize him before the light went out. Ellshaw's face was wet with the river water that had been slopped over him to help him back to unhappy consciousness, but there was something else on his face besides water—a pale clammy fright that made his oversized red nose stand out like a full-blown rose against the blanched sickliness of his cheeks.

The match spun from the Saint's fingers into the water with an expiring hiss, dropping the curtain of blackness between them again, and the Cockney's adenoidal voice croaked hysterically through the curtain.

"I carn't tell yer nothing, guv'nor—strike me dead if I can!"

"I shouldn't dream of striking you dead if you can," said the Saint kindly. "But if you can't . . . well, I really shouldn't know what to do with you. I couldn't just let you run away, because then you might begin to think you'd scored off me and get a swollen head, which would be very bad for you. I couldn't adopt you as a pet and take you around with me on a lead, because I don't like your face so much. I couldn't put you in a cage and send you to the Zoo, because the other monkeys might object. And so the question would arise, brother, how would one get rid of you? And of course it would always be so easy to get hold of your skinny neck again for a while, and hold you under water while you blew bubbles."

"Yer wouldn't dare!" panted Ellshaw.

"No?" The Saint's voice was just an infinitely gentle challenge lilting out of the darkness. "Did you get a good look at me when I struck that match, by any chance? You knew me well enough when I dropped in to see you in Duchess Place. And you talked as if you'd heard all about me, too. Did somebody ever tell you there was anything I didn't dare?"

He could hear the racking harshness of the man's breathing.

"Yer wouldn't dare," Ellshaw repeated as if he was only trying to convince himself. "That . . . that 'ud be murder!"

"Yeah?" drawled the Saint. "I'm not so sure. You tell me the answer, brother, out of that vast general-knowledge fund of yours—is it legally possible to kill a man who's already dead? Because you are dead, aren't you? You were murdered nearly a year ago."

It was a shot literally in the dark, but the sharp catch of the other's breath was as clear an answer to him as if he had had a searchlight focused down the boat. His thumb-nail gritted across another match, and the flame cut the pitiless buccaneering line of his face out of the gloom for as long as it took him to light a cigarette. And then there was only the red tip of the cigarette glowing in the intensified dark, and his voice coming from behind it: "So how on earth could I murder you again, brother? I could only make you stay dead, and I don't think anybody's ever laid down the law about a crime like that."

"I don't know nothing," persisted Ellshaw hoarsely. "Honest I don't."

"Honest you do," said the Saint persuasively. "But I didn't even ask for your opinion. Just you come through with what's on your mind, and I'll let you know whether I think it was worth knowing."

Ellshaw did not answer at once, and Simon went on quite calmly, with a matter-of-fact detachment that was more deadly than any bullying bluster: "Don't kid yourself, sonny. If I had to toast your feet over a hot fire to make you talk, it wouldn't be the first toasting party I'd been out on. If I ever felt like wiping you off the face of the earth, I'd do it and never have a sleepless night on account of it. But just for this one occasion, I'm liable to be as good as you'll let me. When I came out here to catch a man, I told Chief Inspector Teal I'd bring him back with me, and I'd just as soon bring him back alive. What Teal will do to you when he gets you depends a whole lot on how you open your mouth first. Get wise to the spot you're sitting in, Ellshaw. It isn't everybody's idea of a good time to get himself hanged, but nobody who did a good job of King's Evidence has ever been strung up yet."

"They couldn't do it," said Ellshaw sobbingly. "They couldn't 'ang me. I ain't done nothing—"

"What about your wife?" said the Saint ruthlessly.

"She's all right, guv'nor. I swear she is. Nobody's done 'er no 'arm. I can tell you all abaht that."

"Tell me."

"Well, guv'nor, it was like this. When she spotted me in Duchess Plyce, an' I 'ad to get rid of 'er, we thought afterwards she might go blabbin' abaht 'aving seed me, so we 'ad to keep 'er quiet, see? But she ain't dead. She just got took off to some other place an' kep' there so she couldn't talk. We couldn't 'ave people lookin' for 'er, though, an' kickin' up a fuss, so we 'ad to give out she was dead, see?"

"Did you have to get the police to fish her dead body out of the Thames as well—just to make it more convincing?" asked the Saint coldly.

He was not quite sure what answer he expected—certainly he had not looked at the question as a vital thrust in the argument.

The reaction which it obtained startled him, and he was surprised to find that he could still be startled.

For some seconds Ellshaw did not speak at all, and then his voice was shockingly different from the defiant whine in which he had been talking before.

"Go on," he said huskily. "Yer carn't tike me in wiv a yarn like that."

"My dear sap," said the Saint slowly, "I don't want to take you in with any yarn. I'm only telling you. Your wife's body was taken out of the river last night. It was supposed to be suicide at first, but now they're pretty sure it was murder."

There was another silence at the opposite end of the canoe, and Simon Templar drew his cigarette to an instant's bright gleam of red in which the lines of his mouth could be seen as intent and inexorable as a stone mask, and went on without a change in the purring level of his voice.

"If you keep your mouth shut I wouldn't give you a bad penny for your chance. You can put a lot of things over on a jury, but somehow or other they never take a great shine to a fellow who kills his own wife. Of course, they say hanging isn't such a bad death . . ."

Ellshaw was making queer noises in his throat, as if he was struggling to do something with his voice.

"Oh Gawd!"

His feet shuffled on the bottom. His breath was whistling through his teeth with a weird harshness that chilled something dormant in the Saint's heart.

"You ain't tryin' to scare me, are yer? Yer just tellin' me the tile to make me talk. She ain't . . . dead?"

"I'm afraid she is."

Ellshaw gulped.

"My Gawd . . ." His voice went shrill. "The dirty lyin' swine! The rat! He told me—"

There was a sound as if he flopped over athwart. In another moment he was sprawled across the Saint's feet, clutching aimlessly at Simon with crazy shaking hands.

"I didn't do it," he blubbered. "I swear I didn't! I didn't wish 'er dead. I believed wot I told yer. I thought she was just 'idden away somewhere, like I was. I ain't never murdered nobody!"

"Didn't you know that Lord Ripwell was to be murdered?" said the Saint relentlessly. "Didn't you know that I was to be murdered?"

"Yes, I did!" shouted the other wildly. "But I wouldn't 'ave murdered Florrie. I wouldn't 'ave stood for killin' me own missus. That filthy double-crossin'—"

Simon gripped him by the shoulders.

"Will you squeal, Ellshaw?"

He could feel the man's stupefied eyes straining to find him in the darkness.

"Yes, I'll squeal. My Gawd, I'll squeal!"

"You're a bright boy after all," said the Saint.

He pushed the demented man away and took up his paddle again. Driving the canoe back up the stream with cool steady strokes, he felt a great ease of triumph. It was the same quiet thrill that a chess-player must feel on mastering an intricate problem. He realized with a touch of humour that it was one of the very few episodes in which success could not conceivably bring him one pennyworth of boodle, but it made no difference to his satisfaction. He had taken one of his impulsively wholehearted likings to Lord Ripwell.

The red light in the back upper window swam into view again past a clump of trees, and he turned the canoe into the bank and drove the paddle-blade into the shallow river bed to hold it. Ellshaw was still moaning and muttering incoherently, and, for his own sake, Simon hauled him up out of the canoe and shook him vigorously.

"Snap out of it, brother. This is your chance to get even—and shift yourself off the high jump at the same time."

"I'm going to squeal," repeated Ellshaw dazedly.

The Saint kept hold of him.

"Okay. Then come up to the house and let Teal listen to it."

He rushed the trembling man over the rough lawn and up the side of the house to the French window of the living-room. There was an exclamation somewhere in the middle distance, and heavy feet pounded after him. The beam of a bullseye lantern picked him up.

"Oh, it's you, sir," said the police guard, illuminatingly. "I thought—Gosh, what have you got there?"

"A tandem bicycle," said the Saint shortly. "Get back to your post."

Teal, startled by the noise, was on his feet when he thrust his prize into the room. The detective's jaw hung open, and for a second or two he stopped chewing.

"Good Lord . . . is that—"

"Yes, it is, Claud. A new gadget for punching holes in Cellophane. If I could go on thinking up questions like that, I might be a policeman myself. Which God forbid. Don't you know your boy friend?"

For once in his life Chief Inspector Teal was incapable of being offended.

"Ellshaw! Was he outside?"

"No, he was baked into the middle of a sausage-roll in the pantry perfectly disguised as a new genius from Scotland Yard."

"How did you know he'd be there?"

"Oh, my God!" Simon pushed the harvest of his brain work into a chair like a sack of beans, and subsided against the table. "Have I got to do everything for you? All right. It was only this morning that I crashed into Duchess Place. I ought to have been killed last night.

Since that failed, they hoped to get me this morning when I went nosing around. When that fell through, they had to make a quick getaway. I assumed that they were so far from expecting trouble that they hadn't got a spare bolt-hole waiting to move into. Therefore they had to do something temporary. The Grand Panjandrum couldn't have been a Grand Panjandrum at all if he hadn't known that Ellshaw was a bit of a dim bulb. Therefore he wouldn't want to risk letting him far out of his reach. He knew he was coming down here this afternoon, so naturally he'd park Ellshaw somewhere locally where he could get in touch with him, while he figured out what they were going to do next. Having made up his mind, he'd have to tell Ellshaw. Therefore Ellshaw would have to come to him for instructions—it would probably be easier than him going to see Ellshaw, and at the time he'd think it was just as safe. Therefore Ellshaw had to come here. Therefore he probably had to come here soon. Therefore he'd probably come tonight. And even if he didn't, I couldn't do any harm by waiting. Therefore I waited. QED. Or do you want a dictionary to help you out with the two-syllable words?"

Teal swallowed.

"Then he was—"

His eyes travelled to a carefully corked bottle on a side table. Simon knew at once that it must be a sample of whisky corked for analysis, and smiled faintly.

"You needn't bother with that," he said. "I can tell you what's in it. It's nitroglycerine . . . as used in making the best bombs. If Irelock hasn't coughed it all up you could drop him down the stairs and blow up the house, but it's a deadly enough poison without that. No, I don't think Ellshaw did it. He wouldn't have known. But the man who made our two bombs might have."

"Then do you mean it isn't Ellshaw—"

"Of course not. It's much too big for him. There he is. Look at him. There's the guy that all the commotion's about—the great million-pound mystery that people had to be killed to keep. But he isn't the brains. He couldn't do anything at all. He's dead!"

Mr Teal blinked, staring at the red-nosed snivelling man who lay sprawling hot-eyed in a chair where Simon had thrown him. He looked alive. The low-pitched gasping noises that broke through his lips sounded alive.

"How is he dead?" Teal asked stupidly.

"Because he's been murdered. And don't forget something else. He's King's Evidence—I promised him that, and you haven't a case to go to a jury without him."

The detective hesitated.

"But if he had anything to do with murdering his wife—"

"He didn't. I believe that, and so will you. He was double-crossed. After his wife had seen him, he was told she'd got to disappear in case she shot her mouth. He thought she was just going to be kept somewhere in hiding, like he was. He'll tell you all about it. The Grand Panjandrum knew he'd never stand for killing his wife, so that was the story. And that's why he's going to squeal. You are going to squeal, aren't you, Ellshaw?"

The man licked his lips.

"Yes, I'll talk. I'll tell everythink I know." His voice had gone back to its normal level, but it was coarse and raspy with the blind vindictiveness of the passion that was sweating down inside him. "But I didn't kill Florrie. Nobody 'ad to kill 'er. I didn't know nothink about it. I'll tell yer."

The Saint lighted a cigarette and drew the smoke down into his lungs.

"There you are, Claud," he murmured. "Your case is all laid out for you. Shall I start the story or shall Ellshaw?"

Teal nodded.

"I think we'd better wait a moment before we begin," he said. "Our police methods are useful sometimes. We've got young Nulland."

"You have?"

"Yes." Mr Teal was beginning to recover some of his habitual bored smugness. "He was held up with a puncture just outside Sunningdale, and a motor-cycle patrol spotted him—I had a phone call while the doctor was here last. He's being sent back under guard—they ought to arrive any minute now."

Simon raised his eyebrows.

"So you know that he wasn't kidnapped after all?"

"It doesn't look like it," replied the detective stolidly. "Anyhow, there was nobody with him when he was found, and he hadn't any convincing story to tell. We'll soon know, when he gets here."

The Saint let go a trickle of smoke, but before he could speak again a car hummed slowly up the road and stopped opposite the house. He sat up, with the careless lights wakening in his blue eyes, and listened to the tread of footsteps coming up the drive.

"Didn't I tell you we were going to have fun?" he remarked. "I think your police are wonderful."

Mr Teal looked at him for a moment, and then went out to open the front door.

Simon's glance followed him, and then turned back to the man who sat quivering in the arm-chair. He swung his legs off the table.

"You're the exhibit, aren't you?" he said softly.

He turned the chair round so that Ellshaw faced the door and must be the first person whom the returning prodigal would see when he entered the room. Then he went back to his perch on the table and went on with his cigarette. Outwardly he was quite calm, and yet he was waiting for a moment which in its own way was the tensest climax of the adventure. Out of the twisted tangled threads, in breathless pauses between the shuttling of move and counter-move and unexpected revelation, he had at last built up a pattern and a theory. All the threads were in place, and it only wanted that last flash of the shuttle to bind them all irrefragably together—or tangle the web once more and set him back to the place where he began.

Inspector Oldwood came first; then the Honourable Kenneth Nulland; last of all came Teal, completing the party and closing the door behind him. Presumably the guard who had brought Nulland over from Sunningdale had been dismissed, or told to wait outside.

Simon did not so much as glance at the two detectives. His eyes were fixed on the pale fish-like face of Lord Ripwell's son and heir.

He saw the face turn whiter, and saw the convulsive twitch of the young man's hands and the sudden glazing of his eyes. Nulland's lips moved voicelessly once or twice before any sound came.

"Oh God," he said, and went down without another word in a dead faint.

Simon Templar drew a deep breath. "Now I can tell you a story," he said.

9

Nulland sat on the sofa after they had brought him round. He sat staring at Ellshaw as if his brain was still incredulously trying to absorb the evidence of his eyes, and Ellshaw stared back at him with dry lips and stony eyes.

"I think this all began more than a year ago," said the Saint.

Chief Inspector Teal searched for a fresh wafer of chewing-gum and unwrapped it. It was significant that at this time he made no attempt to assert his own authority to take charge of the proceedings, and, after one curious glance at him, Inspector Oldwood pulled out his pipe and found his way to a chair without interrupting.

"The idea, of course, was to get hold of Ripwell's money," Simon went on, lighting a cigarette. "Probably any other millionaire's money would have done just as well, but Ripwell was the obvious victim close at hand. The question was how to do it. Ordinary swindling could be ruled out: Ripwell was much too keen a business man to let himself be diddled out of anything more than paltry sums. That left, on the face of it, one other chance—extortion. Well, that was tried, in a tentative sort of way. Ellshaw came here with some minor secret out of Ripwell's past, and the result was just about what one would expect. Ripwell laid a trap for him, gave him a good scare, as he thought, and then didn't bother to prosecute him."

"How on earth did you know that?" asked Oldwood, with some surprise.

"From your cop outside—I was having a chat with him, and it just happened to come out. But I recognized Ellshaw from the description of this attempted blackmailer, which you probably couldn't have done, and that made a lot of difference. But even so, it was only incidental evidence. It just clinched an explanation of why the blackmail had to be tackled afresh in a more roundabout way. I don't think Ellshaw's little effort was ever meant to succeed. It was meant to give a direct line on the way Ripwell could be expected to react to a bigger proposition, and it washed him out pretty completely. So that was when the real plot started."

"You mean, to murder Lord Ripwell?" said Teal hesitantly.

"Yes. Of course, wilful murder was a much bigger proposition, but it had to be faced. And it was about the only solution. If Ripwell's money couldn't be extorted out of him, it could still be inherited. I'll give our friend all the credit for looking at it cold-bloodedly, facing the facts, seeing the answer, and making the best possible use of the bare material at his disposal. Take a look at Nulland for yourselves—weak, vain, rather stupid, a gambler, capable of extraordinary viciousness when he's in liquor—"

Mr Teal's cherubic pink face seemed to go a shade less rubicund.

"But—good God!" he said. "To murder his own father—"

Simon looked at him oddly.

"You know, Claud, there are times when I ask myself whether anyone could possibly be so dumb as you try to make yourself out," he remarked compassionately. "All I'm doing is telling you the facts about Nulland's character as I had them from Martin Irelock, and he ought to know what he's talking about. He does know, too, and he could prove it. Naturally he wouldn't think of doing it, and I'm not too prejudiced, and I've got Ellshaw for a witness. Irelock wants to cover up Nulland. That's why he put down that fake bloodstained handkerchief tonight, to make it look more positively like kidnapping—and I'm ready to bet that he actually told Kenneth to run away in the first place—because he could see that Nulland was shaking in his boots at the idea of being surrounded with detectives, even a wretched imitation of a detective like you, Claud. Irelock knew that Nulland couldn't get through the rest of the evening, let alone the week-end, without getting caught out, and he was ready to go to any lengths to save him. He's been setting himself up as a shield all along. Anywhere between last week and a year ago, when Nulland thought he'd killed Ellshaw, Irelock played guardian angel."

"Do you mean Irelock was in it with him?" stammered Mr Teal blankly.

The Saint's lips twitched helplessly, but he held back the scathing retort which they were shaping automatically. His keen ears had caught an infinitesimal sound outside the room, and in one amazing soundless moment he had hitched himself off the table and crossed over to the door. He turned the handle and whipped it open, and his long arm shot out and caught Martin Irelock as the secretary was turning away.

"Come in," said the Saint's gentlest voice. "Come in and help me finish my story."

Irelock came in because he had to. With the Saint's iron grip on his arm, he had no option. He was in his pyjamas and a thick camel-hair dressing-gown, and his unnaturally old doll-like face was even greyer than it had been when he had swallowed his recent glassful of whisky and nitroglycerine. Simon closed the door again and stayed with his back to it.

"What's the matter?" demanded Irelock, in a strangely weak voice. "I heard somebody arrive—"

"Lots of people have been arriving, dear old fruit," said the Saint heartily. "In fact, the whole cast is more or less assembled. We were only waiting for you to complete the party. And now I want you to tell all these nice kind policemen how you set out to get hold of Ripwell's millions."

"I don't know what you're talking about," said Irelock throatily.

"No?" The Saint's voice returned to gentleness. "Well, you've got a lot of good precedents for that remark. I think nearly all the best murderers have said it. But this time we know too many of the answers. In fact, I think I could almost finish the job without any help from you. We all know how, when you first got the idea of making yourself rich, you tried Ripwell on blackmail—through Ellshaw here. And we were just starting to reconstruct your next move. We've seen how you must have figured out that if you couldn't get anything out of Ripwell, it'd be a damned sight easier to get it out of his son. We've got a good idea of how you set about it. Using Ellshaw again, you must have engineered Kenneth into a gamble with him. You knew Kenneth's weaknesses. You fed him plenty of drink at the same time. Ellshaw is such a damn bad card-sharper that people see through him even when they are tight, as Teal told me. Kenneth saw through him. There was a quarrel, then a fight. Ellshaw got laid out—as you'd planned. And then you sobered Kenneth up and told him Ellshaw was dead. You said you'd find a way to get rid of the body and cover up the evidence, and later you told him you'd done it. And from that moment he was in your power to do what you liked with—while you were making him believe, all the time, that you were his best friend. All you had to do was to hide your partner—Ellshaw—away, while you got rid of Ripwell, and then, after Kenneth had inherited the money, everything was set for you to start putting on the screw."

"That's right, guv'nor," Ellshaw broke in savagely. "That's wot 'e told me. An' I shammed dead, an' everythink. And then the dirty double-crossin' swine—"

"The man's raving," said Irelock unsteadily.

"Nuts," said the Saint crisply. "You're through, and you know it. Kenneth's here to tell the world how you kidded him you were saving him from the gallows. Ellshaw's here to tell us that that's the plot as you put it up to him. And Ellshaw's here as well to tell us how you double-crossed him by killing his wife!"

Ellshaw was coming up out of his chair with a red flame in his eyes. His fingers were curled and rigid like claws.

"Yes, that's wot you did," he snarled. "You told me she wouldn't come to no 'arm—you swore you was only goin' to 'ide 'er away somewhere. And you killed 'er! You murdered my wife. You told me a lot of lies. You knew I wouldn't've let yer do it if I'd known. And you were goin' to keep me workin' in with you, 'elpin' yer to mike money an' playin' all yer dirty games, when all the time you'd got Florrie's blood on yer 'ands. My Gawd, if 'anging isn't too good for yer—"

His voice went into a sort of shriek. Oldwood, who was nearest, wrapped powerful arms round him and held him back.

"That's the swine as did it!" screamed Ellshaw. "'E told me wot 'e was up to, 'ow 'e was goin' to kill Lord Ripwell an' then put the black on 'is son fer 'aving killed me in a fight. I know all about it! An' I can tell yer 'ow 'e meant to kill Mr Templar in Duchess Place—"

"Take it easy," said Oldwood, struggling with him.

Teal thrust himself forward at last, a massive figure of belated officialdom coming into its egregious own. He looked at Nulland.

"Is that true?"

The young man swallowed.

"Yes," he said in a low voice. "At least, the part about me is."

"You ran away tonight because you thought we were after you?"

The other nodded without speaking, and Teal turned back to Irelock.

"Have you got any answer to make?"

Irelock stood silent, looking from face to face. His mouth tightened, making his Kewpie face seem even more grotesquely grown up, but he did not open it to reply. The detective waited; then he shrugged.

"Very well. I shall have to take you into custody, of course. I had to warn you that anything you say may be taken down and used in evidence against you."

For the first time since he had come into the room, Irelock met his eyes. He even smiled slightly.

"That's hardly necessary, Inspector," he said. "You seem to have plenty of evidence already. I think I can flatter myself that it took a clever man to catch me." His gaze wandered significantly over to the Saint. "When did you first . . . suspect me?"

"When you saw a face at the window," Simon told him, "and the party broke up at a very psychological moment. I hadn't anything definite even then, but I began to wonder."

Irelock nodded.

"That was bad luck, of course," he said matter-of-factly. "But I had to do something to stop Kenneth finding out that Ellshaw had been seen alive. Then, after I'd started a scare, I thought I might as well go on with it. If I'd been lucky, I might have got you and Ripwell in the garden—as it was, you nearly got me." He touched his forearm, where the bullet had grazed him. "But it made my story more circumstantial. It was only afterwards that I realized that Kenneth might be suspected, and I had to try and manufacture some evidence in his favour."

"Why did you drink your own poison?"

"Partly because Teal wouldn't drink, and by that time I knew I'd got to get rid of both of you together. Partly because you'd just been saying things which showed me that you were fairly hot on my trail—I didn't know what you might have said to Teal already. It was the only time I lost my nerve. I tried to turn the idea into a way of throwing you off the scent again."

"Do you realize the meaning of all you're saying?" asked Teal grimly.

Irelock sighed.

"Oh, yes. Quite well. But there doesn't seem to be much point in giving you any more trouble. After all, you've got other witnesses. You ought not to have Ellshaw, but that's another piece of bad luck. I told him that if he saw a red light in my window he was to keep away, but apparently he didn't keep away far enough."

"One more question," said the Saint. "Why didn't you kill me in Duchess Place?"

"Because I hadn't got a gun," answered Irelock simply. "I never set out to go in for that sort of crime—not till it was thrust on me. I notice that murderers in books always have guns, but they aren't really easy for the amateur to get hold of. I should have got rid of you like I got rid of Mrs Ellshaw—knocked you out and sunk you in the river while you were unconscious. It was only when things began to happen down here that I got hold of Ripwell's old revolver. And of course he did have some ammunition, but he'd forgotten it."

"Have you still got this gun?" Teal asked quickly.

Irelock's lips moved in a wan smile, and he put his right hand into the breast of his dressing-gown. Three of them at least caught the sudden cunning shift of his eyes, and realized too late what was coming—it was queer, Simon reflected afterwards, how completely they had been taken in by his implied surrender, when every one of them should have known that the murderers who make a full and calm confession at the moment when they are unmasked are as rare as fresh pineapples in Lapland.

What Ellshaw knew, or what he guessed, none of them ever discovered. It is only on record that he was the first of them to move, the only one to get up and go straight for Irelock. Twice the room rocked to the crash of the heavy gun, and Ellshaw staggered at the impact of each shot, but he held on his course. He must have been dead on his feet, but in some uncanny way he caught Irelock at the door and fell on his arm, dragging the revolver down so that it could only aim at the floor. It took two men to unlock the clutch of his fingers on Irelock's wrist, and the bruises of that dying grip were still stamped on the other's flesh a fortnight later, when he stepped down from the dock to wait for the answer to the greatest mystery of all.

THE CASE OF THE

FRIGHTENED

INNKEEPER

1

Business took Simon Templar to Penzance, though nobody ever knew exactly what he had to do there. He took Hoppy Uniatz with him for company, but Hoppy never saw him do it. Simon parked him in the bar of a convenient pub for an hour, and that was that. For all that this story can record, he may have spent the hour in another pub across the street, talking to nobody and watching nothing. The Saint's business was as irregular as himself and directed by the same incalculable twists of motive: he was liable to do a great many important things with apparent aimlessness, and a great many unimportant things with the most specious and circumstantial parade of reasons.

It is about two hundred and eighty miles from London to Penzance, which the Saint drove in five hours, including one break for a cigarette and a drink in Taunton, and after that one hour for which Hoppy Uniatz was alone, he climbed back into his car as if he was cheerfully prepared to drive the same two hundred and eighty miles home without further delay.

The chronicler, whose one object it is to conceal no fact which by its unfair suppression might deceive any one of the two hundred and fifty thousand earnest readers of this epic, is able to reveal that this performance had never entered Simon Templar's head, although the Saint would have done it without turning a hair if it had happened to be necessary. But he did not say so, and Mr Uniatz, citizen of a country whose inhabitants regard a thousand-mile jaunt in much the same light as the average Londoner regards a trip to Brighton, would have been quite unperturbed whatever the Saint had announced for his programme. Hardly anything was capable of perturbing Mr Uniatz except a call for mental effort lasting more than five consecutive seconds, and that was an ordeal to which he had never been known to submit himself voluntarily.

He sat placidly at the Saint's side while the huge snarling Hirondel droned eastwards along the coast, chewing the butt of an incredibly rank cigar in a paradise of intellectual vacancy which allowed his battered features to relax in a calm that had its own rugged beauty, being very much like something that Epstein might have conceived in a sportive mood. They left the rocks of Cornwall behind them and entered the rolling pastures and red earth of Devon, diving sometimes through the cool shadows of a wood, sometimes catching sight of a wedge of sea sparkling in the sunlight between a fold of the hills. Simon Templar, who was constitutionally unable to regard the highways of England as anything but a gigantic road-race circuit laid out for his personal use, did nothing to encourage a placid relaxation in anybody who rode with him, but Hoppy had sat in that car often enough to learn that any other attitude could lead only to a nervous breakdown. Only once was he jarred out of his phlegmatic fatalism, when the Saint sounded his horn and pulled out to pass a big speeding saloon on a straight stretch beyond Sidmouth. As they swept up alongside, the saloon swerved out spitefully: the Saint's face hardened under a sheath of bronze, and he held grimly on, with his offside wheels on the very edge of the road. They got through with a shrill scraping of wings, and then Simon swung the Hirondel sharply in, and heard Hoppy's breath hiss through his teeth.

"Geez, boss," said Mr Uniatz uncertainly, "I t'ought we was finished den." He felt around at his hip. "Say, why don't ya stop de wagon an lemme go back an' shoot up dat god-damn son of a witch?"

Simon glanced at the driving mirror, and smiled rather gently.

"He has been shot up, Hoppy," he said, and Mr Uniatz looked back and saw that the saloon had stopped far behind, tilting over at a perilous angle with its near-side wheels buried in a deep ditch.

They roared over four more hills, whipped around half a dozen more corners in hair-raising skids, and thundered past a gaunt grey building in a barren hollow, close to the road. Simon took the cigarette from between his lips and pointed to it.

"Do you know what that place is, Hoppy?" he asked.

Hoppy screwed his neck round.

"It looks like a jail, boss," he said, and the Saint grinned.

"It is a jail," he murmured. "With that eagle of yours, you go straight to the bullseye. That noble pile is Larkstone Prison, where the worst of the first offenders go—there isn't anyone in it who's doing less than seven years. Chief Inspector Claud Eustace Teal has often told me how much he'd like to see me there."

They climbed another slope, and dropped down with surprising contrast into Larkstone Vale. In an instant the rather monotonously undulating agricultural country through which they had been travelling disappeared like a mirage, and they were coasting down a mild gradient cut into one wall of the valley towards the sea. A glimpse of thatched cottages clustering along the borders of the estuary blinked through the trees which cloaked the slope, and a broad shallow stream wound southwards in the same direction a little way below them. It was one of the least known beauty spots in the South West, still unspoiled even in those days, and the setting sun, abruptly cut off by the rise which they had just crested, left it in a pool of peaceful dusk which made all the tortuous alleys of lawlessness where the Saint made his career, and where the men in the drab prison over the last spur of hill had been less fortunate, seem momentarily ridiculous and unreal.

Simon trod on the brake and brought the great car to a smooth standstill on the upper ledge of the village.

"I think this will do us for the night," he said.

"We ain't goin' back to London?" asked Mr Uniatz, putting two and two together with a certain justifiable pride in his achievement.

The Saint shook his head.

"Not tonight, Hoppy. Perhaps not for days and days. I like the look of this place. There may be adventure—romance—a beauteous damsel in distress—anything. You never know. They may even have some good beer, which would do me almost as much good. C'mon, fella—let's have a look round."

Mr Uniatz disentangled himself from the bucket seat in which his muscular form had been wedged, and stepped stoically into the road. He was not by nature or upbringing a romantic man, and the only damsels in distress he had ever seen were those he distressed himself, but he had been afflicted since adolescence with a chronic parching of the gullet, and the place where they had stopped looked as if it might be able to assist him on his endless search for relief. It was an old rambling house of white plaster and oak timbering, with dormer windows breaking through a thatched roof and crimson ramblers straggling up the walk: a carved and painted sign over the door proclaimed it to be the Clevely Arms. Entering hopefully, Mr Uniatz saw the Saint drawing off his gloves in a sort of lounge hall with a rough-hewn staircase at the far end, his dark head almost touching the beams and his blue eyes twinkling with an expectant humour that might well have been worn by an Elizabethan privateer standing in the same spot three hundred and fifty years ago. But no Elizabethan privateer could have had more right to that smile and the twinkling eye with it than the Saint, who had carved his name into the dull material of the twentieth century as a privateer on a scale that would have made Queen Elizabeth dizzy to think of.

"Over there," he said, "I think you'll find what you want."

He swung across the hall and ducked under a low lintel on one side into a small but comfortable bar. A pleasant-looking grey-haired man with glasses came through a curtain behind the counter as he approached, and bade them good evening.

"I should like a pint of beer," said the Saint, "and half a bottle of whisky."

The grey-haired man filled a pewter tankard from the wood, and turned back with it.

"And a whisky?" he queried.

He had a quiet and educated voice, and the Saint hated to shock him. But his first duty was to his friend.

"Half a bottle," he repeated.

"Would you like me to wrap it up?"

"I hardly think," said the Saint, with some regret, "that that will ever be necessary."

The landlord took down a half-bottle from the shelf behind him, and put it on the counter. Simon slid it along to Mr Uniatz. Mr Uniatz removed the cap, placed the neck in his mouth, and poured gratefully. His Adam's apple throbbed in rhythmic appreciation as the neat spirit flowed soothingly through the arid deserts of his throat in a stream that would have rapidly choked anyone with a less calloused oesophagus.

Simon turned again to the landlord, who was watching the demonstration in a kind of dazed awe.

"You see why I find it cheaper to buy in bulk," he remarked.

The grey-haired man blinked speechlessly, and Hoppy put down the empty bottle and wiped his lips with a sigh.

"You ain't seen nut'n yet, pal," he declared. "Where I come from, dey call me a fairy."

It was the first time he had spoken since they entered the house, and Simon was utterly unprepared for the result.

All the colour drained out of the grey-haired man's face, and the ten-shilling note which Simon had laid on the bar, which he had just picked up, slipped through his shaking fingers and fluttered down out of sight. He stared at Hoppy with his nostrils twitching and his eyes dilated in stark terror, waiting without movement as if he expected sudden death to leap at him across the bar.

It only lasted for a moment, that startling transformation into terrified immobility, and then he stooped and clumsily retrieved the fallen note.

"Excuse me," he muttered, and shuffled out through the curtain behind the counter.

The Saint put down his tankard and fished out a cigarette. Not even the most shameless flatterer had ever said that Hoppy's voice was vibrant with seductive music: such a statement, even with the kindest intentions, could not have been made convincingly about that rasping dialect of New York's Lower East Side which was the only language Mr Uniatz knew. Hoppy's voice was about as attractive and musical as a file operating on a sheet of jagged tinplate. But the Saint had never known it to strike anyone with such sheer paralysed horror as he had seen the landlord reduced to for that brief amazing moment.

Mr Uniatz, who had been staring at the curtained opening with a blank fish-like expression which in its own way was no less cataleptic, turned perplexedly towards him, seeking light.

"Dijja see dat, boss?" he demanded. "De guy looked like he was waitin' for us to turn de heat on him! Did I say anyt'ing I shouldn't of?"

Simon shook his head.

"I wouldn't know, Hoppy," he answered thoughtfully. "Maybe the bloke doesn't like fairies—you can never tell, in these great open spaces."

He might have said more, but he heard a footstep beyond the curtain, and picked up his tankard again. And then, for the second time, he put it down untouched, for it was a girl who came through into the serving space behind the bar.

If there was to be a beauteous damsel in distress, Simon decided, the conventions insisted that it must be her role. She was tall and slender, with dark straight hair that took on an unexpected curl around her neck, steady grey eyes, and a mouth to which there was only one obvious way of paying tribute. Her skin reminded him vaguely of peaches and rose-petals, and the sway of her dress as she came in gave him a suggestion of her figure that filled his head with ideas of a kind to which he was quite amorally susceptible. She said "good evening" in a voice that scarcely intruded itself into the quiet room, and turned to some mysterious business with the shelves behind her.

Simon let a drift of smoke float away from his cigarette, and his blue eyes returned with a trace of reluctance to the homely features of Mr Uniatz.

"What would you think," he asked, "of a girl whose name was Julia?"

Out of the corner of his eye he saw her start, and turned round to face her with that gay expectant smile coming back to his lips. He knew he had been right.

"I came right along," he said.

Her gaze flashed to Hoppy Uniatz, and then back to the Saint, in a second of frightened uncertainty.

"I don't understand," she said.

Simon picked up a burnt match-stick from the floor and leaned his elbows on the bar. As he moved his tankard to make room, it spilt a tiny puddle of beer on the scarred oak. He put the match-stick in the puddle and drew a moist line down from it towards her, branching out into a couple of legs. While he did it, he talked.

"My name is Tombs." He drew a pair of arms spreading out from his first straight line, so that the sketch suddenly became an absurd childish drawing of a man with the original spot of liquid from which it had developed for a head. "I booked a room the other day, by letter." He dipped the match again, and drew a neat elliptical halo of beer over the head of his figure. "Didn't you get it?" he asked, with perfectly natural puzzlement.

She stared down at his completed handiwork for a moment, and then she raised her eyes to his face with a sudden light of hope and relief in them. She picked up a cloth and wiped the drawing away with a hand that was not quite steady.

"Oh, yes," she said. "I'm sorry—I didn't recognize you. You haven't stayed here before, have you?"

"I'm afraid not," said the Saint. "But then, I didn't know what I was missing."

Once again she glanced nervously at Mr Uniatz, who was gazing wistfully at a row of bottles whose smug fullness was reawakening the pangs of his incurable malady.

"I'll get the man to take your bags up," she said.

Taking in the grace of her slim young suppleness as she turned away, Simon Templar was more than ever convinced that he was not wasting his time. He had been lured into no wild-goose chase. In that quiet inn at the foot of Larkstone Vale there was a man in whose eyes he had seen the fear of death, and a damsel in distress who was as beautiful as anything he had seen for many moons; that was more or less what he had been promised, and it was only right that the promise should have been so accurately fulfilled. The dreary cynics were everlastingly wrong; such joyously perfect and improbable things did happen—they were always happening to him. He knew that he was once more on the frontiers of adventure, but even then he did not dream of anything so amazing as the offer that Bellamy Wage had made on the day when he was sentenced to ten years' penal servitude after the Neovision Radio Company failed for nearly two million pounds.

2

"Say," blurted Hoppy Uniatz, broaching a subject which had clearly been harassing him for some time, "is anyt'ing de matter wit' me?"

"I shouldn't be surprised," said the Saint pitilessly, from the basin where he was washing the dust of travel from his face. "All that whisky you sluice your system with must have its effect some day, even on a tin stomach like yours. What are the symptoms?"

Mr Uniatz was not talking about ailments of that kind.

"De foist time I open my mout' in dis jernt, de barman looks at me like he t'inks I'm gonna take him for a ride. When de goil comes in, she looks at me just de same way, like I was some kinda snake. I ain't no Ronald Colman, boss, but I never t'ought my pan was dat bad. Have all dese guys here got de jitters, or is anyt'ing de matter wit' me?" he asked, working back to his original problem.

The Saint finished drying his face with a chuckle, and slung the towel round his neck. He took a cigarette from a packet on the table and lighted it.

"I'm afraid I've rather led you up the garden, Hoppy," he confessed.

"De garden?" repeated Mr Uniatz dimly.

"I've been kidding you," said the Saint, hastily abandoning metaphor, in which Mr Uniatz was always liable to lose his way. "We aren't stopping here just because I saw the place and thought we'd stay. I came here on purpose."

Hoppy Uniatz digested this statement. Simon could watch the idea percolating gradually into his skull.

"Oh . . . I see . . . So when you says de name is Tombs—"

"That's the name I'm using here, as long as it takes in anybody. And don't you forget it."

"I get it, boss. An' de room you booked—"

Simon laughed.

"That requires a little more explanation," he said.

He took up his coat from where he had thrown it over a chair, and slipped out an envelope from the breast pocket. The lamplight gleamed on a ripple of his bare biceps as he sprawled himself over the bed with it.

"Listen to this," he commanded:

Dear Saint,

I've no right to be writing this letter to you, and probably you'll never even read it. I've never met you, and I don't even know what you look like. But I've read about some of the things you've done, and if you're the sort of man I think you are you might listen to me for a minute.

This is an old sixteenth-century inn which belongs to my uncle, who's a retired engineer. My father died in South Africa five months ago, and I came here to live because there was nowhere else for me to go.

Queer things have been happening here, Saint. I don't know how to go on, because it sounds such utter nonsense.

*But I've heard people walking around the place at night,
when I know perfectly well there's nobody about, and
sometimes there are sort of rumbling noises underground
that I can't account for. Lately there have been some horrible
men here—I know you must be thinking I'm raving already,
it sounds so childish and hysterical, but if only I could talk
to you myself, I might be able to convince you.*

*I can't go on writing like this, Saint. You'll just think,
"Oh, another neurotic female who wants a good smacking,"
and throw it into the wastepaper basket. But if you're ever
travelling this way, and you have a little time to spare, I'd
give anything to see you drop in. You can stay here as an
ordinary guest, and find out for yourself whether I'm crazy.
My uncle says I am, but he's frightened too. I can see he is,
even though he won't admit it.*

*Something's growing up in this place that must mean
trouble: and it might be in your line. I wish I could hope
that you'd believe me.*

Julia Trafford

The furrows of painful thought grooved themselves into Mr
Uniatz's brow again.

"Julia?" he said. "Was dat de dame we spoke to downstairs?"

"I take it she was."

"An' she wrote you dat letter?"

"To which I replied saying that I should come here as soon as
I could, armed to the teeth and probably masquerading under the
suggestive name of Tombs."

"So we come here today on poipose—"

"To find out whether the girl really is nuts, or whether there are fun and games in the offing that might keep us out of mischief for a while."

Mr Uniatz nodded. The layout was becoming clearer. Only one major point remained obscure.

"Whaddas it got to do," he asked, "wit' de garden?"

The Saint groaned helplessly, and rolled off the bed to rake out a clean shirt from his Oshkosh. Buttoning it at the open window, he looked out through a loose grille of trees, over the red and grey roofs of the village towards the sea. The tide was out, and the estuary was a tongue of glistening reddish mud, veined with tiny rivulets, that licked in between the hills and drank up the flow of the river. On either edge of it a narrow strip of shingle broke straight up into irregular red cliffs capped with velvet grass. The mud was littered with dinghies and stranded buoys, and the broad hulls of a half-dozen fishing boats lay canted over along the line of the deepest channel, with a man or two moving on the decks about the ordinary business of checking tackle and sorting nets. There was a sense of peace and patience about the place, an atmosphere of changeless simplicity and homeliness, that made him wonder once again what sinister racket could possibly find food in such surroundings. But that was what he had come there to discover.

He picked up his coat with a good-humoured smile.

"I'll murder you later," he promised Mr Uniatz kindly.

Leaving Hoppy to perform his own ablutions, he went downstairs again and strolled out into the road. He wanted a map from his car to gain a more detailed knowledge of the topography of the district, and on his way back he collected another item of information from the legend painted over the door in the traditional style: *MARTIN JEFFROLL, Licensed to Sell Wines, Beer, Spirits, and Tobacco.* The superscription was not new, but it revealed traces of an older name which had been blacked out. Presumably Mr Jeffroll was the grey-haired man who had been so strangely frightened by the sound of Hoppy Uniatz's discordant voice.

Simon went back into the little bar off the hall and lighted a fresh cigarette. It was Jeffroll who came through the curtains and civilly declined the Saint's invitation to join him in a drink. Simon ordered a pink gin, and was served with unobtrusive courtesy: the panic-stricken creature whom he had glimpsed in Jeffroll's shoes a short while ago might never have existed, but the landlord had withdrawn behind a wall of indefinable reserve that was somewhat discouraging to idle conversation. Having served the drink, he retired again through the curtain, leaving the Saint alone.

Simon took up the glass and solemnly drank his own health in the mirror behind the bar, and he was setting the glass down again when the same mirror showed him a man who had just come into the hall. Quite spontaneously he turned round and scanned the newcomer as he came on under the low arch—it was purely the instinctive speculative scan of a lone man at a bar who considers the approach of another lone man with whom he may exchange some of the trivial conversation that ordinarily breaks out on these occasions, and he was unsuspectingly surprised to notice that the other was coming towards him with more than speculative directness.

There was hardly time in the short distance that the other had to cover for the Saint's curiosity to grow beyond the vaguest neutrality, and then the man was standing in front of him.

"Is that your car outside?" he asked.

His voice was harsh and domineering, and the Saint did not like it. Studying the man more closely in the waning light, he decided that he didn't care much for its owner, either. He had never been able to conceive an instant brotherly regard for ginger-headed men in loud-checked ginger plus fours, with puffy bags under their small eyes and mouths that turned down sulkily at the corners, particularly when they spoke with harsh domineering voices, but even then he was not actually suspicious.

"I have got a car outside," he said coolly. "A cream-and-red Hirondel."

"I see. So you're the young swine who drove me into a ditch outside Sidmouth."

The Saint ceased to be perplexed. A genial smile of complete comprehension lighted up his face.

"Good Lord!" he exclaimed happily. "Have you been all this time getting out?"

"What did you say?" snarled the man.

"I asked whether you'd been all this time getting out," Simon repeated, with undiminished affability. "Or was that a rude question? Is your car still in and did you walk from there?"

The man took another step towards him. At those still closer quarters, he did not look any more attractive.

"Don't give me any of your lip," he rasped. "Do you know you nearly killed me with your dirty driving?"

"I rather hoped I had," said the Saint calmly. "I like killing road-hogs—it makes the country so much more pleasant to move about in."

"Say that again?"

Simon raised his eyebrows. The ginger-haired man, even without knowing the Saint, might have been warned by the imperturbable leisureliness of that gesture alone, but he was too close beside himself with rage to perceive his own foolishness.

"My dear hog," said the Saint, "are you deaf or something? I said—"

It has already been mentioned that the ginger-haired man was incapable of perceiving his own foolishness. Otherwise he could not possibly have been tempted as he was by the half-glass of gin and angostura which Simon Templar was poising in his left hand while he talked. Even though he might have known the toughness of his own two-hundred-pound frame, and might have guessed that the debonair young man in front of him weighed no more than a hundred and seventy-five pounds, he need not have allowed his undisciplined temper to make him such a sempiternal sap. But he did.

His hand smacked up in an insolent swipe, and the glass of pink gin was knocked up through the Saint's fingers to splash its contents over Simon's face and the front of his coat.

Simon glanced at the mess, and started to take out his handkerchief. He was smiling again, and the Saint was as dangerous as a Turk when he smiled.

"That was rather rash of you," he said, and suddenly his fist shot out like a bullet from a gun.

The ginger-haired man never even saw it coming. Something that was more like a lump of brown rock than a human fist leapt towards him through the intervening space and collided smashingly with his nose in a punch that sent him reeling back in a blind gush of agony to fetch up jarringly against the wall behind him. Hauling himself forward again with a strangled oath, he saw the Saint's gentle smile again through a crimson mist, and launched a vicious swing at it that would have been worth all his trouble if it had connected. But in some unaccountable way the smile omitted to keep the appointment. It swayed unhurriedly aside at the very moment when the swing should have met it, and the violence with which his fist bludgeoned the empty air threw the ginger-haired man off his balance. In technical language, he led off for the next blow with his chin, and that same astonishingly hard fist was there in exactly the right place to meet his lead. The only difference was that on this encounter he felt no pain. His teeth scrunched shudderingly together under the impact, and then every raw and vengeful thought in his head was wiped out by a ringing of heavenly bells and a vast soothing darkness that merged indistinguishably into dreamless sleep . . .

Simon picked up his handkerchief again and quietly mopped the sticky dampness off his clothes. Jeffroll had come through into the bar again, and he realized that the girl Julia was standing in the low archway that connected with the hall. But it was not until he noticed how silently they were staring at the recumbent slumber of the ginger-haired man that he realized that the delightful episode which had just taken place had an implication for them that he would never have suspected.

3

Jeffroll was the first to look up. "What happened?" he asked.

The Saint shrugged.

"I haven't the faintest idea," he replied blandly. "The bloke seemed a bit excited, and I think he banged his head on something. It doesn't look like a very exhilarating pastime, but I suppose there's no accounting for tastes. Was he a pal of yours?"

Jeffroll let himself out from behind the bar and dropped on one knee beside the prostrate ginger-clad body, without answering. Simon's coolly observant eyes noticed that his hands were trembling again, and that his actions contained an essence of something more than the natural solicitude of a conventional innkeeper whose premises have been desecrated by an ordinary breach of the peace. The Saint put away his sodden handkerchief and considered whether he had left anything undone that might improve the shining hour, and then he saw the startled face of Hoppy Uniatz peering over Julia Trafford's shoulder, and went across to him.

Mr Uniatz's mouth hung open—and, hanging open, it was an amazingly large mouth. The light of battle was peeping tentatively out of his eyes like spring sunshine through a cloud.

"What ya hit him wit', boss?" he asked wistfully. And then, as the merest afterthought, "Who is dat guy?"

"The guy we ditched near Sidmouth," explained the Saint under his breath. He grasped Hoppy firmly by the arm. "And now shut your face for a bit, will you? I guess I'm about ready to eat."

The dining-room was a low raftered room looking out on to a tiny garden cut out of the sheer hillside. Simon steered Mr Uniatz briskly into it before that unrivalled maestro of tactlessness could drop any heavier bricks in the hearing of the chief protagonists, but when he reached his sanctuary he found that it was considerably less invulnerable than he had hoped it would be. The room only held four tables, and it was so small that the four of them might have been joined together in one communal board for all the privacy they afforded. Moreover, one of the tables was already occupied by a party of four men who fell curiously silent at the Saint's entrance.

They were in their shirtsleeves, and their shapeless trousers had an air of grubby masculine comfort, as if they were placidly prepared to crawl about on their knees or sit down on a heap of loose earth without any qualms about its effect on their appearance. At first sight they might easily have been taken for a quartet of hikers, and yet, if that was what they were, they must have started on their pilgrimage very recently, for their bare forearms were practically untouched by the sun. Their hands, in contrast to that unexpected whiteness of arm, were coarsened with the unmistakable rough griminess of manual labour, which could hardly overtake the average holiday tramper before exposure had left its mark on his skin. It was that minor contradiction of make-up, perhaps, rather than their unfriendly silence, which made Simon Templar pay particular attention to them, but there was no outward and visible sign of his interest. He took them in at one casual glance, with all their individual oddities—a big black-haired man who had not shaved, a thin fair-haired man with a weak chin, a bald burly man with a vintage-port complexion, and an incongruously small and nondescript man with a grey moustache and pince-nez. And beyond that one sweeping survey there was nothing to show that he had taken any more notice of their existence than he had of the typical country-hotel wallpaper adorned with strips of pink ribbon and bouquets of unidentifiable vegetation with which some earlier landlord had endeavoured to improve his property. He dumped Mr Uniatz in a seat at a corner table, taking for himself the chair which commanded a full view of the room, and cast a pessimistic eye over the menu.

It offered one of those seductive bilingual repasts with which the traveller in England, whatever he may have to put up with during the day, is so richly compensated at eventide.

POTAGE BIRMINGHAM

—

BOILED COD AU BEURRE

—

LEG DE MOUTON RÔTI
POMMES CHIPS
SPINACH

—

SUET PUDDING
FROMAGE—BISCUITS

Simon put down the masterpiece with a faint sigh, and opened his cigarette-case.

"Did I ever tell you," he asked, "about the extraordinary experience of a most respectable sheep I used to know, whose name was Percibald?"

It was plain from the expression on Mr Uniatz's homely pan that he had never heard the story. It was equally plain that he was ready to try dutifully to discover its precise connexion with the shindig in hand. The convolutions of painful concentration carved themselves deeper into his dial.

"Boss—"

"Percibald," said the Saint firmly, "was a sheep of exceptionally distinguished appearance, as you may judge from the fact that he was once the innocent cause of a libel action in which a famous Cabinet Minister sued the president and council of the Royal Academy for damages on the grounds that a picture exhibited in their galleries portrayed him in the act of sharing the embraces of a nearly nude wench with every evidence of enjoyment. On investigation it was found that the painting had only been intended for a harmless pastoral scene featuring a few classical nymphs and shepherds, and that the artist, feeling that shepherds without any sheep might look somewhat stupid, had induced Percibald to pose with one of the nymphs in the foreground. This, however, was merely an incident in Percibald's varied career. The extraordinary experience I was going to tell you about . . ."

He burbled on, hardening his heart against the pathetic perplexity of his audience. It is one of the chronicler's major regrets that the extraordinary experience of Percibald is not suitable for quotation in a volume which may fall into the hands of ladies and young children, but it is doubtful whether Mr Uniatz ever saw the point. Nor was the Saint greatly concerned about whether he did or not. His main object was to shut off the spate of questions with which Mr Uniatz's hairy bosom was obviously overflowing.

At the same time, without ever seeming to pay any attention to them, he was quietly watching the four men in the opposite corner. After their first silence they had put their heads together so briefly and casually that if he had actually taken his eyes off them for a moment he might not have noticed it. Then an exchange of whispered words opened out into an elaborately natural argument which he had no trouble to hear even while he was talking himself.

"Well, I know it's on the road to Yeovil. I've been there often enough."

"Damn it, I was born and brought up in Crewkerne, and I ought to know."

"I'll bet you a pound you don't."

"I'll bet you five pounds you're talking through your hat."

"Well, you show it to me on a map."

"All right, who's got a map?"

It turned out that none of them had a map. The big unshaven man finished loading his pipe and got up.

"Perhaps the landlord's got a map."

"He hasn't. I asked him yesterday."

The extraordinary experience of Percibald reached its indelicate conclusion. Mr Uniatz looked as if he was going to cry. The Saint scanned his memory rapidly for another anecdote, and then the big man moved a little way down the mantelpiece and cleared his throat.

"Excuse me, sir—do you happen to have a map of the country around Yeovil?"

Simon put aside a plate containing a small piece of lukewarm blotting-paper which was apparently the translation of Boiled Cod au Beurre.

"I've got one in the car," he said. "Are you in a hurry?"

"Oh, no. Not a bit. We just want to settle an argument. I don't know if you know the district?"

"Vaguely."

"Do you know Champney Castle? I say it's between Crewkerne and Yeovil, and my friend says it's in the other direction—on the way to Ilchester."

The Saint had never heard of Champney Castle, and he was even inclined to doubt whether such a place existed, but it never occurred to him to interfere with anybody's innocent amusements.

"I know it quite well," he replied unblushingly. "There's an entrance from the Ilchester Road and another from the Yeovil Road. So you're both right."

The man looked convincingly blank for a moment, and then a chuckle of laughter broke out from his companions, in which he joined. Cordial relations having thus been established, the other members of the party turned their chairs to an angle that subtly gathered up the Saint and Hoppy into their conversation. It was all very neatly and efficiently done, with a disarming geniality that would have melted the reserve of anyone less hoarily aged in sin.

"Are you staying here long?" inquired the fat man with the fruity face.

"I haven't made any plans," answered the Saint carelessly. "I expect we'll hang around for a few days, if there's anything interesting to do."

"Do you like fishing?"

"Sometimes."

"You get some pretty big conger off Larkstone Point."

Simon nodded.

"I should think they'd be good sport."

The small man with the grey moustache polished his pince-nez industriously on a napkin.

"Dangerous, of course, if you don't know your business," he remarked. "You don't want to loop the gaff on your wrist—if you did that, and made a slip, I don't suppose we'd ever see you again. But lots of things are much more dangerous."

"I suppose so," agreed the Saint gravely.

"Lots of things," repeated the thin fair-haired man, apparently addressing the tablecloth.

"For instance," said the fat fruity man thoughtfully, "I've never been able to make out why everybody in America seems to be so frightened of gangsters. If any of them tried to do their stuff over here, I'm sure that would be very dangerous . . . for them."

The big unshaven man struck a match.

"Wouldn't stand an earthly, would they, Major? I don't know how the police would react to it, but personally I wouldn't have any compunction about tying 'em to a rock at low tide and leaving 'em there."

"Nor would I," echoed the one with the fair hair, to his audience of bread-crumbs.

"Serve them right if we did it," said the grey moustache clearly. "I haven't any sympathy for common thugs who try to shove their noses into other people's business."

Not even Mr Uniatz's most ardent admirers, if he ever had any, could fairly have flattered him on his lightning grasp of conversational trends, but he had a definite talent for assimilating a simple idea if it was pushed under his nose several times in a sufficient variety of ways. Even then, he was still far from knowing exactly what was going on, but it was dimly percolating into the misty twilight of what for want of a better word must be loosely termed his mind *(a)* that the four men at the other table were saying something uncomplimentary, and *(b)* that their attitude included some general disparagement of the manners and customs of his native land. It would be untrue to suggest that he knew the meaning of more than half of these words, but they would have served to convey a fairly accurate description of his psychic impressions if he had known them. It was also a matter of elementary knowledge to him that a guy does not get uncomplimentary to another guy without being prepared to shoot his best insults out of a rod, and that was a stage of the proceedings at which Mr Uniatz could make up a lot of lost ground in the way of repartee. He began to grope frowningly around his hip, but Simon kicked him under the table and smiled.

"You do sound bloodthirsty," he murmured.

The bald fruity man got up. Standing on his feet, he looked big and solid in spite of his rich complexion and extensive waistline.

"Oh, no. Not particularly bloodthirsty. Just four old soldiers who got used to being shot at quite a long while ago. I really don't think we'd be the best people for any gangsters to pick on—some of them would certainly get hurt. It's worth thinking about, anyway!"

A waitress came in with the next course of the Saint's dinner. She went over and whispered something to the grey-moustached man, who dropped his pince-nez and spoke in an undertone to the fair-haired man with the receding chin. The other two looked at them as they got up.

"You must excuse us," said the grey moustache, rather abruptly.

He went out, and the others followed him after a second's hesitation. Hoppy Uniatz stared at the closing door blankly—he was experiencing some of the sensations of an early Christian who, having braced himself for a slap-up martyrdom, has been rudely sniffed at by a lion and then left high and dry in the middle of the arena. Coming on top of the other incomprehensible things that had happened to him since he arrived there, this was not soothing. He turned to the Saint with a rough sketch of these complex emotions working itself out on his face.

"Boss," he said awkwardly, "dis place makes me noivous."

4

Simon Templar chuckled, and probed a tentative fork into the section of warm rawhide crowned with a wodge of repulsive green mash which was apparently the local interpretation of Leg de Mouton under the influence of spinach.

"I can't imagine it, Hoppy," he said.

Mr Uniatz's frown deepened.

"Ja see dose guys take a run-out powder on us?" he demanded, starting methodically at the beginning.

"They do seem to have breezed on."

"Maybe dey see me goin' for my Betsy," said Mr Uniatz, passing on to the more nebulous realms of theory.

"They could hardly have helped it."

"Well, where dey t'ink dey get off pullin' dat stuff an' beatin' it before we say anyt'ing?"

The Saint grinned.

"I think we can say we've been very politely warned off. In fact, I don't think I've ever seen it done in a more classical style—those birds must have been reading the smoothest detective stories. How's your spinach? Mine tastes as if they'd been mowing the lawn this afternoon."

He struggled through as much more of the meal as his stomach would endure, and lighted a cigarette. Mr Uniatz was finished some time before him—Hoppy's calloused maw would have engulfed a plateful of live toads dressed with thistles and wood-pulp without noticing anything extraordinary about the menu, even in normal times, and when he was worried he was even less likely to observe what he was eating. Simon pushed back his chair and stood up cheerfully.

"Let's take a walk," he said.

Mr Uniatz licked his lips yearningly.

"I could just do wit' a drink, boss."

"Afterwards," said the Saint inexorably. "I want to look over the lie of the land."

There was no sign of the four genial diners when they went out, nor of the unpleasant ginger-haired man who had been foolish. A couple of obvious local inhabitants were poring over tankards of beer in the bar parlour off the hall—Simon caught a mere glimpse of them as he went by, but he did not see Martin Jeffroll, and there was nothing visible or audible to suggest that anything worth the attention of a modern buccaneer had happened there for the last two hundred years.

He got into his car and drove it round to the garage, a ramshackle shed dumped inartistically on to the north wall of the inn. It had never been designed to give a comfortable berth to cars of the Hirondel's extravagantly rakish proportions, and there was a big grey lorry parked along one side which forced the Saint to go through some complicated manœuvres before he could get in. He managed to squeeze himself into the available space with some accompaniment of bad language, and rejoined Hoppy on the road.

"We'll go down to the waterfront and smell some ozone."

There was a rough grey stone promenade where the lowest houses straggled along the edge of the bay, and at one end of the village a similar stone causeway sloped down from it and ran out for some distance along the edge of the channel through which the river found its way seawards through the mud. Apparently it had been laid out at some time to give easier access to the boats moored in the channel at low tide. The usual fishing village's collection of miscellaneous hardy craft was scattered out across the inlet, with here and there a hull whose brighter paint and more delicate lines spoke of some more fortunate resident's pleasure. A little way out on the darkening water he could see a few scraps of sail, and a curiously shaped vessel at anchor which looked like a dredger.

He was rather surprised to see a signpost on the quay—one arm pointed to Seaton, the other to Sidmouth. He had not known that there was another through road besides the one by which he had arrived. Later that evening he looked it up on a map and found that there was an alternative route along the coast which took a big loop seawards, rejoining his own road near Lyme Regis.

The knowledge did not immediately give him any clue to the mystery. He sat on a bollard and watched the tide lap in through the gathering dark, smoking a steady series of cigarettes and trying to co-ordinate his meagre information. There was a girl who did not look particularly hysterical, who had heard strange things at night. There was an innkeeper who was undoubtedly a badly frightened man. There was a red-haired road-hog who seemed to have something to do with something. There were four hikers untouched by the weather who talked like traditional conspirators in the accents of Sandhurst. He could see one rather obvious theory which might somehow embrace them all, but it failed to satisfy him. Larkstone was some way east of the historical smugglers' country, and in any case the popularization of aerial transport had changed all the settings of that profession.

Mr Uniatz had no theories. He had been trying very hard to work several things out for himself, but after a while the effort gave him a headache and he laid off.

It was quite dark when they strolled back to the hotel. Jeffroll was locking up. He bade the Saint a distantly polite good night, and Simon remembered the lorry which was taking up more than its fair share of the garage.

"Do you think it could be moved?" he asked. "I'm likely to be here for two or three days."

The landlord pursed his lips apologetically. "As a matter of fact, it was left here on account of a debt by a man I've never seen again. It won't go—the propeller shaft is broken. And it's too heavy to push. I don't want to spend any money on repairing it, and I'm trying to sell it as it stands. I'm afraid it is a bit of a nuisance, but I'd be very much obliged if you could put up with it."

Simon went upstairs with the knowledge that he was unlikely to get much sleep that night, but the prospect did not trouble him. He had gone without sleep before, and could give the appearance of going without it for phenomenal periods, although by cat-napping at appropriate moments he could secure more rest than many people gain from a night's conventional slumber. At the same time he wished that he could have heard more from Julia Trafford first, and it might have been a telepathic fulfilment of his unspoken thought when the door of his bedroom opened again almost as soon as he had closed it and she came in.

Almost every woman has some setting in which she can look astonishingly beautiful: for Julia Trafford, wide-trousered crêpe-de-Chine pyjamas and a flimsy silk wrap, with the shaded lights striking unexpected glints of copper from her dark hair, was only one of many. Hoppy Uniatz, who had no natural modesty, stared at her dreamily. The Saint could have thought of many more interesting things to talk to her about than the troubles of her frightened uncle, but he hoped she was not going to fall in love with him, which was one of the most serious risks he ran when succouring damsels in distress.

"I had to see you," she said. "That letter I wrote was so stupid—I didn't believe you'd pay any attention to it at all. Are you really the Saint?"

"Scotland Yard is convinced about it," he said solemnly, "so I suppose I must be."

He made her sit down and gave her a cigarette.

"What exactly is this all about?" he asked.

"I don't know," she said helplessly. "That's the trouble. That's why I wrote to you. There's something ugly going on. My uncle's terrified, even though he won't admit it. I've begged him to tell me several times, but he keeps on saying I'm imagining things. And I know that isn't true."

The ginger-haired man, apparently, had been there before, and on his second visit he had been accompanied by two others whose descriptions sounded equally unpleasant. Each time he had seen Jeffroll alone, and each time the interview had left the innkeeper white and shaking. After both occasions she had made attempts to gain his confidence, but he had only denied that there was any trouble, and refused to talk about it any more. She knew, however, that since the second visit he had taken out a licence for a revolver, for the local police sergeant had come in with it one afternoon when he was out.

"Do you think he's being blackmailed?" she asked.

"I don't know," said the Saint mildly. "What about these noises you hear at night—would they be the blackmailers painting up their armour?"

"They're—well, I told you nearly all I could in my letter. This is a very old place, and a lot of boards creak when they're stepped on. Sometimes when I've been lying awake reading at night I've heard them, even when I know Uncle Martin's gone to bed and nobody else has any business to be moving about. At first I thought we were being burgled, but I went downstairs twice and I couldn't find anybody."

He raised his eyebrows.

"You thought there were burglars in the place, and you went down to look for them alone?"

"Oh, I'm not nervous—I think most burglars would run for their lives if they thought anybody was coming after them. But that was before that red-haired man came here."

"And the noises have been going on—how long?"

"Nearly all the time I've been here. And then there's the rumbling. It sounds like a train going by, very close, so that the house vibrates, but the nearest railway is five miles away." She looked at him with a sudden youthful defiance. "You don't believe in ghosts, do you?"

"I've never seen one yet," he said coolly. "Certainly not a ginger-haired one in ginger plus fours."

He finished his cigarette and lighted another, strolling thoughtfully about the room. He did believe in neurotic women, having been pestered by more than his share, but he knew no species which panicked over imaginary terrors and at the same time went single-handed in search of burglars. Besides, he had seen certain things for himself. The landlord's startling reaction to Mr Uniatz's rasping voice, for instance—it had puzzled him considerably at the time, but he realized now that a man who had had disturbing interviews with a bloke like Gingerhead might have some reason to be frightened of a stranger who looked and talked like the most blatantly typical gangster that ever stepped. Obviously Jeffroll was being threatened, but ordinary blackmail was a very inadequate explanation, and the cruder forms of extortion were not likely to reach a small innkeeper in an obscure Devonshire village.

"Who are the Four Horsemen?"

She was baffled for a moment.

"Oh, you mean the men who were having dinner? They were here before I came. My uncle seems to be quite friendly with them. They go out fishing every night—you never see them about before dinner."

The fat fruity man, he learned, was Major Portmore; the big black-haired man was Mr Kane; the grey moustache and pince-nez were worn by Captain Voss; and the thin man with the deficient chin who always talked to the table was blessed with the name of Weems.

"They've always been perfectly nice to me," she said.

"I'll believe you," he murmured. "I thought they were most refined. A bit sinister in their line of backchat, but very British. What happened to the ginger bloke?"

She didn't know. Jeffroll had carted him into his private office to revive him, leaving her in charge of the bar, and later on had announced that the patient had recovered and departed quietly. He had seemed pleased, and this was understandable.

The Saint smiled.

"I suppose there must be a good deal of head-scratching going on about us by this time," he said. "First of all we're taken for a couple of Gingerhead's strong-arm guys, and then I sock Gingerhead on the jaw and put the whole thing cockeyed. I wonder if Uncle is tying himself in knots over it, or whether he thinks the whole show was a piece of low cunning especially staged to put him off the scent."

"I couldn't tell you, but I'll let you know if I do find out. You've spoken to Major Portmore, then—what did he have to say?"

"He was quite pleasant. They told us they didn't like gangsters, and gave us a few ideas about what they'd feel like doing if any hoodlums tried to muscle in on their preserves. It was all very nicely done, and if I'd been an ordinary thug I might have been quite impressed. Possibly. But I'll agree with you that they seem pretty harmless fellows at heart, and that only makes things more complicated. If they're quite innocent, why the hell don't they get some policemen to deal with Gingerhead and me?"

He scowled over the enigma for a few moments longer, and then he shrugged.

"Anyway, I suppose we'll find out. I'm going to do my sleeping in the daytime like the Four Horsemen—the night has a thousand eyes, and mine are going to be two of 'em."

He got up out of the arm-chair into which he had thrown himself, with a quick smile that wiped the hard calculating lines out of his face in a flash of careless friendliness that was absurdly comforting. She really was rather beautiful, even if that moment found her at a loss for anything but the conventional answer.

"I don't know why you should take so much trouble—"

"It's no trouble. Most of us have to earn our living, and if there is any useful racket working around here I shall get my percentage out of the gate. I'll let you know where I get to, and you can keep in touch with me. I haven't made up my mind yet what part I'm going to try to put over, so you'd better not take a lot more risks like this in case anybody got wise to us. If I want to tell you anything, I'll leave a note"—he glanced swiftly about the room—"under that corner of the carpet. And you'd better park your mail in the same place. Unless it's desperately urgent. Don't worry, kid—Hoppy and I are rough on rats, and when the ungodly think up a game that we didn't play in our cradles . . ."

He left the rest of the sentence in the air, with the hairs at the back of his neck tingling.

While he talked, he had become faintly aware of a queer vibration that was at first too deep in its choice of wavelength to be perceptible to any ordinary faculty. And then, gradually, it grew strong enough to be felt. A glass upturned over the neck of

217

the carafe on the washstand trilled in a sudden shrill relay of the impulse. He listened, in utter silence, and heard something like the rumble of wheels roll through the earth and come to a thudding stop far underneath his feet.

5

Julia Trafford's face was suddenly white in the dim light which robbed the tapestry covering of the chair-back behind her of much of its hideousness. Her lips parted breathlessly.

"That's it," she whispered, with her grey eyes widening against his. "You heard it yourself—didn't you? That's what I've been hearing."

The lamplight cut dark lines and piratical masses of shadow out of his brown face and brought up the glint of blue steel in his mocking gaze. He stood checked in precarious stillness, with the white scrap of his cigarette clipped between steady fingers, and the lamp threw his shadow towering up the wall so that his head and shoulders stooped over the low ceiling.

"How far away is this railway?" he said.

"The line's about five miles inland—the nearest station is Colyford."

He nodded.

"Go back to your room, bright eyes," he said, and his hand touched her shoulder as she stood up. "And don't lose any sleep over it. Whatever this racket is, I'll take it apart and see what makes it go."

He closed the door after her, and found Hoppy Uniatz gaping at it with the glazed otherworldly look of a man who is going to be seasick. For a couple of seconds he studied the phenomena in fascinated silence, and then he cleared his throat tactfully, and Mr Uniatz came out of his trance with a guilty start.

"I could give dat dame a tumble sometime—when I ain't got nut'n better to do," he said, in a tone so overpoweringly blasé that the Saint blinked at him in considerable awe.

Simon would have liked to probe deeper into this remarkable statement, but he reserved his curiosity for a more leisured date.

"I think I'll wander about the place and look at the architecture," he said.

"Okay, boss." Mr Uniatz roused himself finally out of his dreams, and dragged out his Betsy. He slid back the jacket and inspected the cartridge in the chamber with unromantic stoicism. "Wit' you an' me on de job, I guess dis racket is on de skids."

"With me on the job, it may be," said the Saint calmly. "You're going to stay here and snore for both of us—and that ought to be a pushover for you."

He was firm about this, in spite of Hoppy's injured protests. For a partner in a gun-fight, Simon would have asked nobody better, but for a tour of stealthy investigation he would as soon have chosen a boisterous young bison.

"I want you to look after Julia," he said craftily, and Mr Uniatz brightened. "Where are you going?"

"Ant'ing you say goes, boss," said Hoppy, with his hand on the door-knob.

"You don't have to go," said the Saint coldly. "I said look after the girl, not at her. Her room's just down the passage on the other side, and if she's in trouble you'll be able to hear her. When she wants you in her bedroom I'm sure she'll ask for you."

He left Mr Uniatz brooding happily over this consoling thought, and went out into the dark corridor. At such times of emergency the Saint's fluency of shameless inventiveness was unparalleled—he had not the faintest idea where Julia Trafford's room was actually situated, and the fear of what might happen if an amorous and impatient Mr Uniatz went prowling hopefully into the bedchamber of a hysterical cook was perhaps one of the most disturbing thoughts in his mind at that moment.

The passage was more or less, rather less than more, lighted by the wavering gleam of a small oil lamp hung in a bracket on the wall—from the beginning he had noticed this prevalence of primitive illumination in the hotel, for he had seen the silver pylons of the national electric supply grid spanning the valley as he drove down. Downstairs it was quite dark, but on these ventures he carried his own illumination which was less conspicuous in any case than switching on the ordinary lights in any place he wanted to explore.

The dim beam of an electric flashlight in his hand, irised down to the thinnest useful pencil of luminance by a circle of tinfoil pasted over the lens, guided him about the ground floor. No creaking boards betrayed his movements, for he had a tread like a cat when he chose to use it, and an uncanny instinct for treacherous footings. He covered the rooms which he had seen before, hall and dining-room and lounge bar, and others which he had not seen but which were roughly what he would have expected to find. The kitchen was behind the dining-room, a big stone-flagged room like a barn, which must have served for a staff dining-room as well, and might well have held even more distinguished company in the days when eating was a heartier and more earnest business. Opening off the kitchen was a long paved passage which seemed to run the length of the building. He tried the different doors, each with the same care and silence, and reviewed a series of sculleries, pantries, lavatories, coal and wood cellars, wine and beer stores, and a small staff sitting-room. The last door, at the end, appeared to lead out into a yard at the back—it was locked on the inside, and when he turned the key he found himself in the open under the shadow of the garage.

He was retracing his steps when he heard the dull vibrant rumble under his feet again. It was much more distinct than it had sounded upstairs, with a definite metallic harshness, but even then it was not so loud that he could fix it clearly in his mind. If he had been there as an ordinary unsuspecting guest, it might not have attracted his attention at all—he would probably have put it down subconsciously to a heavy lorry passing on the road outside, and would never have felt urged to probe into it further. Also, the place being what it was, he would very soon have been in bed and asleep, and there was nothing sufficiently startling about the muffled noise to wake him. But he was not asleep and he was not unsuspecting, and he knew that the sound was not quite the same as that of a passing lorry.

He opened another door in the passage and found himself in another short length of corridor—it was scarcely large enough to be called an inner hall. On one side was a door carrying the painted word "Private"; it was locked and he guessed that this was Jeffroll's own sanctum. On the other side was a red curtain, and when he went through it he discovered himself back in the diminutive lounge, but on the serving side of the bar.

There was one obvious thing to do there, and the Saint was nerveless enough to do it. He paid the money scrupulously into the till and sat on the bar with his modest glass and a completely brazen cigarette, waiting and listening in silence. Twenty minutes later he heard the noise again.

This time it seemed to give birth to three faint echoes—they were about sixty seconds apart, and each of them was sharper and crisper in tone than the original sound. The effect was something like that of three slow spaced rollers of surf sweeping up a shingle beach. Again the noise was not startlingly loud, but it was closer and clearer.

Simon ran thoughtful fingers through his hair. The rumble passed again, seeming to recede into the distance, and then the stillness settled down again. His watch told him that it was nearly midnight, but he had no superstitions.

He slid down to the floor, broke up the stub of his cigarette, and washed the fragments down the sink under the bar, dried his glass on a cloth and replaced it on its shelf, and picked up his torch. He was, for the moment, irritatingly stymied, but he felt that something ought to be done. He had verified the last fraction of Julia Trafford's story, and he was baffled to find any natural explanation. On the other hand, up to that moment he had also failed to find an unlawful solution. Secret passages of some kind were manifestly indicated, but to measure every room and corridor and draw up plans of the building to locate discrepancies in the sum total was a lengthy job for which he had very little patience and, prosaically enough, no implements at all.

There remained the locked door of Jeffroll's private office, and he thought he could cope with this. Curiously enough it gave him an unaccountable difficulty, and he had been working on it for a couple of minutes before he discovered that the thing that was obstructing his skeleton key was another key left in the lock on the inside.

He changed his instrument for a pair of thin-nosed pliers and turned the key quite easily, but with even greater caution. A key on the inside of a locked room, except in fictional murder mysteries, vouches for someone on the inside to turn it, and yet he could not see so much as a glimmer of light in the cracks between the old badly-fitting oak door and its frame. Then, as he took up the pressure of the latch with delicately practised fingers, he heard a limp sort of dragging scuff of movement which no normal ambusher would have made, and a grunting moan of stertorously exhaled breath which removed the last of his hesitation.

The nape of his neck prickled, but he went in boldly—he had an intuitive certainty of what he would find there, and he did not gasp when the beam of his torch shone full into the dilated eyes of the man with ginger hair.

6

Simon swept his flashlight round in a quick survey of the rest of the room. There was no other visible exit than the door which he had just opened, unless the door of a large built-in safe in another wall concealed unconventional secrets. There was a desk with a swivel chair behind it, a typewriter on a side table, a filing cabinet, a shelf littered with books and papers, an armchair, and a few faded and nondescript prints on the walls—the conventional furnishings of a small country hotel office. He had no doubt that some of these superficially innocuous fittings might repay closer investigation, but he turned back to the ginger-haired man as a more obvious feature of interest.

"Do you do this for fun, or are you practising a vaudeville act?" he murmured pleasantly.

The other made no answer, for the very good reason that his mouth was blocked by an amateurish but effective gag. Nor, as he might well have been tempted to do, did he get up and make another attempt to destroy the symmetry of the Saint's face, because the lengths of wire bound tightly about his wrists and ankles made any such hearty greeting impossible.

Simon enjoyed the sound of his own voice, but in those circumstances he was prepared to be generous. He squatted down and loosened the gag sufficiently to remove one of Gingerhead's disadvantages, but not so thoroughly that it could not be speedily replaced if necessary. When the cloth was pulled down he saw that the man's mouth was twitching with fear.

"What are you going to do?"

Simon tilted up his flashlight to show his own face.

"What would you do to a bloke who was very rude to you and spilt your drink?" he asked.

The man licked his lips.

"I didn't mean to do that. I lost my temper. I didn't know—"

"What didn't you know?"

"I didn't know you were—one of them. You've got to let me out. You can't do anything to me. There's a law in this country—"

Simon thought quickly, and came to a decision.

"Let you out, Ginger Whiskers? You're a bit of an optimist, aren't you?"

"I could make it worth your while," said the other feverishly. His voice was not harsh and domineering now, but its quavering terror was perhaps even more unpleasant. "I'll give you anything you like—a thousand, two thousand—"

"Go on."

"Five thousand—"

The Saint clicked his tongue reproachfully.

"Ten thousand pounds," said the man shakily. "I'll give you ten thousand pounds to let me go!"

"This is getting interesting," drawled the Saint. "Have you got all this money in your pocket?"

"I can get it for you." The man dropped his voice lower, although neither of them had spoken far above a whisper.

The Saint sighed.

"Sorry, brother, but this is a cash business."

"You could have it first thing in the morning—before that, if you wanted it."

"Where is it coming from?" asked the Saint, with calculated scepticism. "Will you go down into the village and hold out your hat, or are you going to burgle the bank?"

"I know where I can get it. I've got to meet a man—tonight!"

"Where are you going to meet him?"

The man glared at him silently, with narrowing eyes, but Simon stuck to his point.

"Let me go and meet this man," he said slowly. "If he'll pay ten thousand quid to save your life, I'll come back and see about it."

"How do I know you will?"

"You don't," Simon admitted sadly. "But you can take it from me that unless I do see this bird and his money I'm not going to do anything for you. And then the uncertainty would be so much more trying. Instead of wondering whether I was going to help you or not, you'd only be able to wonder whether you were going to be buried alive under the public bar or fed to the congers off Larkstone Point."

He kept his light focused on the ginger-haired man's blotched, puffy face, and read everything that was going on in the mind behind it.

"He'll be waiting on the road to Axminster, exactly three miles from Seaton," came the reply at length. "He'll do anything to get me out. For God's sake, hurry!"

Simon doubted whether God would really be deeply concerned, but he allowed the invocation to pass unchallenged. He bent forward and replaced the gag as it had been when he came in, and switched out his light on the ginger-haired man's mutely terrified eyes.

"If they have fed you to the congers when I get back, I'll go fishing," he murmured kindly.

He left the office on this encouraging note, and let himself out into the back yard by the door at the end of the kitchen passage. The garage doors had been left open, and after a second's hesitation he began to manœuvre his car out of its place by hand. It was a task that taxed all his strength, but he preferred the hard work to the risk of starting the engine where it might be heard by someone in the hotel. Fortunately the garage was built on a slight slope, and after a good deal of straining and perspiration he manhandled the big Hirondel into a position where he could get in behind the wheel and coast out of the yard and down the hill until it was safe to touch the self-starter. At the first corner he turned round, and sent the great purring monster droning back up the grade towards the Seaton Road. He was well on his way before he remembered that he had not even waited to tell Hoppy Uniatz where he was going.

There was something else which he had forgotten, but he did not recall that until much later.

He was conscious of a deep and solemn exhilaration. The sublime good fortune that was always spreading itself so prodigally over all his adventures showed no signs of shirking its responsibilities. Destiny was still doing its stuff. One got a letter, one went somewhere, one exchanged a few lines of affable badinage with a selection of mysterious blokes, one dotted an ugly sinner on the button, and forthwith the wheels began to go round. It might have been a coincidence that he had had cause to smite Ginger Whiskers so early in the proceedings, but from then on everything had unwound like clockwork. The presence of Ginger Whiskers, bound and gagged, in that locked office, was only part of the machinery—obviously, when Jeffroll had come out and seen him slumbering peacefully and harmlessly on the floor, the opportunity to put him away must have seemed far too good to miss. Simon would have grabbed at it himself, and he guessed that that decision was the cause of the message which had summoned the Four

Horsemen from the dining-room and broken up their friendly exchange of compliments. Everything, up to that point, was clear: the mystery of what it was all about remained. But the eccentric philanthropist who was willing to pay ten thousand pounds for the life of a blister like Gingerhead might offer some more hints on that subject.

He understood the ginger-haired man's psychology to three places of decimals. Whatever the outcome of this interview might be, the waiting accomplice would at least learn what had happened to his confederate, and Ginger Whiskers was doubtless banking far more heavily on the advantages of getting his message through than on the Saint's desire to help him. If their positions had been reversed, the Saint would have gambled on the same horse. But before that bet was decided he hoped to become much wiser himself—he had forgotten that in certain circles he was one of the best-known men in England.

The trip meter on the dash was just turning over the third mile from Seaton when he picked up a red light stationary by the side of the road. As his headlights drew nearer to it he saw that it was the rear light of a small saloon of a popular make. He dimmed his lights and pulled in just in front of it, and a man came up, walking with quick jerky steps.

"Is that you, Garthwait?"

Simon gathered that this was the name by which Ginger was known to the police. He hunched his shoulders and tried to remember Garthwait's rasping voice.

"Yes."

The light of a powerful torch was flashed on his face, and he heard the unknown man's hissing breath.

"At least," he said quickly, "Garthwait sent me—"

"Mr Simon Templar, isn't it?" said the other gently. "I know your face quite well."

For a moment the Saint almost recanted his views on the lavish publicity which the newspapers had given to some of his exploits although for many years that disreputable fame had been one of his most modest vanities. But he smiled.

"You do know your way round, don't you, dear old bird?" he remarked.

"That is my business," said the other dryly, as if he was making a very subtle joke. "Please keep your hands on the steering-wheel where I can see them. I've got you covered, my friend, and I could shoot you long before you could reach your gun."

His voice had a dusty pedantic quality which was the last intonation Simon Templar would ever have expected from a man who spoke of unlawful armaments and sudden death with so much self-possession.

"You're welcome," said the Saint amiably. "My life is insured, and I'm considered to be an A.1 risk. I wish I could say the same for Comrade Garthwait. There seems to be some sort of idea that he would be Good for Contented Congers, but he said you'd pay ten thousand pounds to keep him on dry land, and I thought it might be worth looking into. I suppose love is blind, but what you can see in a wall-eyed wart like that—"

"Where is Garthwait?"

"When I saw him last, he was gagged up and tied together with wire, meditating about the After Life."

"Where was this?"

"In the Old House."

"The hotel?"

"Oh, no," said the Saint carefully. "It was too risky to keep him there. Don't you know the Old House?"

The man behind the flashlight did not pursue the subject.

"And he told you I'd give you ten thousand pounds to let him out?"

"That's what he said. I'm afraid I thought he was a bit optimistic at the time, but I didn't like to discourage him. After all, when there's so much money at stake—"

"How do you know that?" asked the other sharply.

The Saint smiled.

"Garthwait told me."

"Did he tell you about last night's job?"

"Yes, he told me that, too," answered Simon coolly, and knew in the next instant that he had made a fatal mistake—the man he was talking to was as alive to all the tricks of the trade as he was himself.

"That's interesting," said the dry stilted voice, "because there was never any such thing as 'last night's job.' You had better get out of that car, Mr Templar. If Garthwait is really in danger, it would doubtless be diminished if your friends knew that you were in a similar predicament."

Simon thought very swiftly. He had set out cheerfully to try his luck, and the luck had gypped him very neatly. At the same time, he couldn't let it have everything its own way. In a kindly and impartial spirit, he reviewed the pros and cons of the not so philanthropic philanthropist's suggestion for continuing the game, and decided that it lacked any really boisterous humour.

He had not stopped his engine when he stopped the car, but it was throttled down to a mere whisper which might not have forced itself upon the philanthropist's attention. While he appeared to deliberate whether he should obey or not, he made a rapid deduction from the flashlight of the probable position of the man behind it. Then, with a faint shrug, he opened the door.

The light moved out of the way, towards the rear of the car, as he had expected. Turning as if to get out, his left hand found the switch which controlled the car's lights; he had already flipped the car into gear, and his feet were resting on the clutch and accelerator pedal. In one concerted movement he snapped out every light against which he might have been silhouetted, roused the engine to a sudden roar of power, and banged in the clutch.

Something crashed deafeningly behind him and left his ears singing, and then he was crouched low over the steering-wheel, swerving away up the road with the seat pressing forcefully into his back under the urge of the Hirondel's terrific power. The open door slammed into latch in the slipstream: his ears caught the thin shred of another more vicious slam behind him that might have been an echo of the door and was not, and his teeth flashed in a Saintly smile before he whirled round the next corner and was out of range.

He was still smiling when he ran down the hill into Larkstone and cut his engine before swinging round to glide up to the garage beside the inn. Even after that minor miscalculation he remained the blithest of optimists—he hadn't once caught sight of the face of the man to whom he had spoken, but he would know that dry pedantic voice anywhere, and he had found men before with less to identify them than that.

He had his next surprise when he turned his wheels towards the garage and prepared to repeat his earlier strenuous performance by manhandling the car back into its berth, for as his dimmed lights panned round he saw that he had an unobstructed run in. The lorry that had blocked his way before, which Jeffroll had told him was out of action with a broken propeller-shaft, had vanished.

7

So had Garthwait—he discovered that when he went indoors and opened the door of the manager's office. The mere fact that the door opened without any manipulation reminded him that he had not turned the key from the outside when he left, and then he remembered that he had also left behind the pliers with which he had turned it in the first place—they were still lying on the floor where Garthwait had been, and he recollected that he had put them down when he loosened the gag and had forgotten to pick them up again. The pliers, like most similar instruments, were also wire-cutters, and there were four severed strands of wire lying near them to show how they had been used.

For a man who had made so many mistakes in one night, the Saint went to bed very lightheartedly. He heard the same queer subterranean rumbling twice more before he fell asleep, but he did not allow it to disturb his rest.

The faithful Mr Uniatz had been snoring serenely in his chair when Simon turned in, and he was still snoring on the same majestic note when the Saint woke up. He leapt up like a startled hippopotamus when the Saint shook him, and then he blinked sheepishly and lowered his gun.

"Sorry, boss . . . I guess I must of fell asleep."

"After all, a brain like yours must rest sometimes," said the Saint handsomely.

It was eight o'clock, and the morning was clear and bright. Sitting squeezed up in the diminutive bath of the hotel's one rudimentary bathroom, he told the story of his night's adventure in carelessly effervescent sentences—at least, the tale bubbled on exuberantly enough, in the flamboyant inconsequential idiom which was his own inimitable language, until he noticed that his audience was not following him with all the rapt breathlessness which he felt his narrative deserved. He stopped, and regarded Mr Uniatz speculatively. Mr. Uniatz coughed.

"Boss," said Mr Uniatz, waking out of his reverie as if the whole tedious business of noises in the night, gagged men in locked rooms, pedagogues with pop-guns, and disappearing lorries had now been satisfactorily disposed of, and the meeting was free to pass on to more spiritual pursuits. "What rhymes wit 'goil'?"

"'Boil,'" suggested the Saint, after a moment's poetic reflection.

Mr Uniatz pondered the idea for a while, his lips moving as if in silent prayer. Then he shook his head dubiously.

"I dunno, boss—it don't sound quite right."

"What doesn't sound quite right?"

"Dis voice of mine."

"I shouldn't let that prey on my mind, Hoppy," said the Saint encouragingly, although he was finding the train of thought more and more obscure. "After all, you can't have everything. Maybe Caruso wasn't so hot with a Roscoe."

Hoppy Uniatz frowned.

"I don't mean de verse I talk wit', boss; I mean de voice I'm makin' up when I fall asleep last night. It starts dis way:

"You're so beautiful, you're like a rose,
I'm tellin' ya, an' I'm a guy who knows:
Your eyes are like de shinin' stars,
Dey remind me of my Ma's:
I t'ink you are a swell kind of goil—"

He hesitated.

"I bet a neck like yours never had a berl."

He concluded, scratching his head. "It don't sound right, somehow, but I never had no practice makin' up pomes."

Simon dried and dressed himself in stunned silence.

He strolled out into the road in the strengthening sunshine, and found his steps leading him almost automatically down towards the harbour, although he had no need of the walk to sharpen his appetite for breakfast. Down on the quay he found a blue-jerseyed old salt smoking his pipe on a bollard and gazing out to sea with the faraway bright-blue eye which is popularly supposed to express the sailor's unquenchable yearning for the great open waters, but which can actually be quenched with the most perfunctory dilution of water. It was a very conventional politeness to exchange good mornings, easy enough to pass on to some more explicit appreciations of the weather, and from there to a broader discussion of life in those parts. The man had the easy garrulousness of his kind, and perhaps he also scented a future customer for fishing expeditions.

"Aye, there was more life here when I wurr a boy. Fordy ships there wurr in the fishing fleet then—now, there ain't 'aardly a dozen. What with the 'aarbour fillin' up now an' everything, it do zeem as if we'll all have to take up vaarming afore long." He poked the stem of his pipe towards the horizon. "That dredger out yonder, she been workin' here for three months gone tryin' to keep us open, but it keeps fillin' up."

Simon gazed out at the thread of smoke rising from the dredger's funnel against the pale blue sky.

"You mean the sea's going back on you?"

"Aye, it do zeem that way zometimes. You zee that channel down there where the boats lay—down there by the causeway? That's where she's woorst. Seems to come up with the tide, like every night, an' it gets caught there like it would by a breakwater, or else the river brings it down an' the tide catches it an' throws it back. It's all we can do to keep 'er clear." The man's voice held a certain personal pride, as if he himself had gone out with a spade and established the enormity of the disaster at first hand. "It's due to the world goin' round the sun, that's what it is—just as you could walk across on dry land once from here to Fraance . . ."

He grumbled on into a startlingly abstruse geological theory which was apparently designed to prove that such things did not happen when the earth was flat—only returning from his flights of imagination when the time came to point out, as the Saint had suspected, that he was the owner of the best boat for fishing on the coast, and that his services could be secured at any time for a purely nominal fee.

Simon made vague promises, and went thoughtfully back up the hill. Nestling into the bank of a cool green, with the stippled shadows of the overhanging trees stirring lazily across it, the rambling black-timbered inn looked more than ever like the sort of place where the most sensational mystery should be a polite and courtly, seventeenth-century ghost with a clanking chain and a head under its arm, and he wondered if that was one reason why it had been so ideally chosen.

He did not go indoors at once, but continued his stroll round to the garage. The lorry was back in its place, exactly as if it had never been moved, and it would not have required much self-deception to persuade him that he had dreamed its absence. But the Saint did very little dreaming of that kind, and he touched the radiator and felt that it was warm. He put his foot on one of the rear wheels and pulled himself up to inspect the interior of the truck. There was a dusty layer of red earth on the bottom, and particles of the same soil clung to the sides: he smeared one between his finger and thumb, and it was damp.

"All very interesting," said the Saint to himself.

He squeezed in between the lorry and the wall, and saw other sprinklings of earth on the concrete floor. The wall against which the truck was parked was an exterior wall of the hotel itself—the bare oak beams and timbering and the rough yellowish plaster seemed to stare out miserably at the cheap modern brickwork and corrugated iron which had been stuck on to them to produce the garage. He spent some minutes in a minute examination of the wall, and used the blade of his penknife to make sure.

When he came out again he was humming gently under his breath, and his blue eyes were twinkling with a quiet and profound delight. The yard straggled off into a long grass slope flimsily cut off by a staked wire fence. He ducked through the wire and sauntered up the hill until he reached a slight prominence from which he had a considerable view of the road which ran past the inn, and the upper country towards which it led. He could see where the straight march of the silver power pylons dropped over the main ridge of hill, stepped carelessly over the road three hundred yards away, and sent its glistening wires in a long sweep over the gladed valley to climb sedately over the rise on the other side. For some time he stood with his hands in his pockets and the dreamiest ghost of a smile on his lips, gazing out over the landscape. There was a ditch at the foot of the hill, beside the road, and it was this that he made for when he walked down again. The bottom of the ditch was overgrown with weed and couch-grass, but he felt about with his hand, and found what he had expected to find—a heavy insulated cable. He knew that he would find one end of the cable leading to the pylon nearest the road, if he cared to follow it. Walking slowly back to the inn, he came to a place where a slight hump in the road border indicated a comparatively recently filled excavation. It disappeared at the end of the concrete lane that led to the garage, and he knew that the insulated cable reached its destination somewhere very near.

At that moment he knew half the answer to the riddle of the Clevely Arms, and the solution staggered him.

Hoppy Uniatz was already in the dining-room, endeavouring to persuade a giggling waitress that a pound of fried steak garnished with three eggs and a half-dozen rashers of bacon was a very modest breakfast for a healthy man.

"Get him what he wants, Gladys," said the Saint, sinking into the other chair. "And call yourself lucky he's on a diet. If he was eating properly he'd spread you on a piece of toast and swallow you for an hors-d'œuvre."

"Dat bale of straw is fifty in de deck," growled Mr Uniatz cryptically, reaching for the solace of the bottle of whisky which he had foresightedly brought into the room with him. "Where ya been, boss?"

Simon lighted a cigarette.

"I've been exploring. We'll go on and see some more when you've finished."

"I dunno, boss." Mr Uniatz stared vacantly at the pink floral motif on the opposite wall. "Dis ain't such a bad flea-box. Whadda we have to pull de pin for?"

"We aren't pulling the pin, Hoppy," said the Saint. "This is just some local scenery we're going to take a look at. We may be staying here a long time—I don't know. Life has these uncertainties. But I think the trouble is coming fairly soon."

How soon the trouble was to come he had no means of knowing.

He went up the hill again, with Hoppy, after breakfast, but not in the same direction as he had gone before. This time he climbed the steeper slope due west from the back of the hotel. They struggled through winding paths among the trees and undergrowth to a muttered accompaniment of strange East Side expletives from Mr Uniatz, who never took exercise out of doors, and presently broke clear of the patch of woodland into a broad bare tract of grass that rolled up to an undulating horizon against the blue sky. From the top of this rise he could see patches of the roof of the inn through the branches, but he was more interested in the view on the opposite side of the hill. He stood looking at this for a little while in silence while Mr Uniatz recovered his breath, and then he sat down on the grass and took out his cigarette-case.

"If you can take your mind off poetry for a while and concentrate on what I'm saying, it may be useful," he said. "I want you to know what this is all about—just in case of accidents."

And he went on talking for about half an hour, sorting out the facts and putting them together with infinite deference to the limitations of Mr Uniatz's cerebral system, until he had made sure that even Hoppy had assimilated as much of the secret as he knew himself. He had never expected to produce any sensational reactions, but Mr Uniatz bit the end from a cigar and spat it out with a phlegmatic practicality which was equivalent to the flabbergasted incoherence of any lesser man.

"Whadda we do, boss?" he asked.

"We hang round," said the Saint. "It may happen tonight or it may happen a month from now, but we can take it as written that a job like this isn't planned and worked out on that scale without there's something pretty worthwhile in it, and when the balloon goes up we'll be round to inspect the boodle."

He had a cool estimate of his own danger. The Garthwait outfit had acquired bigger and better reasons to dislike him, whatever part they had decided he was playing in the pageant. The Jeffroll fraternity might be equally puzzled about his status, but in the next ten minutes he had three separate indications of their esteem.

While he sat talking on the hill his keen eyes had caught the stirring of a bush at the edge of the wooded patch below him, and he had seen the movement of a scrap of white behind it. Walking down again as casually as if he had noticed nothing, he let the path lead him towards the place where he had seen the watcher. It was Major Portmore, leaning against the bole of a tree where the shrubbery almost hid him from the hilltop—but for the flash of his white shirt, he might have been passed unobserved while he stood still. He had a pipe between his teeth and a shot-gun under his arm, and he nodded unconcernedly when the Saint greeted him.

"Thought I might get a rabbit," he said amiably. "You often see them sunning themselves up there."

Simon raised a faintly quizzical eyebrow.

"I should have thought tigers would have been more in your line," he murmured.

"Tigers," said the Major, taking out his pipe, "or rats. It's all the same to me."

The Saint let his eyes dwell gently on the other's shepherd's-warning complexion.

"If the rats are pink ones, on bicycles," he said gravely, "don't shoot."

He left the gallant Major a shade darker in colour, and bore thoughtfully to the left, towards the garage. Slipping into his car, he adjusted the throttle and ignition, and pressed the starter. The engine turned over several times without firing, and he abandoned the effort to save his batteries. Doubtless an expert investigation would show what had been done to put it out of action, but it required no investigation to tell him that Major Portmore's sudden transfer of interest from fishing to rabbiting had the same reason as the disabling of the Hirondel.

He wandered round to the front of the hotel, and found Captain Voss sitting on a bench beside the door with a newspaper on his knee, his face wrinkled up against the glare till he looked like a grey-haired lizard. He said "Good morning" briefly in answer to the Saint's cheery nod, and returned to his paper, but the Saint knew that he did not read another line until they had passed on into the hall.

Simon Templar went into the lounge and sat on a window seat with his feet up, considering these three tributes with the aid of a cigarette. The change of attitude since last night was not lost on him. Then, the principal idea had been to persuade him to move on, and he had gathered that if he moved on without fuss everybody would have been quite happy and asked no questions. Now, even if the idea was not actually to keep him there, it was at least plain that he was not to go anywhere without being watched—the tampering with his car fitted in with that scheme equally well, for it was flagrantly a hopeless car for anyone to try to follow. Simon sat thinking it over with profound interest, while Hoppy Uniatz sat beside and chewed one end of his cigar and smoked the other in a sublime complacency of unhelpfulness. He heard a small car grind fussily down the road and stop with a squeak outside, without letting it interrupt his meditations, and then, through the half-open window over his head, he heard something else that stiffened him into attention with a jerk.

"Morning, Voss—is Jeffroll inside?"

It was the thin desiccated voice of the man he had met on the Axminster Road in the small hours of that morning—the man who, according to Garthwait himself, might have paid ten thousand pounds for the rescue of that prodigious pimple on the cosmos.

8

There was no doubt that his bald use of Voss's surname, without prefix, was not meant impertinently; equally beyond question was the implied acceptance of the familiarity in Voss's pleasant reply:

"He's in the office—sorry I can't come in with you."

"Not at all," said the dry voice punctiliously.

Simon was peering between the curtains, trying to catch a glimpse of the owner of the voice, and then he heard footsteps in the hall and sank back hurriedly, snatching out a handkerchief to cover his face. Pretending to blow his nose vigorously, but not so noisily as to make himself the object of undesirable curiosity, he saw the man come through the archway which communicated the lounge and the hall. It was a small man, who walked easily under the low beams, and the chief impression it gave was one of studied and all-permeating greyness. Everything about him seemed to be grey—from the top of his baldish head and the parchment pallor of his face, down through his rusty swallowtail coat and striped trousers, to his incongruously foppish suède shoes. He carried a small black brief-case in a grey-gloved hand, and Simon searched for a moment for the one unmistakable thing that linked his whole appearance to his dry dusty voice. In another moment he got it. The Saint refused to believe that anyone who looked and dressed and spoke so exactly like a rather seedy lawyer could possibly have any other reason for existence.

And this grey old bird was the mysterious unknown who had recognized him on the Axminster Road. Simon's eyes narrowed fractionally as he remembered the parched undertone of humour in the man's accounting for that recognition. "That is my business . . ." Undoubtedly it was—but why was this bloke, whom Garthwait promptly called upon in his emergency, calling in such a friendly fashion on the men who had tied Garthwait up and apparently planned to fatten eels on him?

Simon bit his lip. He would have given much to overhear what was happening in the office, but his explorations had already revealed that there were only two approaches to Jeffroll's sanctum, either through the back of the bar or along the passage from the kitchen, and a moment's reflection showed both of those routes to be impracticable. The Saint swore comprehensively under his breath, damning and blasting everything about the hotel, from the amblyopic architect who had first conceived its fatuous layout down to the last imbecile grandchild of the paranoiac plumbers who had inexplicably omitted to drown themselves in its drains, and when he took out his cigarette-case again for the soothing compensation of tobacco, it was empty.

He got up restlessly, and went out again to the road. An ancient Morris stood outside, and he recognized it as the car he had met during the night—the identification of the grey dry man was absolutely complete, beyond question. But what the hell was it all about? The lawyer knew that he had been associated with Garthwait, must have known that his voice was easily recognizable; if he had been on such friendly terms with the hotel garrison as his approach and reception seemed to prove, he seemed to be taking an insane risk in coming back to see them after having been caught in his duplicity. Or was it something more than an insane risk? The Saint realized that unless that action were absolutely insane, the danger might be transferred to himself. He had to catch up with the development and put himself in front of it again, quickly. He still wanted a cigarette . . .

"Going for a walk?" said a quiet voice at his elbow. "Mind if I come with you?"

He had set off to walk down to the village almost automatically, remembering a tobacconist's shop that he had noticed on his earlier stroll, and he had been concentrating so fiercely on his new problem that for the instant his mind had let slip the knowledge that he was under very thinly veiled surveillance.

"I'm only going out for some cigarettes," he said.

"That's just what I want," replied Captain Voss blandly.

For a moment Simon coldly considered whether he should pick up the wizened little man and throw him forcefully over Larkstone Point into the sea, but he controlled himself. He did only want a packet of cigarettes just then, and it would be time enough to start throwing his weight about when he had something more important on hand. But he stopped a little way down the hill to make a pretence of tying his shoelace, and looked back at the hotel. The big black-haired man, Kane, was sitting outside now, exactly as Voss had been sitting, turning the pages of the same newspaper. The door was still guarded while Hoppy remained inside—Voss must have given some signal to call out the reserve watch-dog when he left his post.

Simon bought a packet of cigarettes, while Voss made a similar purchase, and turned back up the hill. He was walking slowly, but his brain was tearing along, trying to place itself inside the minds of at least three people at once. In spite of that, while he had built up and demolished a score of theories, he hadn't a single settled hypothesis standing at the end of his quarter of an hour's walk.

Someone else had thought ahead of him—he saluted the fact grimly as he came up to the door of the inn again. The lawyer's car was still standing outside, but the man himself was not in sight. Jeffroll was. He was standing beside Kane, watching them approach, and he nodded as the Saint came up.

"Good morning, Mr Tombs—could you spare me a moment?"

"Any number," said the Saint coolly.

At that moment he was tense and alert, keyed to a hair-trigger watchfulness, although there was not a trace of uneasiness to be read on his brown face.

"Come into the office," said Jeffroll.

Simon realized that his face was curiously strained and haggard, his mouth twitching unconsciously as it had been the previous evening. Whatever this conversation was to be about, quite definitely it held something that the Saint hadn't included in any of his theories.

Perhaps that was the principal reason why Simon Templar's vigilance relaxed at that crucial moment. He had shrewdly summarized Jeffroll as a man who would never be a good actor, and he knew that that drawn anxiety was utterly genuine. He followed the landlord through the lounge and the curtains behind the bar, with his imagination whirling through a fresh burst of frantic effort to encompass this new and unexpected twist, but without the same grim vigilance, although he knew that Voss had come in also and was following behind him. That is, and ever after was, the only excuse he could make for himself, and the mistake might have cost him his life.

Jeffroll opened the door of the office, and stood aside for the Saint to go in. Simon went in with a languid stride—Portmore and Weems were there, but the lawyer was surprisingly absent. Then something hard jabbed into his back, and he began to appreciate his error.

"Put up your hands."

It was Jeffroll's voice, behind him, speaking with a half-hysterical menace that held the Saint studiously motionless where a more callous and seasoned intonation might have encouraged him to lazy backchat or even a swift attempt to retrieve the situation. But he was old enough in outlawry to know that the innkeeper's forefinger was as uncertain on the trigger as only the finger of a panic-stricken man can be, and he stood very still.

The weight of his automatic came off his hip-pocket, and then he was pushed forward. Only then, when he could turn round and see Jeffroll's face, and keep a wary eye on the man's reactions, did he venture to indulge in any conversational amenities.

"Bless my soul," he remarked mildly. "Do you know, for a moment I thought you were going to kiss me."

Major Portmore reached down under the desk, where he was sitting, and brought up the shot-gun which he had been carrying in the wood that morning.

"Get over against the wall and shut up," he ordered harshly.

Simon got over against the wall.

"Now, then," said Jeffroll, over the sights of his revolver, "where is Julia?"

The Saint's mouth hardened as if it had been turned to stone. Then that was the explanation of the landlord's strange whiteness. Ideas drummed through his brain—Hoppy Uniatz asleep, Garthwait who had escaped while he was away, the lawyer's visit . . . But he scarcely had time to pin down one of those speeding flashes of fact before Jeffroll's voice was shrilling into his ears again.

"Hurry up, damn you! I'm going to count up to ten. If you haven't answered by that time—"

"What happens?" asked the Saint, in his quietest voice. "You can hang yourself off that beam without bothering to shoot me—or would you rather have it done legally? And where does it get you, anyhow?"

Portmore nodded.

"That's right," he said impersonally. "I told you shooting was too quick, Jeffroll. Voss—Weems—you tie him up, I'll see if I can make him talk."

Weems got up limply out of his chair and produced a coil of wire. The Saint's arms were twisted behind his back, and the wrists quickly and efficiently bound; then his ankles were similarly treated. Jeffroll's mouth worked as if he was tempted to refuse interference and stick to his original threat, but he said nothing.

Portmore got up and came round the desk. He handed the shotgun over to Voss and stood in front of the Saint.

"Will you answer that question, or have I got to thrash it out of you?" he demanded.

Simon looked at him steadily. Placed as he was, it required a superhuman effort to hold back the obvious defiance. Only the fact that he could understand and sympathize with the feelings of his inquisitors helped him to check his temper—that, and the knowledge that the same liberties could not be taken with a crazed amateur that could be taken with dispassionate professionals.

"Don't you think it might have been worthwhile asking me the question in a normal manner, before you were reduced to all this Lyceum stuff?" he replied evenly.

For a second they were taken aback; then Portmore blustered back into the breach.

"All right—if you're going to answer the question, you can answer it now."

"I haven't the vaguest notion where Julia is," said the Saint immediately. "But I expect Garthwait could tell us."

"Because he helped you take her away," chattered Jeffroll.

"You're wrong there," said the Saint, as equably as he could. "I've told you that I had nothing to do with it. Will you tell me when you think she was taken?"

The landlord's white tragic face was in grotesque contrast to the murderousness of his eyes.

"You know that. You let Garthwait out of this office—you only pretended to fight him because you thought we'd be taken in by you. You took her away between you, last night. You took your car out of the garage—"

"You saw that when you came out to drive a lorry-load of earth from your tunnel down to the quay and tip it into the harbour," said the Saint.

If he had expected to cause a sensation with that blunt challenge, he was disappointed. Not one of the men showed any more reaction than if he had shown that he knew the hotel had a thatched roof, and Jeffroll babbled on: "You took her away in your car, and then Garthwait telephoned this morning—"

"This is wasting time," snarled Voss. "Let him do the talking, old man, and if he doesn't talk we'll see what we can do to make him."

"I'm waiting for a chance to talk," retorted the Saint curtly. "I guess there are plenty of explanations to be made, and I don't want to waste time either. I'll put my cards on the table and trade them for yours, if you can stop making damn fools of yourselves for five minutes."

"Get on with it, then," said Portmore. "And don't call me a damn fool again, or I'll hurt you."

Simon looked him in the eyes.

"Hitting a man who can't hit you back would naturally prove you weren't a damn fool, wouldn't it?" he said icily.

"Oh, leave him alone, Portmore," drawled Weems. "Let's hear what he's got to say first."

"Thanks." Simon held the Major's gaze as long as the other would meet it; then he relaxed against the wall. "What I've got to say won't take long. To start with, my name isn't Tombs. It's Templar—Simon Templar. You may have read about me in the newspaper sometimes. I'm called the Saint."

This time he did get a reaction, but for about the first time in his life he did not pause to bask in the scapegrace glow which his own notoriety usually gave him.

"I came down here because I heard there was something mysterious going on, and poking my nose into mysterious goings-on is my business. I'd never met Garthwait in my life, never heard of him, till we had that argument in the bar last night and I pushed his face in. I know most of the crooks in this country, but I can't know all of them. I came prowling about last night because I heard noises, and I found Garthwait tied up in here—"

"And let him out."

"No. I admit it was my fault that he got out, but it was unintentional. I opened the door with a pair of wire-cutting pliers, and I left them behind, accidentally, when I went out again. Before that, he'd told me that he was supposed to meet a guy on the Axminster road, and that this guy would give me ten thousand quid to let him loose—from the way he talked he seemed to think I was one of your party. I pushed off to keep the date with this guy—"

"And he gave you ten thousand pounds to let Garthwait go," said Voss flatly.

Simon shook his head.

"He didn't—for one reason, because he was a bit wiser in sin than you fellows, and he recognized me."

"But you'd have done it if he had given you ten thousand pounds."

"I don't know," said the Saint candidly. "It isn't my party anyhow, and I've a pretty open mind, but on the whole I doubt it. Anyway the question doesn't arise. I went out to keep this date because I was hoping to collect some more information on this racket you've got here. On account of the guy on the road recognizing me, I didn't get much more than a couple of bullets whizzing past my ear, but I did hear his voice, and I've heard it again this morning. I can't help it if you think this is a tall story, but the guy on the road—Garthwait's pal—was your lawyer friend who just called."

There was a moment's silence, and then Weems sniffed loudly.

"Oh, quate," he said, and Simon Templar, who reckoned that he himself could do almost anything with his voice, had to acknowledge that he had never heard such a quintessence of sneeringly bored incredulity expressed in two syllables.

"You're the worst liar I've ever listened to," rasped Portmore, more crudely. "Why, you bloody crook! Yestering told us you'd probably have some slippery story—"

"I notice he didn't stay to listen to it," said the Saint.

For a second he had them again, and in that second he got several things straight. Yestering hadn't taken such an insane risk after all—the lawyer had simply come to the hotel with two strings to his bow and an arrow on each of them, ready to use whichever one his reception told him to. If it had been hostile, he would have known at once that the Saint really was in cahoots with the inn garrison, but Julia Trafford would still remain as an effective hostage. The reception having been friendly, Yestering would have realized that the Saint was sitting in with a lone hand: to pass on the job of getting rid of him to Jeffroll & Co. was the most elementary tactical development. But there was one thing the lawyer had forgotten—or, rather, had never known about—one cogent argument that might still be thrown in in time to break the back of Jeffroll's insensate vengefulness before his fear drove him too far beyond the reach of reason. Seizing his momentary advantage without relaxing a fraction of his iron restraint, the Saint used it.

"I can give you a certain amount of proof," he said. "It doesn't back up every word I say, but it's something. I didn't come down here entirely off my own bat. I was asked to come—by someone on the spot who was definitely worried about what was going on."

"Who was that?" asked Voss sceptically.

"Julia."

They stared at him hesitantly—even Portmore looked doubtful. Then Jeffroll's trembling hand brought up the revolver again.

"That's a lie! Julia didn't know anything—"

"That's why she wrote to me," said the Saint. "The letter's in my breast pocket—why don't you read it?"

Portmore took it out and passed it over.

"Is that her writing?"

Jeffroll nodded.

"My God," he said stupidly.

Voss took the letter from him, glanced through it, and handed it to Portmore. They looked at each other rather foolishly. Portmore dropped the letter on the desk in front of Weems, who turned it over with a limp hand and rubbed the place where his chin would have been if he had had a chin. An awkward kind of silence settled upon the congregation and scratched itself reflectively, as Job might have done on discovering a new and hitherto unsuspected boil.

Weems was the first to break it.

"That does seem to make things look a little bit different," he admitted, gazing vacantly at the inkwell.

Portmore cleared his throat.

"What was your story again?" he asked.

The Saint repeated it, in greater detail, and this time there were no interruptions. When it was finished, the four men looked at one another almost bashfully, like members of a Civic Reform committee who have caught each other buying nudist magazines. Something compromising had certainly been done. There had, perhaps, been a slight technical departure from the canons of good form and unblemished purity. But nothing, of course, that had not been done with the most impeccable motives—that could not, naturally, be explained away with a few well-chosen words delivered in an austere and dignified and gentlemanly tone.

The other three turned automatically to Jeffroll, tacitly appointing him their spokesman, but perhaps this failure to respond immediately was understandable. The innkeeper had lowered his gun some minutes before, but the strained pallor of his face had altered only in degree.

"Then . . . then that means Garthwait has got her!" he stammered. "And if Yestering . . . if Yestering's gone over to him . . . or he may even have been the man who put Garthwait on to us—nobody else knew. Then it'll all have been for nothing—they'll use our work and divide the money . . ." Suddenly, absurdly, his weak pathetic eyes turned to the Saint in helpless appeal. "What are we going to do?"

Simon smiled.

"I'd like to help you," he remarked lazily, "but I'm afraid it always cramps my style when I'm tied up."

"Sorry, old boy," drawled Captain Voss, for after all he was an officer and a gentleman, and had once played cricket for Oxford.

He stepped forward to undo the wire, but he had barely started fumbling with it when there was a scutter of quick lurching footsteps in the passage outside, and the door burst open with a crash.

It was the big black-haired man, Kane, who reeled in under the startled eyes of his companions. His shirt was ripped into two great trailing fragments, and he was clutching one side of his head dizzily. A small trickle of blood ran down his cheek from under the heel of his hand. He stared at the scene for a moment and then nodded weakly, sagging against the jamb of the door.

"Good," he said huskily. "We've still got one of the swine, anyhow."

"What the hell are you talking about?" demanded Portmore, with the reaction of his nerves indexed in the unnecessary loudness of his voice. "This fellow's all right—we made a mistake. What's happened?"

Kane glared at him with bloodshot eyes.

"Who made a mistake?" he rasped. "That pal of his—that Yankee thug—came out just now. After Yestering. He tried to hit me with the butt of his gun—did it, too. Laid me out. When I woke up I was lying in the hall—and he'd got away!"

9

Simon Templar wriggled his cramped limbs into the most comfortable position he could find, and tried to doze. There was really nothing to encourage him in this relaxation, for even the most ascetic of mortals might find it difficult to fall into a peaceful sleep while lying on a hard floor with his hands tied behind his back, and the mental serenity which might have made these physical discomforts tolerable was noticeably lacking. The Saint scratched an itching part of his nose by rubbing it against the edge of the carpet, and contemplated the inscrutable capriciousness of Life.

Six hours ago he had been on the very point of removing himself from under the aim of a thunderbolt with masterly adroitness and aplomb. Five and three-quarter hours ago he might have been in complete control of the situation, with Jeffroll and the Four Horsemen sitting in eager humility at his feet while he planned and ordered their counter-attack with crisp and inspiring efficiency. But during that vital quarter of an hour things had gang, as they had with Robert Burns' immortal mouse, distressingly agley.

They had, fairly enough, given him a chance to explain the conduct of Mr Uniatz, but for once in his life the Saint felt as if he had been hit below the belt. He had been swatted with the full force of the sort of situation which he had himself so often used on Chief Inspector Teal, of Scotland Yard, and he admitted the poetic justice of the reversal without enjoying it any the more for that.

"The damn fool must have gone off his rocker," was the only thing he had honestly been able to say, and even now, five hours and three quarters later, he could think of no other explanation. The psychological motivations of Hoppy's mind remained, as they always had been, shrouded in the impenetrable darkness of the Styx. Down in the forest of Mr Uniatz's fog bound brain, something occasionally stirred, and only God Almighty could predict what would develop from one of those rare bewildering feats of cerebral peristalsis.

Simon tried to derive some consolation from the fact that he was not dead yet.

On the other hand, he wasn't far off it. Major Portmore, in his bluff healthy way, had been the first to advocate a resumption of threats of violence, but he had been overruled. At least their previous conversation had done something to shake the meeting's confidence in itself, and to restore a tendency to sober and judicial thinking. And Julia Trafford's letter remained as one unshaken scrap of evidence in the Saint's favour. Jeffroll was sure it wasn't a forgery, and Voss admitted that to call it a forgery would have postulated an almost unbelievable amount of foresight and cunning on the Saint's part. Weems said, "Oh, absolutely. But—" and continued to stare vacuously at his fingernails. Kane, with his head still bloody and aching from the impact of the butt of Hoppy's Betsy on his temple, was pardonably inclined to side with Portmore, but Jeffroll had lost some of the fire which had temporarily wiped out his natural self. During the argument a little information came out. The big moment, it appeared, was actually scheduled for that very night: everything had been done, the work finished, everything prepared, and Yestering in his lawful capacity of a solicitor had visited the prison the previous afternoon to warn his client. The Saint listened quietly, co-ordinating what he heard, and his veins tingled. It was too late for the hotel confederacy to turn back, and they would gain nothing by doing so. Luck had timed his arrival at the Clevely Arms on the very peak of eventfulness, but whether that luck was good or bad seemed to be highly doubtful.

"What's the use of finding out where Julia is?" Jeffroll summed up the situation. "Even if we knew we were getting the truth. Garthwait told us what'd happen if we tried to get her back, and I believe he'd be capable of it. I'd rather lose everything than risk that."

"What about the police?" Portmore suggested awkwardly, but the innkeeper shook his head.

"Garthwait's threat would still hold good—he'd be all the more vicious. Besides, if they got him, he'd be sure to let out the rest of it, just for revenge. That'd mean we should all suffer. There's no need for all of you to be sacrificed—oh, I know you're going to say you don't care, but I wouldn't allow it. No. We can still go on, and get Julia back in exchange for B. W. . . . And after that, if we've still got this fellow, we may be able to drive another bargain in exchange for him."

His grim hurt eyes turned back to the Saint with a sober implacable resentment that was perhaps more terrible than his first frantic passion, and Simon Templar remembered that look, and Kane's significant grunt of acquiescence, during all those hours in which he had nothing else to do but estimate his own nebulous prospects of survival.

They had at least allowed him to eat—a plate of cold meat and somewhat withered-looking salad had been brought to him at two o'clock. His hands had been untied, but Kane and Portmore—Portmore re-possessed of his shot-gun—had stood over him while he ate it. The Saint had no doubt that Portmore would have had a fatal accident with the gun—"not knowing it was loaded"—if he had made any attempt to escape, and he saved his strength for a better opportunity. Neither of the men spoke a word while he was eating, and for once Simon had no time to spare on polishing the lines of backchat with which he would ordinarily have amused himself in goading his jailers to the verge of homicide—he was wise enough to know that homicide must be already close enough to the forefront of their minds. After the meal was finished, his wrists were bound again, and he was left to resume his uncomfortable contemplations.

Rolling over on his back and squinting up, he could watch time creeping round the face of the clock on the mantelpiece. Five o'clock went to six, six to seven, seven to eight. From time to time he experimented with different schemes for releasing himself, but the wire with which he had been bound was strong and efficiently tied, and his movements only served to tighten it till it cut into his flesh. He would cheerfully have given a hundred pounds for a cigarette, and another hundred for a tankard of beer. Eight o'clock crawled on to nine. He began to suffer another acute physical discomfort which had always been romantically ignored in all the stories he had read about people who were tied up and kept prisoner for prolonged periods . . .

It was past ten o'clock when his captors returned. They wore the shabby trousers and drab shirts in which he had first met them, but the whiteness of their arms no longer puzzled him, for there is no sunshine underground.

Jeffroll went over to the door of the big built-in safe and unlocked it. He turned a switch, and an electric bulb lit up inside. There were no shelves behind the door, but where the shelves should have been he saw a black emptiness and the first rung of a ladder. The Saint was not startled, for that was what he had more or less guessed last night. Even the electric light did not surprise him; he had been putting the final touches to his theory when he looked for the cable that tapped the cross-country grid, and he was sure that the stolen current provided heavier labour besides surreptitious lighting.

The innkeeper turned back and inspected his wrists and ankles again to reassure himself that the Saint was still securely trussed.

"For the last time, will you tell us the truth?" he asked, and there was a hoarseness in his voice that seemed to be resisting a temptation to turn the demand into an appeal.

"I've told you the truth," said the Saint angrily, "and I can't alter it. I'm sorry for you, but you hurt my feelings and I hate being tied up. When I get out of here I'm afraid I shall have to charge you a lot of money for all the fun you've had out of being such a blithering fathead."

"If you get out," said Portmore unpleasantly.

He was carrying a long coil of flex and a couple of sticks of dynamite, and these things answered yet another of the few remaining questions in the Saint's mind. To blow up the tunnel after work was done would effectively solve the problem of delaying pursuit and hampering the tracing of the rescuers while they extended their flying start to really useful dimensions.

The men passed through the steel door and went down the ladder, disappearing one by one. Presently they had all gone, but the safe door was left open and the electric light burned dimly at the top of the dark shaft.

Simon twisted again at his bonds, gritting his teeth at the self-inflicted torture. After a while he felt his hands throbbing and going numb as the tightening metal cut off the circulation, but still he was no nearer to freedom. And no kindly accident had placed a pair of wire-cutters within his reach. He lay back at last breathlessly, and considered his fate as calmly as he could. Julia Trafford, who might have helped him, was kidnapped; Hoppy Uniatz had vanished on the trail of some crazy and incomprehensible inspiration. Nobody else knew where he was. Barring one of those miracles on which his career had already made so many arrogant demands, he could look ahead and see the doors opening for his last and most adventurous journey.

How soon would it be time to go?

Probably there would still be a little more work for the men who had gone into the tunnel to do, a few final preparations to make for the triumphal moment. By this time it was twenty minutes to eleven. Between then and midnight it would happen almost certainly. He watched the minute hand crawl maddeningly up the dial of the clock, begin to drop equally slowly down the other side . . .

Somebody walked with distinctly audible caution down the passage and stopped outside the door, breathing loudly. The handle rattled faintly, but the door had been locked on the inside when Jeffroll and company came in. There was a brief pause, and then a strident whisper grated through the panels.

"Is dat you, boss?"

"Good old Hoppy!" gasped the Saint joyfully.

10

He was not altogether without the power of movement: humping himself inelegantly across the floor like a sort of caterpillar he was able to reach the door, and then, on his knees in front of it, he managed to detach the key with his teeth and push it under the door with his feet. Hoppy unlocked the door and stood beaming down at him like a schoolboy who has come home with a prize.

"Hi," said Mr Uniatz, in comradely greeting.

He stepped forward and untied the Saint as casually as he would have offered him a light for a cigarette, and it only needed this casualness to remind Simon that this complacently grinning bonehead was, after all, the cause of more than half the trouble.

"Where the bloody hell have you been?" he demanded, with an ominous cooling off of his first grateful enthusiasm.

Mr Uniatz blinked at him reproachfully, like a dog who has proudly laid a fresh-killed rat at his master's feet, only to receive a clout over the ear. Something, Mr Uniatz began to suspect, seemed to have come between him and the Boss. The perfect harmony which had hitherto bound them together, their zusammengehörigkeitsgefühl, as the Germans so succinctly put it, seemed to have come unstuck.

"Well, boss, I listen outside de door," he said, with a generous attempt to clear up the entire misunderstanding in a sentence.

"Outside what door?" asked the Saint patiently.

"Outside dis door here," said Mr Uniatz, no less patiently—he felt that for the first time in their acquaintanceship his deity, the boss, was found wanting in rudimentary intelligence. "I hear de udder guys have got de snatch on Julia, an' you told me dis mornin' de attorney was in de racket. So when de guy comes out I bean de guy wit' my Betsy an' go after de guy," explained Mr Uniatz, making everything translucently clear.

Fortunately the Saint had inside information which enabled him to distinguish one guy from another, but this was about as much as he did understand.

"Let me get this straight," he said. "When I came in here, you followed and listened outside the door?"

"Yes, boss."

"And nobody caught you at it?"

"I didn't t'ink about dat, boss," said Hoppy worriedly, as if he feared that he might yet be caught in that past act of eavesdropping.

The Saint wiped his forehead. He could remember himself wishing that he could listen outside that door, and discarding the idea as hopelessly impracticable, but a fool had ambled in where a Saint had certainly feared to tread.

"And you heard about Julia being kidnapped?"

"Yes, boss."

"You got steamed up about it, and pushed off to give somebody the works."

"Well, boss—"

"And then the lawyer came out."

"Yeah. He came t'ru de dinin'-room. I go after him, an' de udder guy tries to stop me, so I bean him wit' my Betsy."

"And then what?"

"De lawyer is gettin' into his heap, an' he don't know I beaned de udder guy. So I climb up in de rumble seat, an' we hit de grit."

Simon nodded, chafing his hands to ease the pain of returning circulation.

"Where did you go?"

"I dunno, boss. Foist we go down to de harbour, an' dis guy gets in a boat an' blows off. I can't find anudder boat to follow him, an' I guess he'd of seen me comin' on de water anyhow, so I sit in de car an' wait. He goes off to a yacht outside an' goes on board. He stays on de yacht t'ree-four hours, an' I begin t'inkin' he ain't comin' back my way. I gotta toist like nobody's business, an' de fishin' guys start lookin' at me an' one of 'em comes up an' asks if I want to rent a boat. After a bit de guy comes back from de yacht, an' I duck in de rumble an' we screw. We go maybe six miles, an' he turns in de drive of a house dat's got a board outside For Sale. Maybe de house is for sale at dat, because I take a gander t'ru de windows an' it ain't got no foinitchure inside. De red-haired guy is inside wit' a coupla gophers, an' I go in t'ru de door, which is not locked, an' dey lamp my Betsy an' stick 'em up."

"They didn't try to shoot it out with you?"

"Say, when I get a hist on a guy he don't have no chance to shoot it out," said Hoppy indignantly. "So I pull deir teet'—lookit, I got de rods here." He fished about in his pockets and produced an assortment of weapons which explained the curious bulges that Simon had noticed on his person. "Well, I say, 'What youse guys done wit' Julia?' Dey don't say nut'n."

"So what?"

Mr Uniatz scratched his head.

"Well, boss, I give dem a message."

Simon's fingers had recovered sufficiently for him to be able to get out a cigarette. He lighted it without interrupting—it seemed better not to inquire too closely into the methods of persuasion to which an old-timer like Hoppy Uniatz would naturally have turned to squeeze information out of reluctant mouths.

"I have to work a long time," said Mr. Uniatz hesitantly. "But after a bit, when I get started on de lawyer, he squawks."

The Saint's irritation had subsided again. He was hanging on Hoppy's narrative with a growing ecstasy of excitement.

"You've found out where Julia is?"

"Yes, boss," said Mr Uniatz sheepishly. "She's upstairs in dis empty house all de time—all I gotta do is go an' look for her."

Simon stared at him for a moment, and then he leaned back and went limp with silent laughter. There was something so climactically cosmic about the picture he saw that it was some time before he could trust his voice again.

"What did you do then—apologize for troubling them?"

"Well, boss, I put 'em all in de flivver an' we come back here. I send Julia up to her room when I come in, an' look for you. De udder guys are still tied up outside."

The Saint got up and walked silently about the room. The time was racing away now, but he expected to hear the warning explosion of Portmore's dynamite before the rescue party returned, and he wanted to get everything worked out before the final showdown.

"Did you find out anything else while you were giving these guys your—er—message?" he asked.

"Yeah," said Mr Uniatz, not without pride. "I finished de job."

He told everything that he had learnt, and Simon listened to him and filled in all the gaps in his own knowledge. The last details of the most amazing plot he had ever stumbled upon fell into place, and he knew the extent of his own sublime good fortune.

"Did you get hold of this chequebook?" he asked, and Hoppy produced it.

He also took over two of the automatics which Hoppy had brought back with him as trophies, and carefully checked the loading of both of them before he put them away, one in each side pocket of his coat. Then he lighted himself another cigarette, and he was smiling. He punched Hoppy thoughtfully in the stomach.

"Next time I make any rude remarks about your brain, I hope you'll hang something on my chin," he said. "All the boodle in this party belongs to you, and I hope you won't spend it on riotous living. Now shove off and keep an eye on the birds outside while I'm busy. Recite some of your poetry to them and cheer them up."

There was no need for him to go down into the tunnel, but he was curious to see the amazing work that Jeffroll & Co. had done, with his own eyes. The ladder inside the safe door took him down through a short shaft into a broad natural cave, and at once he saw how circumstances had helped the rescuers with their undertaking. Some subterranean river, long since dried up, had done half their work for them, but even so he had to admire the thoroughness with which they had carried on that prehistoric excavation.

On the other side of the cavern, which was lighted at intervals by bulbs slung from the low roof, he saw a hydraulic lift at the foot of another shaft that disappeared vertically upwards into darkness, and he guessed that this was the route by which the excavated earth was removed. At the top of this shaft he knew, without looking for it, that he would have found the door cunningly concealed in the timberings and plaster of the outside wall of the inn through which the soil was tipped out into the lorry that stood in the garage close up to that very wall. Running away from the lift into the depths of the cave was a pair of rusty lines professionally laid on sleepers. A small mine truck stood on the rails close to the lift; that was how the earth was brought up from the head of the tunnel, and it would be the explanation of the strange rumblings underground which had troubled Julia Trafford and brought him on to the trail of the mystery.

Following the guiding rails, he came at the end of the cavern to the beginning of the artificial tunnel. A mound of shining machinery abandoned close by he was able to identify as some kind of electric excavating drill which had made this terrific task possible to such a small number of workers: the heavily sheathed power cable, still left in place, beside the truck lines, confirmed all his guesses.

After a moment's hesitation he started into the tunnel. It was barely six feet high, so that he had to stoop slightly to move along it. Throughout the length he saw, it was neatly and expertly buttressed, but all these things were possible with an experienced engineer, which he knew Jeffroll to be, in charge, and four intelligent confederates to help him, of whom two at least must be retired sapper officers. The same electric bulbs dangled at long intervals along the sap, so that in between them there were patches of deep gloom practically amounting to complete darkness. Even so, the technique that must have been required to bring out the far end of the tunnel exactly under a predetermined cell in Larkstone Prison was one of those astounding exercises of scientific ingenuity at which the Saint, as an uninitiated layman, would always have to gape in speechless awe.

As he moved deeper into the warren, he began to pick his steps more cautiously, until he was travelling almost noiselessly, a mere foot at a time. Then he heard a patter of scurrying feet somewhere ahead of him, and Portmore's voice boomed hollowly down the echoes with eerie distinctness.

"Look out!"

Instinctively the Saint spun off the track and pressed himself against the wall, freezing into immobility in the middle of the deepest patch of darkness he could find. The running men came nearer, and then there was a sudden crash of sound that thundered down the tunnel like the crack of doom. A blast of air like a tornado struck him down the whole side of his body, lifted him, off his feet, and hurled him a dozen yards down the passage as if he had been hit by an express train.

He struggled up again, deafened and half stunned, and listened to the patter of falling stones loosened from the roof by the detonation. All the lights had been shattered by the explosion, and when he felt round for the truck lines to get his bearings he found them half buried in the debris. But the buttressing had been good, and the thousands of tons of earth which might have sunk down from overhead had not fallen.

He heard Jeffroll's voice now, startlingly near.

"Are we all right?"

"I am," said Voss, and one by one the others chimed in reassuringly.

There was a sixth voice among the responses, a voice which the Saint had not heard before. A moment later somebody switched on an electric torch, and the owner of the voice was picked up by the beam, scarcely three yards away—a fleshy sallow-faced man who still wore the drab uniform of His Majesty's prisons.

Simon felt in his pocket and drew out one of his guns; his other hand slipped out a tiny flashlight from his breast pocket—it looked very much like a cheap fountain pen, and it had escaped observation when he was searched.

He drew a careful bead on the other torch, and at that range he was quite an accurate shot. The crisp smack of the report as he pressed the trigger synchronized with the sudden return of utter darkness, and then the beam of his own flashlight stabbed out and swept over the five men.

"I hope you will all say your prayers before you ask to die," he murmured politely, and then he turned his light on the sixth stranger again. There might be a few minor gaps in his acquaintance with the underworld, but this man was not exactly of the underworld, and his photograph had appeared in every national newspaper in England for six consecutive days during a certain week eighteen months ago. "Mr Bellamy Wage, I believe?" said the Saint.

11

They were so stunned that he had the stage to himself, but the Saint had no complaint to make about this, for there were times when he liked talking.

"You were sentenced at the Old Bailey to fourteen years' penal servitude on one charge of forgery and two charges of conspiracy to defraud. The Neovision Radio Company went down the drain to the tune of nearly two million quid, and about a million and a half of that was never accounted for except on the general theory that you must have hidden it away somewhere. Altogether you seem to have been pretty smooth at collecting potatoes, and if somebody had given you the wire to pull your freight a month earlier, I'm sure you'd have turned up later as the hell of a big shot somewhere in South America and had the whale of a time on your old age pension."

His torchlight panned warningly over the rescuers again, and nobody moved.

"But even when you were caught, you weren't finished," he went on chattily. "You had Yestering, a smart crook lawyer, and when he couldn't find enough perjurers to lie you out of the dock you gave him another idea. Through him, you offered a reward of half a million pounds to anyone who could get you out of Larkstone, and you would pay all the expenses, signing the cheques he brought when he visited you. He got hold of these men—trained engineers, down on their luck, and willing to take a sporting risk for a fortune. They did this work, but Yestering was too greedy. He wanted more than his fee. When everything was nearly ready, he got hold of a gorilla named Garthwait to try and muscle the others out of here—the idea was that Garthwait should bring off the actual rescue, and claim to have done all the work from the start, and then the two of them would split the reward. Jeffroll and the others knew they were up against it, but Garthwait didn't quite succeed in scaring them off, so Jeffroll's niece was kidnapped last night and held for a hostage. She was to be returned in exchange for you, and Garthwait was still to go on and claim the beauty prize. Unfortunately for everybody except me, I butted in."

Bellamy Wage clenched his fists. He was pale and trembling with fear.

"Who are you?" he asked shakily.

"I am Simon Templar, known as the Saint, and I expect it will be fun for you to meet an honest man after all these twisters you've had round you. I've done a lot of good work on this business myself," said the Saint modestly, "and put up with a good deal of rudery and discomfort, for which someone is going to have to console me. Jeffroll has misunderstood me from the beginning. I suppose there was some excuse for him, but I don't know." He turned the ray of his torch slightly. "By the way, brother, Julia is back."

The innkeeper stood looking at him with his mouth twitching mutely.

"That happens to be true," said the Saint quietly. "My friend—the Yankee thug, I think you called him—rescued her and brought her back. You'll be able to check up on that. And now let's move on—

269

there's no scenery here, and I have an aunt somewhere round who is calling me in a loud voice."

He shepherded the party back along the tunnel, after taking over Jeffroll's revolver—the others were unarmed. At that stage of the proceedings he was making no foolish mistakes, and his flock had no chance whatever to dispute his orders. When the last of them had come up the ladder into the office, he sat down at the desk and laid out his armoury on the blotter.

"You can go and say hullo to Julia, Uncle Martin," he said. "We'll wait for your report."

He waited, tranquilly smoking a cigarette. Weems sat down in another chair and stared at the carpet. Voss finicked with his moustache. Portmore breathed stertorously. Kane leaned against the wall, glowering at him in sulky silence.

Jeffroll came back, and the four men turned to look at him. The answer was in his face, before he nodded.

"It's true," he said. "Julia's back. Mr Templar—"

"You owe me an apology," said the Saint gently. "Isn't that it? And another apology to Hoppy Uniatz." He sighed. "But after all, what's an apology? Will the Commissioners of Inland Revenue accept it in payment of our income tax? Can we pass a bit of it over the bar and get a drink? No. Therefore I'm afraid we must have more."

"What are you going to do?" sobbed Bellamy Wage, in a kind of panic.

The Saint smiled.

"I'm going to ask you to do a little extra writing, dear old bird," he said. "Here is the chequebook on your old age pension, removed from the custody of Comrade Yestering. In case your memory is getting dim, the account is in the name of Isledon. The reward you offered was five hundred thousand. According to plan it should have worked out at a hundred thousand each, but now it'll have to be split seven ways. That is seventy-one thousand four hundred and twenty-eight pounds eleven shillings and fivepence each, but you can make my share payable to Hoppy Uniatz as well—he's earned it. And you boys," said the Saint, glancing over the other conspirators and shuffling his guns persuasively, "are going to take your loss and like it, being thankful that Hoppy and I aren't naturally avaricious."

Bellamy Wage wrote according to instructions, and Simon picked up one of the cheques and led him outside, to where Mr Uniatz was waiting patiently beside his carload of captives.

"Here's your transport," he said, "and I believe there's a motor-boat waiting for you in the harbour and your own yacht outside. And I hope you'll be seasick . . . Get rid of these blisters, Hoppy, and come back for a celebration. You must be dying of thirst, but they've paid their passage and they're entitled to the ride."

When he returned to the office he found five philosophical men examining their cheques. Portmore was the spokesman.

"How about a drink?" he suggested gruffly, and the Saint was delighted.

"I'm glad we got things straightened out without bloodshed," he said. "I like a good amateur, but there were moments when I thought you didn't appreciate me."

"What do you think Garthwait and Yestering will do?" asked Jeffroll.

He asked this some time later, after Hoppy had returned from his mission of speeding the ungodly on their way. Mr Uniatz, reclining in a corner with a bottle of Johnnie Walker all to himself, had been immersed in a sort of coma, with a scowl of hideous agony on his brow from which Simon deduced that he was thinking about something, but at the sound of Jeffroll's question he awoke sufficiently to reply.

"Dey won't do nut'n," he said, closing the argument to his own satisfaction.

"I don't know," Jeffroll demurred. "They're bound to be pretty vindictive. Ever since Garthwait first came here we've been ready to clear out at short notice, and now we can afford to go—"

Hoppy continued to shake his head.

"Dey won't do nut'n," he repeated emphatically. "Mr Templar tells me to get rid of 'em, an' what de boss says goes."

"What on earth do you mean?" demanded the Saint faintly.

"I mean I take 'em for a ride, like ya told me, boss. We take de motorboat, an' when we're outside de harbour I haul out my Betsy an' give dem de woiks. Dey won't do nut'n." Mr Uniatz stretched himself complacently. "Say, juse guys mind if I take dis bottle upstairs an' finish it? I just finished de last voice of pome I was makin' up on de way back, an' I gotta tell it to Julia before I forget."

PUBLICATION

HISTORY

As with many previous volumes, two of the stories in this book first appeared in the British magazine *The Thriller*. "The High Fence" appeared as "The Man Who Knew" in issue No. 280 published on 16 June 1934, whilst "The Elusive Ellshaw" appeared under the title of "The Race Train Crime" in No. 286 just a few weeks later. "The Case of the Frightened Innkeeper" was written specifically for this book.

The book itself was first published in November 1934 with an American edition following in May 1935. This book, almost uniquely amongst early Saint volumes, has never been retitled.

A Czech translation appeared in 1939 under the title of *Tajemný pan Ellshaw—Kdo je pověstný Svatý?* (Cechie), but it's unclear as to whether this was the full book, or simply the first story. The German translation went by the name of *Der Heilige macht weiter* when it first appeared in 1957 whilst the Italian version went by the title of *Il Santo non si arresta* in 1972. A Norwegian edition *Helgenen går på* appeared in 1964 with a Portuguese version appearing that same year under the logical title of *O Santo continua*.

"The Elusive Ellshaw" was adapted for the first season of *The Saint* television series with Roger Moore and was first broadcast on the 17

October 1963. "The High Fence" appeared toward the end of the season, airing on 20 February 1964, and "The Frightened Innkeeper," as the final story was retitled, aired on 18 February 1965.

ABOUT THE AUTHOR

*I'm mad enough to believe in romance. And I'm sick and
tired of this age—tired of the miserable little mildewed
things that people racked their brains about, and wrote
books about, and called life. I wanted something more
elementary and honest—battle, murder, sudden death, with
plenty of good beer and damsels in distress, and a complete
callousness about blipping the ungodly over the beezer. It
mayn't be life as we know it, but it ought to be.*

—*Leslie Charteris in a 1935 BBC radio interview*

Leslie Charteris was born Leslie Charles Bowyer-Yin in Singapore on
12 May 1907.

He was the son of a Chinese doctor and his English wife, who'd
met in London a few years earlier. Young Leslie found friends hard to
come by in colonial Singapore. The English children had been told not
to play with Eurasians, and the Chinese children had been told not to
play with Europeans. Leslie was caught in between and took refuge in
reading.

"I read a great many good books and enjoyed them because
nobody had told me that they were classics. I also read a great many
bad books which nobody told me not to read . . . I read a great many

popular · scientific articles and acquired from them an astonishing amount of general knowledge before I discovered that this acquisition was supposed to be a chore."[1]

One of his favourite things to read was a magazine called *Chums*. "The Best and Brightest Paper for Boys" (if you believe the adverts) was a monthly paper full of swashbuckling adventure stories aimed at boys, encouraging them to be honourable and moral and perhaps even "upright citizens with furled umbrellas."[2] Undoubtedly these types of stories would influence his later work.

When his parents split up shortly after the end of World War I, Charteris accompanied his mother and brother back to England, where he was sent to Rossall School in Fleetwood, Lancashire. Rossall was then a very stereotypical English public school, and it struggled to cope with this multilingual mixed-race boy just into his teens who'd already seen more of the world than many of his peers would see in their lifetimes. He was an outsider.

He left Rossall in 1924. Keen to pursue a creative career, he decided to study art in Paris—after all, that was where the great artists went—but soon found that the life of a literally starving artist didn't appeal. He continued writing, firing off speculative stories to magazines, and it was the sale of a short story to *Windsor Magazine* that saved him from penury.

He returned to London in 1925, as his parents—particularly his father—wanted him to become a lawyer, and he was sent to study law at Cambridge University. In the mid-1920s, Cambridge was full of Bright Young Things—aristocrats and bohemians somewhat typified in the Evelyn Waugh novel *Vile Bodies*—and again the mixed-race Bowyer-Yin found that he didn't fit in. He was an outsider who preferred to make his own way in the world and wasn't one of the privileged upper class. It didn't help that he found his studies boring and decided it was more fun contemplating ways to circumvent the law. This inspired him to write a novel, and when publishers Ward Lock & Co. offered him a three-book deal on the strength of it, he abandoned his studies to pursue a writing career.

When his father learnt of this, he was not impressed, as he considered writers to be "rogues and vagabonds." Charteris would later recall that "I wanted to be a writer, he wanted me to become a lawyer. I was stubborn, he said I would end up in the gutter. So I left home. Later on, when I had a little success, we were reconciled by letter, but I never saw him again."[3]

X Esquire, his first novel, appeared in April 1927. The lead character, X Esquire, is a mysterious hero, hunting down and killing the businessmen trying to wipe out Britain by distributing quantities of free poisoned cigarettes. His second novel, *The White Rider*, was published the following spring, and in one memorable scene shows the hero chasing after his damsel in distress, only for him to overtake the villains, leap into their car . . . and promptly faint.

These two plot highlights may go some way to explaining Charteris's comment on *Meet—the Tiger!*, published in September 1928, that "it was only the third book I'd written, and the best, I would say, for it was that the first two were even worse."[4]

Twenty-one-year-old authors are naturally self-critical. Despite reasonably good reviews, the Saint didn't set the world on fire, and Charteris moved on to a new hero for his next book. This was *The Bandit*, an adventure story featuring Ramon Francisco De Castilla y Espronceda Manrique, published in the summer of 1929 after its serialisation in the *Empire News*, a now long-forgotten Sunday newspaper. But sales of *The Bandit* were less than impressive, and Charteris began to question his choice of career. It was all very well writing—but if nobody wants to read what you write, what's the point?

"I had to succeed, because before me loomed the only alternative, the dreadful penalty of failure . . . the routine office hours, the five-day week . . . the lethal assimilation into the ranks of honest, hard-working, conformist, God-fearing pillars of the community."[5]

However his fortunes—and the Saint's—were about to change. In late 1928, Leslie had met Monty Haydon, a London-based editor who was looking for writers to pen stories for his new paper, *The Thriller*— "The Paper with a Thousand Thrills." Charteris later recalled that "he said he was starting a new magazine, had read one of my books and would like some stories from me. I couldn't have been more grateful, both from the point of view of vanity and finance!"[6]

The paper launched in early 1929, and Leslie's first work, "The Story of a Dead Man," featuring Jimmy Traill, appeared in issue 4 (published on 2 March 1929). That was followed just over a month later with "The Secret of Beacon Inn," starring Rameses "Pip" Smith. At the same time, Leslie finished writing another non-Saint novel, *Daredevil*, which would be published in late 1929. Storm Arden was the hero; more notably, the book saw the first introduction of a Scotland Yard inspector by the name of Claud Eustace Teal.

The Saint returned in the thirteenth issue of *The Thriller*. The byline proclaimed that the tale was "A Thrilling Complete Story of the Underworld"; the title was "The Five Kings," and it actually featured Four Kings and a Joker. Simon Templar, of course, was the Joker.

Charteris spent the rest of 1929 telling the adventures of the Five Kings in five subsequent *The Thriller* stories. "It was very hard work, for the pay was lousy, but Monty Haydon was a brilliant and stimulating editor, full of ideas. While he didn't actually help shape the Saint as a character, he did suggest story lines. He would take me out to lunch and say, 'What are you going to write about next?' I'd often say I was damned if I knew. And Monty would say, 'Well, I was reading something the other day . . .' He had a fund of ideas and we would talk them over, and then I would go away and write a story. He was a great creative editor."[7]

Charteris would have one more attempt at writing about a hero other than Simon Templar, in three novelettes published in *The Thriller* in early 1930, but he swiftly returned to the Saint. This was partly due to his self-confessed laziness—he wanted to write more stories for *The Thriller* and other magazines, and creating a new hero for every story was hard work—but mainly due to feedback from Monty Haydon. It seemed people wanted to read more adventures of the Saint . . .

Charteris would contribute over forty stories to *The Thriller* throughout the 1930s. Shortly after their debut, he persuaded publisher Hodder & Stoughton that if he collected some of these stories and rewrote them a little, they could publish them as a Saint book. *Enter the Saint* was first published in August 1930, and the reaction was good enough for the publishers to bring out another collection. And another . . .

Of the twenty Saint books published in the 1930s, almost all have their origins in those magazine stories.

Why was the Saint so popular throughout the decade? Aside from the charm and ability of Charteris's storytelling, the stories, particularly those published in the first half of the '30s, are full of energy and joie de vivre. With economic depression rampant throughout the period, the public at large seemed to want some escapism.

And Simon Templar's appeal was wide-ranging: he wasn't an upper-class hero like so many of the period. With no obvious background and no attachment to the Old School Tie, no friends in high places who could provide a get-out-of-jail-free card, the Saint was uniquely classless. Not unlike his creator.

Throughout Leslie's formative years, his heritage had been an issue. In his early days in Singapore, during his time at school, at Cambridge University or even just in everyday life, he couldn't avoid the fact that for many people his mixed parentage was a problem. He would later tell a story of how he was chased up the road by a stick-waving typical

English gent who took offence to his daughter being escorted around town by a foreigner.

Like the Saint, he was an outsider. And although he had spent a significant portion of his formative years in England, he couldn't settle.

As a young boy he had read of an America "peopled largely by Indians, and characters in fringed buckskin jackets who fought nobly against them. I spent a great deal of time day-dreaming about a visit to this prodigious and exciting country."[8]

It was time to realise this wish. Charteris and his first wife, Pauline, whom he'd met in London when they were both teenagers and married in 1931, set sail for the States in late 1932; the Saint had already made his debut in America courtesy of the publisher Doubleday. Charteris and his wife found a New York still experiencing the tail end of Prohibition, and times were tough at first. Despite sales to *The American Magazine* and others, it wasn't until a chance meeting with writer turned Hollywood executive Bartlett McCormack in their favourite speakeasy that Charteris's career stepped up a gear.

Soon Charteris was in Hollywood, working on what would become the 1933 movie *Midnight Club*. However, Hollywood's treatment of writers wasn't to Charteris's taste, and he began to yearn for home. Within a few months, he returned to the UK and began writing more Saint stories for Monty Haydon and Bill McElroy.

He also rewrote a story he'd sketched out whilst in the States, a version of which had been published in *The American Magazine* in September 1934. This new novel, *The Saint in New York*, published in 1935, was a significant advance for the Saint and Leslie Charteris. Gone were the high jinks and the badinage. The youthful exuberance evident in the Saint's early adventures had evolved into something a little darker, a little more hard-boiled. It was the next stage in development for the author and his creation, and readers loved it. It became a bestseller on both sides of the Atlantic.

Having spent his formative years in places as far apart as Singapore and England, with substantial travel in between, it should be no surprise that Leslie had a serious case of wanderlust. With a bestseller under his belt, he now had the means to see more of the world.

Nineteen thirty-six found him in Tenerife, researching another Saint adventure alongside translating the biography of Juan Belmonte, a well-known Spanish matador. Estranged for several months, Leslie and Pauline divorced in 1937. The following year, Leslie married an American, Barbara Meyer, who'd accompanied him to Tenerife. In early 1938, Charteris and his new bride set off in a trailer of his own design and spent eighteen months travelling round America and Canada.

The Saint in New York had reminded Hollywood of Charteris's talents, and film rights to the novel were sold prior to publication in 1935. Although the proposed 1935 film production was rejected by the Hays Office for its violent content, RKO's eventual 1938 production persuaded Charteris to try his luck once more in Hollywood.

New opportunities had opened up, and throughout the 1940s the Saint appeared not only in books and movies but in a newspaper strip, a comic-book series, and on radio.

Anyone wishing to adapt the character in any medium found a stern taskmaster in Charteris. He was never completely satisfied, nor was he shy of showing his displeasure. He did, however, ensure that copyright in any Saint adventure belonged to him, even if scripted by another writer—a contractual obligation that he was to insist on throughout his career.

Charteris was soon spread thin, overseeing movies, comics, newspapers, and radio versions of his creation, and this, along with his self-proclaimed laziness, meant that Saint books were becoming fewer and further between. However, he still enjoyed his creation: in 1941 he indulged himself in a spot of fun by playing the Saint—complete with monocle and moustache—in a photo story in *Life* magazine.

In July 1944, he started collaborating under a pseudonym on Sherlock Holmes radio scripts, subsequently writing more adventures for Holmes than Conan Doyle. Not all his ventures were successful—a screenplay he was hired to write for Deanna Durbin, "Lady on a Train," took him a year and ultimately bore little resemblance to the finished film. In the mid-1940s, Charteris successfully sued RKO Pictures for unfair competition after they launched a new series of films starring George Sanders as a debonair crime fighter known as the Falcon. But he kept faith with his original character, and the Saint novels continued to adapt to the times. The transatlantic Saint evolved into something of a private operator, working for the mysterious Hamilton and becoming, not unlike his creator, a world traveller, finding that adventure would seek him out.

"I have never been able to see why a fictional character should not grow up, mature, and develop, the same as anyone else. The same, if you like, as his biographer. The only adequate reason is that—so far as I know—no other fictional character in modern times has survived a sufficient number of years for these changes to be clearly observable. I must confess that a lot of my own selfish pleasure in the Saint has been in watching him grow up."[9]

Charteris maintained his love of travel and was soon to be found sailing round the West Indies with his good friend Gregory Peck. His forays abroad gave him even more material, and he began to write true-crime articles, as well as an occasional column in *Gourmet* magazine.

By the early '50s, Charteris himself was feeling strained. He'd divorced his second wife in 1943 and got together with a New York radio and nightclub singer called Betty Bryant Borst, whom he married in late 1943. That relationship had fallen apart acrimoniously towards the end of the decade, and he roamed the globe restlessly, rarely in one place for longer than a couple of months. He continued to maintain a firm grip on the exploitation of the Saint in various media but was writing little himself. The Saint had become an industry, and Charteris couldn't keep up. He began thinking seriously about an early retirement.

Then in 1951 he met a young actress called Audrey Long when they became next-door neighbours in Hollywood. Within a year they had married, a union that was to last the rest of Leslie's life.

He attacked life with a new vitality. They travelled—Nassau was a favoured escape spot—and he wrote. He struck an agreement with *The New York Herald Tribune* for a Saint comic strip, which would appear daily and be written by Charteris himself. The strip ran for thirteen years, with Charteris sending in his handwritten story lines from wherever he happened to be, relying on mail services around the world to continue the Saint's adventures. New Saint books began to appear, and Charteris reached a height of productivity not seen since his days as a struggling author trying to establish himself. As Leslie and Audrey travelled, so did the Saint, visiting locations just after his creator had been there.

By 1953 the Saint had already enjoyed twenty-five years of success, and *The Saint Detective Magazine* was launched. Charteris had become adept at exploiting his creation to the full, mixing new stories with repackaged older stories, sometimes rewritten, sometimes mixed up in "new" anthologies, sometimes adapted from radio scripts previously written by other writers.

Charteris had been approached several times over the years for television rights in the Saint and had expended much time and effort during the 1950s trying to get the Saint on TV, even going so far as to write sample scripts himself, but it wasn't to be. He finally agreed a deal in autumn 1961 with English film producers Robert S. Baker and Monty Berman. The first episode of *The Saint* television series, starring Roger Moore, went into production in June 1962. The series was an immediate success, though Charteris himself had his reservations. It reached second place in the ratings, but he commented that "in that distinction it was topped by wrestling, which only suggested to me that the competition may not have been so hot; but producers are generally cast in a less modest mould." He resented the implication that the TV series had finally made a success of the Saint after twenty-five years of literary obscurity.

As long as the series lasted, Charteris was not shy about voicing his criticisms both in public and in a constant stream of memos to the producers. "Regular followers of the Saint saga . . . must have noticed that I am almost incapable of simply writing a story and shutting up."[10] Nor was he shy about exploiting this new market by agreeing to a series of tie-in novelisations ghosted by other writers, which he would then rewrite before publication.

Charteris mellowed as the series developed and found elements to praise too. He developed a close friendship with producer Robert S. Baker, which would last until Charteris's death.

In the early '60s, on one of their frequent trips to England, Leslie and Audrey bought a house in Surrey, which became their permanent base. He explored the possibility of a Saint musical and began writing some of it himself.

Charteris no longer needed to work. Now in his sixties, he supervised the Saint from a distance whilst continuing to travel and indulge himself. He and Audrey made seasonal excursions to Ireland and the south of France, where they had residences. He began to write poetry and devised a new universal sign language, Paleneo, based on notes and symbols he used in his diaries. Once Paleneo was released, he decided enough was enough and announced, again, his retirement. This time he meant it.

The Saint continued regardless—there was a long-running Swedish comic strip, and new novels with other writers doing the bulk of the work were complemented in the 1970s with Bob Baker's revival of the TV series, *Return of the Saint*.

Ill-health began to take its toll. By the early 1980s, although he continued a healthy correspondence with the outside world, Charteris felt unable to keep up with the collaborative Saint books and pulled the plug on them.

To entertain himself, Leslie took to "trying to beat the bookies in predicting the relative speed of horses," a hobby which resulted in several of his local betting shops refusing to take "predictions" from him, as he was too successful for their liking.

He still received requests to publish his work abroad but had become completely cynical about further attempts to revive the Saint. A new Saint magazine only lasted three issues, and two TV productions—*The Saint in Manhattan*, with Tom Selleck look-alike Andrew Clarke, and *The Saint*, with Simon Dutton—left him bitterly disappointed. "I fully expect this series to lay eggs everywhere . . . the only satisfaction I have is in looking at my bank balance."[11]

In the early 1990s, Hollywood producers Robert Evans and William J. Macdonald approached him and made a deal for the Saint to return to cinema screens. Charteris still took great care of the Saint's reputation and wrote an outline entitled *The Return of the Saint* in which an older Saint would meet the son he didn't know he had.

Much of his time in his last few years was taken up with the movie. Several scripts were submitted to him—each moving further and further away from his original concept—but the screenwriter from 1940s Hollywood was thoroughly disheartened by the Hollywood of the '90s: "There is still no plot, no real story, no characterisations, no personal interaction, nothing but endless frantic violence . . ." Besides, with producer Bill Macdonald hitting the headlines for the most un-Saintly reasons, he was to add, "How can Bill Macdonald concentrate on my Saint movie when he has Sharon Stone in his bed?"

The Crime Writers' Association of Great Britain presented Leslie with a Lifetime Achievement award in 1992 in a special ceremony at the

House of Lords. Never one for associations and awards, and although visibly unwell, Leslie accepted the award with grace and humour ("I am now only waiting to be carbon-dated," he joked). He suffered a slight stroke in his final weeks, which did not prevent him from dining out locally with family and friends, before he finally passed away at the age of 85 on 15 April 1993.

His death severed one of the final links with the classic thriller genre of the 1930s and 1940s, but he left behind a legacy of nearly one hundred books, countless short stories, and TV, film, radio, and comic-strip adaptations of his work which will endure for generations to come.

> *I was always sure that there was a solid place in escape literature for a rambunctious adventurer such as I dreamed up in my youth, who really believed in the old-fashioned romantic ideals and was prepared to lay everything on the line to bring them to life. A joyous exuberance that could not find its fulfilment in pinball machines and pot. I had what may now seem a mad desire to spread the belief that there were worse, and wickeder, nut cases than Don Quixote.*
>
> *Even now, half a century later, when I should be old enough to know better, I still cling to that belief. That there will always be a public for the old-style hero, who had a clear idea of justice, and a more than technical approach to love, and the ability to have some fun with his crusades.* [12]

---

1 *A Letter from the Saint*, 30 August 1946
2 "The Last Word," *The First Saint Omnibus*, Doubleday Crime Club, 1939
3 *The Straits Times*, 29 June 1958, page 9

4 Introduction by Charteris to the September 1980 paperback reprint of *Meet—the Tiger!* (Charter), the last ever print edition.

5 *The Saint: A Complete History*, by Burl Barer (McFarland, 1993)

6 PR material from the 1970s series *Return of the Saint*

7 From "Return of the Saint: Comprehensive Information" issued to help publicise the 1970s TV show

8 *A Letter from the Saint*, 26 July 1946

9 Introduction to "The Million Pound Day," in *The First Saint Omnibus*

10 *A Letter from the Saint*, 12 April 1946

11 Letter from LC to sometime Saint collaborator Peter Bloxsom, 2 August 1989

12 Introduction by Charteris to the September 1980 paperback reprint of *Meet—the Tiger!* (Charter).

WATCH FOR THE SIGN

OF THE SAINT!

THE SAINT CLUB

*And so, my friends, dear bookworms, most noble fellow
drinkers, frustrated burglars, affronted policemen, upright
citizens with furled umbrellas and secret buccaneering
dreams that seems to be very nearly all for now. It has been
nice having you with us, and we hope you will come again,
not once, but many times.*

*Only because of our great love for you, we would like
to take this parting opportunity of mentioning one small
matter which we have very much at heart . . .*

—*Leslie Charteris,* The First Saint Omnibus *(1939)*

Leslie Charteris founded The Saint Club in 1936 with the aim of
providing a constructive fanbase for Saint devotees. Before the War, it
donated profits to a London hospital where, for several years, a Saint
ward was maintained. With the nationalisation of hospitals, profits
were, for many years, donated to the Arbour Youth Centre in Stepney,
London.

In the twenty-first century, we've carried on this tradition but have
also donated to the Red Cross and a number of different children's
charities.

The club acts as a focal point for anyone interested in the adventures of Leslie Charteris and the work of Simon Templar, and offers merchandise that includes DVDs of the old TV series and various Saint-related publications, through to its own exclusive range of notepaper, pin badges, and polo shirts. All profits are donated to charity. The club also maintains two popular websites and supports many more Saint-related sites.

After Leslie Charteris's death, the club recruited three new vice-presidents—Roger Moore, Ian Ogilvy, and Simon Dutton have all pledged their support, whilst Audrey and Patricia Charteris have been retained as Saints-in-Chief. But some things do not change, for the back of the membership card still mischievously proclaims that . . .

> *The bearer of this card is probably a person of hideous antecedents and low moral character, and upon apprehension for any cause should be immediately released in order to save other prisoners from contamination.*

To join . . .

Membership costs £3.50 (or US$7) per year, or £30 (US$60) for life. Find us online at www.lesliecharteris.com for full details.

Made in the USA
Monee, IL
01 September 2022

13007350R00173